WOMEN ON A JOURNEY
Between Baghdad and London

Modern Middle East Literatures in Translation Series

WOMEN ON A JOURNEY
Between Baghdad and London

Haifa Zangana
Translated from the Arabic by Judy Cumberbatch
Introduction by Haifa Zangana

THE CENTER FOR MIDDLE EASTERN STUDIES
THE UNIVERSITY OF TEXAS AT AUSTIN

Cover design: Diane Watts
Series editor: Wendy E. Moore

Library of Congress Control Number: 2007921592
ISBN: 978-0-292-71484-7

The Center gratefully acknowledges financial support for the publication
of *Women on a Journey* from the National Endowment for the Arts in
Washington, D.C.

"The Leader" by Roger McGough (Copyright © Roger McGough 1983)
is reproduced by permission of PFD (www.pfd.co.uk) on behalf of Roger
McGough.

To Iraqi women's struggle, resilience, and resistance

TABLE OF CONTENTS

Introduction ix

Women on a Journey 1

Glossary 233

Notes on the Text 237

INTRODUCTION

I finished writing the original Arabic version of *Women on a Journey* in 2000, before the overthrow of Saddam Hussein's regime and the occupation of Iraq by U.S.-led troops. Like my previous two novels, *Through Vast Halls of Memory* and *Keys to a City*, it was published while I was in exile–in London.

Adiba, Sahira, Um Mohammed, Majda, and Iqbal are my five Iraqi women characters in this novel. At literary events, Iraqis often ask me during question time or in secretive whispers on the side whether Adiba is this woman or Sahira that. At one meeting in Sweden, an Iraqi woman stood up to thank me for writing about Iraqi women but, above all, for having written about Adiba, a friend of hers. Needless to say, I hadn't met or heard of her friend. This scene has been repeated many times. (It is worth mentioning that Majda is the exception, though the development of her character is more dramatic than the rest. Her presence is often ignored, by Iraqi readers in particular.) How do you explain why someone identifies with a character to such an extent that she believes she knows the character—or even *is* the character?

To shed light on the complex relationship that leads to this anomaly in which a reader identifies with the person on whom a character is supposedly based rather than on the character, I have to take a journey, a literary/political/social journey, and stop along the way at different points in time to get a partial glimpse of the background that characterizes Iraqi fiction writing.

HISTORICAL BACKGROUND

As an Iraqi writer, it is impossible to escape the temptation to look back at ancient writers. One cannot resist a trip to Sumer, in southern Iraq. There, Enheduanna (2300 BC), the world's first known writer, recorded her poetry in cuneiform on clay tablets that have withstood the test of time. With such an inspiration, it is no wonder that many of the best Arab poets, in particular women, have continued to emerge from Iraq.

Throughout history, poetry has been a powerful tool for conveying political messages. Poets have often enjoyed prestigious positions as spokespeople for their tribes, emirs, sultans, or even as modern rulers. Poetry has traditionally been the dominant literary genre in Iraq.

Therefore, in order to understand the political and social changes in Iraq, and women's roles in particular, it is essential to look at the role played by poetry in both its oral and written forms. Generations of Iraqi women have used oral poetry as an educational tool to complement the Qur'an in teaching their children history, heroic acts, morality, and responsibility. Women have also used poetry for political ends. It is known that women recited poetry during the 1920 revolution to encourage those fighting against British occupation.

While poetry has played an integral role in the region for thousands of years, it wasn't until the twentieth century that the novel became an important part of the Iraqi literary tradition. Since the publication of Mahmud al-Sayyid's *Jalal Khalid*, the first Iraqi novel, in 1928, fiction writing in Iraq has been dominated by a sense of social and political commitment. Writers have refused to accept the bitter social and political reality and have striven, through the fictional world, to establish an imaginary reality. When they lack the skills or the artistic refinement necessary for writing fiction, they have sometimes succeeded only in recycling political and social reality. Socially and culturally, Arab poets, writers, and intellectuals have expressed new ideas for change and searched for identity.

Jalal Khalid is dedicated to "Iraqi youth, on whom we depend in our struggle to establish freedom and justice." It tells the story of a young man from Baghdad who spends a few years in India. On returning home, he faces the aftermath of the collapse of the 1920 revolution against British occupation. His experience drives him to question the role of the intellectuals, so he decides to publish a literary journal. In Iraq, a literary journal is not a periodical strictly devoted to literature. Due to political repression and the dominance of the political over the literary, literary journals have often been used as covers for political activities or as alternatives to political parties. Today, little has changed. Like Jalal Khalid, many Iraqi writers now dream of publishing a literary journal in an attempt to reach others and affect society.

The establishment of the Iraqi Communist Party in 1932 and the spirit of communism and socialist ideas hugely influenced Iraqi writers. Progressive, leftist ideas took root in Iraq. These ideas introduced writers to the world's literature and art, while at the same time sounding the call to revolutionary change. The Communist Party also celebrated the struggle for social justice. Above all else, the establishment and development of the Communist Party offered Iraqis a political identity with which to overcome sectarian, religious, and ethnic divisions. The shortcoming of the party was its lack of engagement with traditional society and heritage, a failing which proved to be more dangerous than most understood. Islamists and nationalists would fill the gap left by the Communist Party and engage with the traditional elements of society, leading decades later to the often violent political divisions within Iraq. All of this found expression in Iraqi literature.

It was also during the 1930s that fiction writing in its modern form finally began to attract Iraqi women. In 1937 Dalal Khalil Safadi became the first woman to publish an anthology of short stories. In order to appease family and traditions, and to continue publishing, some women poets and writers chose to publish under pseudonyms. The poet Um Nizar's real name was Selma al-Malaika; the name of the poet Sadoof al-Obaidiaya' was Fettina al-Naeeb; and Afra's name was Maqboula al-Hili. Most of their writing was published in magazines and newspapers, rather than in books; hence, it is difficult to acknowledge, document, and study.

In the 1940s, the second generation of Iraqi writers, which included Dhul-Noun Ayyoub and 'Abdul Majid Lutfi, wrote realistic novels. They depicted the life of the poor through unpleasant, unhappy scenes and events. They saw fiction as a way of reproducing the reality of life. Their novels dealt with social issues such as school reform, education and health, land reform, and women's rights; they promoted the education of women, an end to forced marriages, and the abolition of the traditional 'abaya.

There was one exception to this pattern: 'Abdul Malik Nouri. Unlike his contemporaries, Nouri looked deeper into human nature, portraying the individual in his social environment and the influences of colonialism and class struggle upon him. Nouri's writings reflect his interest in sociology and psychoanalysis. He in turn influenced Fuad al-Takarli (b. 1927), a prominent writer of the next generation. Both men greatly admired Russian novelist Fyodor Dostoyevsky.

During the 1950s, arguments surfaced about mastering the techniques of writing, and paying more attention to characterization, plot, setting, and developing one's personal writing style. There was a need to be liberated from the rigid forms which enshrined the era's recurrent themes of social reform. This reflected the fiction writer's need to be more than *katib maqala*, an essay writer or a mere reporter.

Though writers in the 1950s moved fiction writing one step further in terms of technique, the interests of society were given priority and the concerns and inner life of the individual were again overlooked. Later these concerns were sacrificed still further in the pursuit of ideology and an emphasis on one-party politics.

Women writers were also active in the literary debates of the 1950s. In 1956 Safira Jamil Hafiz published *Children and Toys*, in which she dealt mainly, like male fiction writers, with social issues. Though at the same time she questioned the meaning of freedom from a woman's perspective.

While the socio-realist novel remained dominant in the 1950s, writers such as al-Takarli came to realize that such an approach limited their imagination and restricted their style. In an article published in *al-Mustaqbal Magazine*, in May 1953, al-Takarli summarized the intellectual argument about the role of the writer in society and art. He dismissed all previous writers, with the exception of 'Abdul Malik Nouri, describing them as reporters of social events and folk storytellers. He concluded that they were not writing fiction, but were merely assembling daily case reports similar to those compiled in police stations.

Taking into account the lack of freedom under British colonial rule, the literary shortcomings of the period are also understandable given that the art of fiction writing in its modern sense was relatively new, and the language employed was quite different from the spoken language, as is the case in all Arab countries. Because of this, the ability to read and write literature added to the writer's responsibility to society. Writers then and now are expected to represent their people, expressing their hopes, dreams, and ambitions and voicing their problems, especially at times of political upheaval. I myself have often been approached by readers and asked to write about education, women's issues, and social changes. In short, writers are expected to play a role that might be far beyond their capabilities.

Some people still confuse writers with the *ardhahalji* (re-presenters); from the earliest times and up to present-day Iraq, illiterate or semi-illiterate Iraqis have relied on the services of humble scribes to write their official requests and complaints in the approved manner. The *ardhahalji* may be able to do no more than read and write legibly. They offer their services for a few pence at a time where they might be needed: on the street corners near any government office. For some readers, then, the writer is a glorified type of scribe.

In the 1960s and early 1970s, a period that most Iraqi writers, poets, and artists remember with nostalgia, experimental writing emerged. Young fiction writers sought new forms of expression and issued one manifesto after another on freedom and creativity. Heavily influenced by Western trends both in thought and style, they produced a mishmash of crude or comic imitations of Sartre, Camus, and Kafka, mixed with socio-realistic novels and the odd masterpiece.

Writers made the most of the last few years of relative freedom that Iraqis enjoyed before the rise to power of Saddam Hussein, which led to wars, thirteen years of the most comprehensive sanctions imposed by Western governments in modern history, invasion, and the present-day occupation. The consolidation in the late 1970s and during the 1980s of the Ba'ath regime resulted in tighter ideological control in the cultural sphere. The denial of freedom of expression led to a steady erosion of basic human rights. Iraqis, including writers, began to escape the country in the thousands, seeking refuge throughout the world.

Writers inside Iraq survived the wars and brutality of the regime either by resorting to silence, or by continuing to write but relying on allegory and mysticism. Their characters were extracted from ancient history. Gilgamesh could be found walking relentlessly in the narrow alleys of Baghdad; Nebuchadrezzar, the warrior-king of Babylon, returned from the ancient past to claim endless victories in the Iran-Iraq War (1980–1988); martyrs tore off their shrouds to recapture rare moments of heroism; and adventurous men and clever women from *The Thousand and One Nights* revisited war-torn Iraq.

During this period, dozens of second-rate novels, with ambiguous themes and meaningless historical symbols, were published. Yet a few remarkable literary works, such as *Basrayatha*, by Mohammed Khudair, also emerged. Additionally, the pain that women suffered—the loss of their loved ones, the harsh years of sanctions, and the political oppression—was conveyed by a new generation of women novelists: the late Nuha al-Radhi (*Baghdad's Diary*), the late Hayat Sharara (*Idha al-ayamu aghsaqat*, or *When Darkness Falls*), and Betool al-Khudhari (*A Sky So Close*).

WRITING HOME

Beginning in the mid-1980s, a new generation of Iraqi writers, in addition to those who were already well-established, started publishing in exile. Encouraged by a newfound sense of freedom, individuality, security, and independence from both ideological slavery and state oppression, writers in exile have enjoyed the freedom to publish at will.

Writing in exile is characterized by the dominance of memory; uprooted from one's country, the writer relies on memory as a vital tool, enabling him or her to recreate everything that happened in the past and preserve it intact. Memory extends to the present and may overshadow the future. For some, memory becomes life itself. Other writers are happy merely to visit it, using it to reflect on their bitter experiences in Iraq. In their first novels, mostly based on memory, they depict their personal experiences, addressing themes such as serving in the army, wars, imprisonment, fear, and the struggle to escape the country.

The most important issue that has faced Iraqi writers in exile has been political involvement. The majority of them were either members of or ideologically allied to the Communist Party, and were involved in direct political action. They had spent their youth as communists, living and breathing the party; their friends were comrades; and their writings reflected the party line. Understandably, their sense of loss after the collapse of the Soviet Union was enormous, and leaving their country doubled their feelings of isolation. All of a sudden they found themselves in a complete ideological and social void.

The second problem for Iraqi fiction writers in exile is that almost all of them have continued to write in Arabic. This means that they have to rely on translation in order to reach their new readership and become recognized, something which has proven to be very difficult.

My Characters

In this complicated panorama, where do I stand? What about my characters? In reply, I maintain that it is very difficult to separate the personal from the political when both are directed at the same immediate objectives. The same applies to both my fiction and non-fiction writing. I believe that writers should strive to find the right balance between the individual and society, creativity and moral responsibility, imagination and reality. While discovering new domains, they need to tread with great care within old territories—emphasizing through their writing the right of the other to be different. But, above all, I keep reminding myself to beware the trap of ideology.

The five women who are my main characters in this novel are Iraqis, though they are from different ethnic, political, and social backgrounds. They are the carriers of Iraqi history, the storehouses of its collective memory; they represent the struggle, political and social commitment, and resilience of Iraqis, as well as having their own personal experiences, traumas, hopes, and ambitions. At the same time they are refugees. They live in London, stepping carefully in the streets of a new country, full of apprehension and a sense of longing for their families and country. They feel lonely in this strange place and new culture, whose only advantage for them is that it provides a sense of security—a feeling that proves to be false. They stand, metaphorically, on al-at'aba (the threshold), unable to return to their country but at the same time unable to settle in the new one. They are united by their fear of loneliness, despair, isolation, and lack of human contact. Most of the time they live in the past, unable to enjoy the present and not daring to think of the future.

Iqbal, being a single mother and unexpectedly pregnant as a result of her relationship with her English boyfriend, feels that she has to stop and examine her life. She contemplates her present and decides to break the pattern of her existence, which has been dominated by the past. Kurdish Um Mohammed is sheltered by her religious beliefs. Her common sense leads her to understand her son's anger toward all Iraqi Arabs and his refusal to speak Arabic at times of crisis. (For months after the bombardment of my city, Baghdad, during the Persian Gulf War in 1991, I couldn't utter a word in English.) Adiba clings to the past, which overshadows every minute of her present. Asked by Dr. Hawkins in one of her sessions, "Do you and your friends talk about Iraq?," Adiba answers, "Do we talk about anything else?"

Sahira lives in the shadow of her husband, who lives in the shadow of a dying ideology. The three are inseparable. 'Abed Kadhim's character, his depression and disintegrating relationship with Sahira, can only be understood in the context of the history of the Iraqi Communist Party and its rapid decline, if not demise, in the aftermath of the collapse of the Soviet Union. Losing the party was much more devastating for Kadhim than being forced to leave Iraq. The collapse of the party meant the loss of his life; it marked his own death. Sahira's obsession with 'Abed Kadhim is also an attempt to recapture her lost youth and love.

As I noted earlier, readers hardly mention or recognize Majda's existence. Despite her strong personality, they choose to ignore her, for one simple reason: she is a Ba'athist. Majda the Ba'athist is too painful to accept. For me, Majda was the most challenging character to write. Like many of my readers, I only met Ba'athists when they were in power. They were hated, feared, and despised. They were the secret police, interrogators, and torturers. They were the tools used by the dictatorship to create a climate of fear and control. It would have been much easier not to have had her as a character. But I felt I could not erase Majda's presence by looking sideways. She had to be dealt with. Perhaps, like Adiba, I felt that I should face my fears. Understanding Majda, looking at her life sympathetically, was an essential part of liberating my characters/myself from the complexities of hate and fear. As I wrote about her, watching her rise to power, then her slow decline into the abyss of death, loss, and finally madness, I had to learn to like her as a character in order to understand the Iraqis she symbolized. I had to understand her, and at certain moments *be* her, to convey her pain as a mother, as a human being.

Now, beyond my characters, in the reality of today's occupied Iraq, a sterile, dark silence extends its shadow over the imaginary. Like most Iraqi fiction writers, I have not written any fiction, not one word, since the war and occupation in 2003. The cruel reality of occupation has turned writing fiction into a meaningless act. Writers are surrounded by death, barbed-wire fences of hypocrisy, and threatened with the loss of their identity, culture, and the erasure of their memory. But, like many Iraqi writers, I miss literary writing. I miss words and the joy of living in the imaginary with my fictional characters. Sometimes, when not writing about the plight of Iraqis under occupation or attending the *aza'a* of friends and relatives who have been killed, slaughtered, or gone missing in Iraq, I dream of writing a sequel to this novel. Judging by our modern history, I know that Iqbal and Sahira would join in the national struggle against occupation and injustice, and for liberation and freedom.

WOMEN ON A JOURNEY
Between Baghdad and London

CHAPTER ONE

They all agreed that it would be a good idea to meet once a month. Four Iraqi women sitting in a crowded café in Hampstead, northwest London.

The idea took root. Enthusiasm grew. Suggestions were offered, questions raised. They busied themselves arranging the details of the meeting. They were pleased with the idea. Phrases flew about. We'll meet out somewhere. It'll be better than at someone's house. We're fed up with being at home. Yes. That's right. Meeting at someone's house means someone has to shop and clean and tidy and cook. They agreed. It's impossible to travel a long way in a city like London without having something to eat, or tea and a biscuit.

They also agreed they didn't need to flaunt their hospitality, or compete over which of them had the nicest house and possessions.

Yes . . . yes, it will be much better to meet elsewhere.

As their enthusiasm grew, they forgot they were in public. They were sitting so close together that they didn't need to talk loudly. It was such a little café that the other customers wouldn't tolerate the sound of raised voices. But they were blind to everything outside their small circle.

How quickly the minute hand moved across the face of the clock. Tick, tock, tick, tock. The big clock on the wall, which was shaped like a man holding a baby, ticked rhythmically. Tick, tock.

Enthusiasm spread among them, but it was a mere fifteen minutes before boredom crept in. The enthusiasm started getting ready to leave. Tick, tock.

The blaze of interest died down. The voices quieted. The bodies, which had huddled together, warming themselves at the idea and nurturing it, began to cool. They busied themselves sipping their tea or coffee. Majda wound the end of her necklace around her finger, moodily jerking the colored beads which provided the one dissonant note in her otherwise completely black attire.

She added two spoons of sugar to her coffee, then stirred it with a plastic spoon, staring down at it as the delicate and translucent oily film on its surface broke up. She was like someone stirring up a stagnant pond.

"We'll pay for ourselves," she said, jabbing a finger at the others.

Sahira sucked a brown sugar lump taken from the little bowl on the table.

"Don't get so het up, Majda," she said maliciously, in an attempt to provoke her. "Is a cup of tea or coffee so expensive that we have to discuss it a month in advance?"

"I know it's not much, but it's better to agree beforehand so that we're free to order what we want. We can choose what we want and pay for it separately. Supposing one of us wants a meal, and someone else only wants a drink of water? Isn't it better to agree in advance than pretend we want to pay for each other? Otherwise, one day you'll accuse me of not paying because I've forgotten."

Silence fell. They could have done without Majda's outburst. Adiba reflected that it was rare to arrive at an amicable arrangement with Majda. However, they had to keep on trying. She raised the subject of a date for the meeting.

"Which day?"

"What do you mean?"

"Which day shall we meet?"

"Let's see. What do you think—the first Wednesday of the month?"

Um Mohammed disagreed in her heavy Kurdish accent.

"The Kufa Gallery, near me, has meetings on Wednesdays which I like to attend."

"The meetings are in the evening," said Adiba. "We could meet during the day."

"I can't go out more than once a day. I get tired. Fridays would be better."

"I can't make Fridays," interjected Adiba. "I have to interpret in the morning, and I've got my exercise class in the evening. What about the beginning of the week? Monday, for example?"

They concurred.

"What time?"

"Six o'clock in the evening?"

"I don't like going home in the dark," Sahira said. "It makes me nervous."

Um Mohammed agreed with her.

"That's true. The roads aren't safe after dark. Two days ago I heard that one of my neighbors who lives in the same block of flats as I do was attacked by a gang of youths. They almost beat him to death. And for what? Three pounds. Poor man. He only had three pounds in his wallet."

Majda shrugged her shoulders derisively.

"Yet the English are so proud of London. Always boasting about how it is the capital of a first world country."

"London opens its door to all sorts of people," Adiba intervened. "As to safety . . . I am sure it's safe."

"You always defend London and its people," Majda sneered. "You talk about safety. Are you saying Baghdad isn't safe? Have you ever heard of a gang of youths attacking an old man in Baghdad for three dinars?"

Adiba sighed as she watched the young waiter joking with the customers at a nearby table, and didn't reply.

Sahira ignored Majda's remarks. "Our street's scary enough during the day, let alone at night. I'd prefer to meet in the afternoon or the middle of the day."

Um Mohammed weighed in with her support.

"The afternoon would be better, since none of us work."

"Iqbal works," Adiba corrected her. "But she has Mondays off."

"Do you think that Iqbal will want to spend her day off with us?" asked Sahira.

"It's only once a month," Majda snapped, putting an end to any further discussion. "She's welcome if she wants to come. If she doesn't, then she's free to meet whom she wants, when she wants."

"Is one o'clock OK?"

"No, it's lunchtime. Everywhere is crowded between twelve and two."

"Two o'clock in the afternoon, then," Majda suggested irritably. "After lunch. We can have a cup of tea or coffee together."

Sahira asked hesitantly, "How long will the meeting last? I mean, when will it end?"

Majda stared at her for a long moment, then abruptly got to her feet, and dramatically and noisily shoved back her chair. The other customers glanced furtively over at her while pretending to carry on with their conversations. The young waiter swiveled around to check what was happening, then got on with clearing a nearby table as soon as he saw there was no reason to be concerned.

Majda laid a pound coin on the table, the exact price of her coffee. Then she put on her black coat and buttoned it up, winding her long black scarf around and around her neck until her head appeared to be mounted on her shoulders through a series of springs like the neck rings of an African tribeswoman.

Her stance gave her an added power as she towered over them, thin, tall, and draped in black. Before concealing her face under a wide-brimmed black hat, she told them:

"I'll see you. At two o'clock. Next month. As we've agreed, there's no need to phone and confirm."

She hurried away.

A heavy silence settled over their circle.

Her abrupt departure put an end to the underlying sense of tension they were unable to express. It left a sudden void. A black hole that absorbed any words they uttered, any sound of laughter.

Tension consists of heavy particles. It doesn't evaporate, doesn't sublimate, but precipitates among souls.

For several minutes after Majda had gone, they continued to stare at the door. She may have been swallowed up by the world outside, but her dark shadow lingered among them long after her departure.

Sahira was elegantly dressed in bright colors and as carefully made-up for her meeting with the women as for a tryst with a lover. Now she hitched the slightly open bodice of her red dress over her cleavage in order to cover up her rounded breasts, which strained against the material and seemed ready to burst out every time she heaved a sigh or groan. She was the first of those left in the now Majda-less circle to speak. She brushed several grains of brown sugar off her dress, and with them, the echo of Majda's presence and her stinging words. She regarded the two women uneasily, then asked,

"Did I say something to upset her?"

"No, no, don't worry," Adiba said sympathetically. "You know what she's like. You can leave the meeting whenever you want. It's not like a party meeting, where you have to be present from start to finish. Why is it all so complicated? We have been meeting like this for months, haven't we? The only thing that's changed is that we are agreeing to meet on a particular day. We shall meet first and spend some time together and then decide what to do. We can go to a local cinema, or we can sit and chat, or go for a walk on Hampstead Heath if the weather's fine. We can do whatever comes up. It's up to us."

"It's not because I don't like being with you all, but I have to tell Kadhim when I'm getting back. He likes to know exactly when I'm getting home so he doesn't worry."

"Why?" Um Mohammed asked.

Sahira shrugged slightly. "I don't really know, to tell you the truth. Perhaps he's worried about my safety! It's strange. When I'm at home, he doesn't notice if I'm there, but as soon as I leave, he starts worrying about me. He wants to know exactly when I'm coming back. Anyway, I'm afraid of staying out late, especially in winter."

"Don't worry," Adiba said. "Even in the depths of winter, it doesn't get dark before four o'clock."

"You live quite close to Majda," Um Mohammed suggested. "You could arrange to go back with her. At least get on the bus together."

"Majda thinks I'm unreliable ever since I was half an hour late for an appointment."

"Spending half an hour in the street in London's awful weather would try the patience of a stone."

Sahira looked at Um Mohammed in astonishment. "In the street? Who said anything about waiting in the street?" she asked. "We had arranged to meet at her flat. I was late. The boiler at home had broken down. The man from the gas board promised to come and mend it in the morning. I waited and waited but he didn't show up until two o'clock in the afternoon. You see, it wasn't my fault."

"Why didn't you phone and let her know?"

"We didn't have a phone, and I couldn't leave the house and call from the public phone box. She got so cross. I don't know why. After all, she was sitting comfortably in her flat."

"Didn't you explain all this to Majda?" Adiba asked. "Did you tell her what had happened?"

"Yes."

"What did she say?"

"She said an appointment was an appointment and it didn't matter whether we'd arranged to meet at home or in the street."

"I don't understand her," said Um Mohammed. "She's strange. Where has she learned such military discipline from?"

Sahira glanced furtively up at the two women.

"From her party," she whispered.

They heard the whisper. They pretended not to. Adiba said,

"She has been through a hard time, and we should try and understand her."

"We've all had a tough time," Sahira said. "Um Mohammed, Iqbal, you. Which of us has lived the nice, quiet life we would have liked? We've all been forced into exile, and had to leave everything, valuable or not, behind. We're all refugees. We've all suffered. But the difference is that we try and tolerate others, like you say. She doesn't think about anyone except herself. She thinks she's the center of the universe. As they say, she thinks she can wipe the floor with everyone else."

"Sahira, 'aini. May I sacrifice myself for your sake!" Um Mohammed interrupted. "You shouldn't speak like that about someone else. Slander's *haram*; it's forbidden."

"We've all had our misfortunes," Sahira continued, her sense of dislike now thoroughly aroused, "but she thinks she has a monopoly on misery. We all have to look after her and coax her out of her unhappiness. If anyone else dares to complain, she glares at her and puts her down. And why? Because apparently she's the only one who's suffered. Do you remember that time when I told you how worried Kadhim and I were about Shakir's job and whether he would get his contract renewed or not? By the name of God, do you remember how she mocked me? Instead of saying something like '*In sha' Allah*, it'll be OK' or 'If God wills, you'll soon get good news' like the rest of you did, she looked at me as if she were a snake and said, 'You're worried about a silly job contract when our homes and lives have been destroyed.'"

She paused for an instant to catch her breath. "I wish I understood ... Why do we ask her to join us?" she added bitterly. She stopped. Tears glistened in her eyes. "I'd much prefer it if we met on our own."

Um Mohammed straightened the white voile scarf that she wore over her silver gray hair, now braided into a single plait.

"It's true that Majda can be difficult," she said, "but she's good-natured and she needs us. She's a foreigner like us. There are only five of us. Why do we have to argue?"

"All I'm saying is ... if she wants to be friends with people," said Sahira, "then she should show some concern for them and be polite; she should praise God and thank him that we're willing to be friends with her." She gestured excitedly. "No, no, Um Mohammed. Just because your circumstances are difficult doesn't mean that you can look down on other people. On the contrary ..."

"We haven't yet decided where we're going to meet," Adiba interrupted, trying to change the subject of conversation and divert the poisoned barbs away from Majda. "What about this café?"

They agreed.

"And when shall we meet? We've agreed to meet on Monday, but which Monday?"

"Let's see. What's the date today?"

Adiba studied her diary.

"Today's Thursday, October 15th. In a month, it'll be Monday, November 16th. Who'll let Majda know about the date?"

Sahira recalled Majda's parting shot.

"She told us there was no need to call!" she shouted.

Adiba sighed. "Well, I'll phone her," she said, and added, "Iqbal didn't come today. I'm sure there was a good reason. Sahira, could you let her know?"

"I'm seeing her on Sunday evening. She called and asked me to look after her son, as she's invited out to supper. I might even spend the night with her, if Kadhim lets me. I'll certainly tell her."

CHAPTER TWO

Majda walked quickly, eyes to the ground. Once she had stumbled across a ten-pound note among the leaves littering the pavement. She had peered at it closely, unable to believe her eyes. Then, after turning around to make sure that no one was watching her, she'd bent down with an agility that belied her years and picked it up. She had shoved it, just as it was, into her jacket pocket, and had not dared to examine it until she was back in her flat. Ever since then she had walked with her head craned forward, hoping to come across another such find.

Each step measured one square of asphalt. She was reminded of childhood. Playing hopscotch in the alleyways with the boys and girls of Souk Hamada, in Baghdad's al-Karkh district. They had drawn the squares with chalk, and jumped from one to another without touching the lines. She had yelled at them: "It's forbidden to step on the lines. Anyone who disobeys is out." She wanted to play the game now, jump her way all along the road without touching the lines around the squares.

She sighed. If only things were that simple. If only we could wish for something and it would come true. But it wasn't that easy. More and more people crowded onto the street and she had to swerve constantly to avoid bumping into children and pushchairs and the mothers behind them. She reminded herself how old she was and recalled her aches and pains. One fall among the squares and her bones would take years to recover.

Her thoughts seesawed between past and present.

Ah!

If only she hadn't grown old, hadn't left her home, if only Sa'id hadn't abandoned her, if only she hadn't lost . . .

Ah! How many times could she repeat this single sad syllable?

It was half past three.

Time for the primary schools and kindergartens to empty out. A difficult time for someone who hated crowds. In the future she would avoid the streets at this time. It was her fault. She hadn't looked at the time when she left the café. She'd fled in a hurry, fearful that one of the others, particularly Sahira, would decide to accompany her for some of the way. Silly Sahira with her whispers and whining, and her tears, and her innocent air, and the way she went on and on about Kadhim and her children. As if she were the only woman in the world who had had children.

"Stupid, brainless idiot," she said out loud.

She had once told Iqbal, "You know, Sahira reminds me of a hissing snake." Iqbal had replied, "Come on, Majda, don't exaggerate. She's got a nice beautiful voice, particularly when she sings. Have you heard her sing the songs of the late Hudhairi Abu Aziz?"

> He greets her with a flicker of his brow,
> A crinkle at the corner of his eye.
> How well he knows how to greet a woman,
> How beautifully he performs.

At the pedestrian crossing opposite Waterstone's bookshop, she made her way across the road. The pavement was littered with fallen leaves. A woman led a group of children of various ages over the road at the same time, heading toward the community center in Hampstead where there was an after-school club for the children of working women. The children would stay there, under the watchful eyes of two attendants, until six o'clock when their mothers returned from work.

Majda stood in front of the bookshop. She pushed the brim of her hat up slightly, and involuntarily brushed the spot on her right cheek where she had Baghdad boil. In happier times, she had had cosmetic surgery to remove the scars, but the spot remained itchy. When she was agitated or irritable, the itching grew worse.

The Baghdad boil had gnawed at her flesh even after she had had it removed. She was branded, like a slave who was forced to bear the sign of her master. Once she'd consulted a doctor about the itchiness and cracked skin. The doctor was interested in her case. He said he'd read about Baghdad boil, or *leishmaniasis*, in a medical textbook, but hers was the first case he'd encountered. He carefully examined her face, then he took a blood sample. He gave her the results several weeks later. He said he hadn't found anything that might cause the itching, arguing that it was probably psychological.

Majda looked into the shop window. Piles of best sellers and other books were arranged enticingly. She hesitated. Should she go in or not? Finally, she entered the shop to get away from the crowds. She decided to remain there until the streets were quieter and the children of the others had gone. She carefully repeated the phrase: the children of the others. And recalled her daughter Huda. The loss of such high hopes.

If Huda was . . .

No, no, she wasn't going to think about Huda. She put her out of her mind. Returned her to the dark recesses of her memory. Raced up the wide staircase to the first floor, taking the steps two at a time. Afraid, fleeing from the mere thought of her daughter.

She passed under a sign saying Fiction. She had made her way to this section because novels were the only books she read. Through the pages of a novel, she was able to slip into a world of make-believe where she could forget herself, her reality, and her sorrows. The bigger the book, the better.

When Majda had first arrived in London, she had almost died of loneliness, grief, and fear. She had bought a secondhand television: a huge black-and-white set, with an enormous screen that looked like one of the air-cooling units they had had in Baghdad. She'd paid five pounds for it. It was so big that, together with the table, which crouched under it, it took up a quarter of the single room in the flat. Sitting room and bedroom combined. A studio. She told herself bitterly: English pimps! They know how to cheat the world. They call a council room in run-down Burnt Oak a flat/furnished studio.

The flat contained a single bed, a two-person sofa, and two wooden chairs. There was a table, which she used for everything: preparing food, writing letters, mending clothes. When she read the newspaper, she rested her elbows on the table and peered out the window onto the street, which led to Burnt Oak Underground station. When she had had enough television, it became an alternate screen on which to watch the passersby, the strangers. A living panorama. A street jam-packed with mean, dirty shops that catered to Indians and working-class English.

And Majda. Forcibly expelled from her nice big house in the Hayy al-Mansour district of Baghdad, and now left peering out from behind the net curtains of her council flat. Concealed in the inner darkness of the room, she watched them and they didn't see her.

After Majda had bought the television, her life changed slightly. She would spend her days shut away in her council flat, sitting in front of the set, staring at the screen with vacant eyes, unable to comprehend the comedy, drama, and news. The television encircled her in a stream of beautiful moving pictures, helping to distance her from the here and now, and as one program followed another, it absorbed her fears.

Then one day, by chance, she discovered Mills & Boon romances. She bought her first novel for five pence from a shop near her flat, which sold furniture, secondhand clothes, and general bric-a-brac. She was aimlessly looking through the contents of a box on an old table outside the shop, which had a For Sale sign on it, when she came across a small book. Its cover reminded her of an Egyptian pocket novel. She looked at the first line. She was pleased. She could understand it. It was simply written. The owner of the shop noticed her pausing to read and pressed the book on her.

"It's only five pence. If you don't like it, then bring it back and I'll buy it from you for five pence. What about it? Is it a deal? Or look, I've got a better idea. You can have the whole box for fifty pence—spoons, knives, tin opener, and novel. What do you think?" He saw her hesitating and frowned. "What else can you get for fifty pence these days? Go on, tell me."

He put down her hesitation to the expense. In fact, Majda was vacillating because she couldn't understand three-quarters of what he was saying. It was difficult enough for her to make out the local dialect without someone speaking quickly as well. She hurriedly concluded the awkward situation by paying five pence and taking the book.

Five pence was what it had cost her to enter the world of romantic fiction. Later, when she was asked what had helped her come to terms with life in those early years in the bitter freezing cold of London, she would say, "It was a Mills & Boon romance."

She spent months on end in this make-believe world that was so safe and comforting. Her reading induced a druglike stupor. From the moment she took up the novel, she clung to it, reading and reading, bypassing sleep until she had finished it. It was like being a teenager all over again. Like those days when she had lived with the novels of Yousef Siba'i and Ahsan 'Abdul Qadous, books such as *There's a Man in Our House*, *The Empty Pillow*, *A Nose and Three Eyes*, and *Don't Put Out the Sun*.

In those days her tears had flowed unchecked and a warm flush had spread over her fickle body at the mere mention of an exchange of glances between hero and heroine, or his unexpected touch on her hand. As a teenager, she remembered, she had lived through an incident like one described in *There's a Man in Our House*.

Majda hastily shook off the memory. She threw the comfort of romance aside. She admonished herself angrily: worry about how you feel now!

Now?

Now her feelings had hardened into small icy cubes in which there was nothing but fear, doubt, and suspicion. What she wanted was what she got from the romances: a few mindless hours.

The Mills & Boon romances rescued her from her desperate, fear-filled days. They provided her with a bouquet of flowers, brightly colored worlds that were safe and a hundred times better than her depressing reality. They raised her several rungs up the ladder that connected the real world to that of the imagination. She became reconciled to herself, at least part of the time.

Thanks to Mills & Boon, she was gradually able to cut down her daily dose of tranquilizers and the sleeping pills she often took at night. She reached a compromise: she would read the romances and only take her pills when she had to.

For several months, she took to visiting the library once a week. She borrowed six books at a time. She finished them and exchanged them for six others, which she started on immediately. Mills & Boon romances no longer had the power to satisfy her greed, and she moved on to longer novels. She got to know the works of Catherine Cookson, Danielle Steel, and Barbara Taylor Bradford. She read quickly, abstractedly, not bothering about words she didn't understand. She rarely consulted the English-Arabic dictionary because the one thing that interested her in the novel was the fate of the heroine. She was like someone gobbling up a dish of food, unaware of its ingredients. A meal to satisfy her. Numb her. Make her forget. Make her sleep.

In the novels section, she flicked through a book by Catherine Cookson. She turned to the back and read the number at the bottom of the page. Five hundred and sixty-six. Great. This book was worth reading. It would take several days. She opened her handbag. Drew out a small notebook. Wrote down the title and the publisher. I'll go to the library tomorrow and ask Sally, the librarian, to get it for me, she thought. Poor Catherine. What a difficult life she's led. If only I could write a book about my life, it would be as full of suffering as hers.

Someone had once suggested that she write her life story. Who was it, exactly, who'd first brought up the idea? She couldn't remember. She'd replied, "I can't write a letter, let alone a whole book. Sa'id's the one who should write his autobiography."

How many times had she told him to be careful for her sake, if not for his own? If only he'd listened to me, she thought. If only he'd once listened to what I was saying, then it wouldn't have happened. She felt the familiar rush of anger surging through her veins. Like mercury in a barometer. A blind, uncontrollable rage. A rage that possessed her whenever she thought about him. She'd heard that anger consumes itself over the years and becomes spent. So why could it still tear her apart twenty years later?

She replaced the book irritably on the table in the middle of the shop and walked toward the stairs. It was too expensive. Beyond her budget. She only got forty-five pounds a week from the social security. She divided up her expenses as follows:

Food
Gas, electricity, and telephone
TV license (black and white)
Laundry and ironing
Stamps and writing paper
Clothing—bare essentials
Transport
Entrance money for the weekly water aerobics and swimming session she attended with Adiba

If she walked from Hampstead to Golders Green and took the bus from there to Burnt Oak, it would take her an hour and a quarter to reach her flat. She would save ninety pence and use up a whole hour and a quarter of useless time. And she would cut down the time she spends alone in her flat by an hour and a quarter.

Those women were mad. They refused to go out in the evening. She preferred to do the opposite.

Majda's Day

Majda spent her day occupying herself in three ways. She moved from one activity to another, varying the time she devoted to each one: Television watching. Window gazing. Walking around the shops. In the last two years, her relationship with her television had gone through a crisis. She was no longer able to watch it, fearful of coming across a reminder of

Iraq on the news or on some other program. The television had become an enemy, something that tainted the image of someone she loved. She'd put it aside. Covered it up with an old black T-shirt and piled it high with letters from the council and gas, electricity, and telephone bills, which came in uniform brown envelopes.

The window, on the other hand, remained a refuge, and she maintained her links with it when the mood took her.

As for her habit of wandering aimlessly around the shops with no real goal apart from passing the time, it dated back to the beginning of 1988. In the ensuing years it had become more and more ingrained. The first time she'd done it, it was the first day of the January sales. She discovered she could spend hours and hours in the big department stores, sorting through the goods on sale, piling them into a basket, then pretending to change her mind and leaving the shop without buying a thing.

At night, as she lay stretched out on her bed, Majda would prepare herself as carefully for the next day as if she were going out on an important date. She would debate whether to go to the Galleria shopping mall or Brent Cross. She would stare up at the ceiling, annoyed at the sight of the cracked and peeling paint and dangling cobwebs, and say to herself, tomorrow I'll use the broom to sweep them away.

The next day arrived and she forgot.

Lying in bed, she would concoct excuses to go shopping. Convince herself that she needed a pair of cotton socks, a new toothbrush, or some dye for her hair. Little things that she could quite easily have bought in the small shops in the neighborhood. When she was done, she would close her eyes, pleased to have found a reason to wake up in the morning, drink her coffee, get dressed, and leave her room.

Usually she selected one of the new shopping malls. She preferred them because they were big and open, and situated in the suburbs, far away from the center of London where other Arabs tended to congregate; this way she would avoid the risk of running into other Iraqis, in particular.

The malls were warm as well, havens from the changeable British weather.

She could spend the whole day at the mall if she wanted to, wandering around, observing, strolling from shop to shop, like someone taking a walk through fields and orchards. But after an hour or two at most, she would become overwhelmed by a sense of incomprehensible grief and melancholy that forced her to scurry back to "the room," the cocoon through whose woven threads she could gaze at the people in the street.

She would return home without buying anything.

Sometimes, seized with a desire to be with people, she would go out to the public library. She would sit among the strangers, reading the free newspapers and magazines. She'd greet Sally warmly. Thirty minutes later, she'd feel suffocated and leave in a hurry, ignoring Sally's wave.

Once she had stumbled across a party for the elderly. She had shrunk away from the false teeth, gaping mouths, trembling limbs, and transparent skin with the tiny veins showing through like twisting, never-ending canals. After a couple of minutes, she had slid out of the room and fled from the library, cursing the moment of weakness that had taken her there and swearing never to go back again.

Majda's Evening

As evening drew in, she would become confused. Voices whispered to her. She whispered in reply. She cried out her fears, unable to understand what she was feeling. At a time when others were returning home to relax after a hard day's work, she longed to escape. If the flat had been her real home, her past home, she would have been happy to stay there forever.

In Baghdad the situation had been different. Her real life had begun at eight o'clock in the evening, when Sa'id returned home from work and hordes of friends descended on them. They held an open house. "What shall we call the gatherings?" she jokingly asked Sa'id. "Sa'id's Salon? Sa'id's Khan? After all, you're just as good as that Egyptian hostess May Ziyada with her literary salon. We'll call the poets and writers and artists who meet here the Poet Sa'id's Salon or, better still, the Happy Salon— as your name means happy. It'll be a lucky omen for those who come seeking Sa'idi joy!"

He looked at her, pleased with her joke, and she laughed joyfully, feeling as if her heart would burst with happiness.

Those had been good evenings.

When was the last time she'd laughed like that? She couldn't remember. Sa'id's face, in particular, was now hidden behind a black cloud that, after extinguishing his poetry, had choked him physically. Bitterness mounted inside her, taking the place of the love and desire she had once felt. It had a corrosive quality that she could taste on the tip of her tongue as it curled upward and coursed through her body, like a stream of lava burning everything in its path.

She sighed out loud.

Now everything had been reduced to ashes. Love. Home. Country.

And it was all their fault.

She put on her gloves and pulled the brim of her hat down over her eyes. She rubbed her nose. Once outside the warmth of the bookshop, she felt like sneezing. How she hated the cold. Having to remove her hat and gloves ten times a day. The way the damp got into her bones. She remembered how on her first trip to London she'd rushed out to buy a white hat, and Sa'id had watched in surprise as she tried on one after another. She squashed the memory now as she would a tick that, gluelike, stuck to her skin. That sucked out her days. The nectar of her life.

She crossed the road opposite the Hampstead Underground station. The women in the group were so silly. She had suggested meeting in the middle of the city but they had refused. They said, "We'll meet somewhere that is easy for everyone to get to." Sahira said, "Getting into central London will cost me four pounds for a day pass." Majda had kept quiet, recognizing deep down that Sahira was right. It was expensive getting about in London. The cheapest bus journey cost seventy pence.

"Poor Sahira ... From the ... !" She realized she had spoken out loud. She hastily bit back the expression of sympathy. *Mesqina?* Poor? No way! She's been spoiled. Still is ... During the troubles ... she wasn't even in Iraq ... She was living outside the country with her husband ... He's still alive. He looks after her ... She's got her children ... A daughter too ... Oh Huda! ... And they've got money, of course. The party gives them money. They're not like me. I had to run away one dark night ... He attacked us. He destroyed our whole life. Father ... Leader ... Comrade Leader. What did we ever do to him?

She walked up to the Horse Pond, the highest point in Hampstead. The water in the pond was shallow. The area was exposed on all sides. She felt a cold breeze sting her face. The scars of her Baghdad boil itched dreadfully.

At the bus stop, she looked back and saw a number 268 approaching, headed for Golders Green. She hesitated. Should she catch the bus or walk home? By the time she had made up her mind and decided to catch the bus, it had gone past. She sighed. Life would be so much simpler if someone else was prepared to make the decisions for you. How much easier it would be to belong to a party or a religion. To be married to a strong man. Anything rather than go through the agonies of hesitation and indecision.

On the other hand ... why did she have to bear the consequences

WOMEN ON A JOURNEY

when someone else made a decision? Just because Sa'id decided to open his doors to all and sundry, without taking proper precautions, why did she have to suffer for his stupidity?

Why did I stay and take the blame when he went away, happy with the decision he had made? *Sa'id!*

Here she was, back at her word games, making puns on Sa'id's name. Had Sa'id really been happy? In the warm bygone days she had spent with him, she had laughed out loud at her own clever puns, but now they only left her with a bitter taste in her mouth.

There was a beautiful park on her left. Golders Hill. She sometimes came here for a walk with Adiba or Iqbal. If her daughter Huda were here, she would have come with Majda.

Last summer, Majda and Adiba had sat in the café in the park—a nice café, prettily arranged. They sat in silence under a big umbrella, watching the old and the young and the dogs stroll by. She drank her black coffee, sweetened with two spoonfuls of sugar, while Adiba ate an almond-flavored ice cream.

In an attempt to push aside the painful curtain of silence that had fallen between them, Adiba asked her,

"What do you do all day?"

Majda shrieked with laughter, then she stopped suddenly, dismayed at her own merriment.

"Every day's the same!" she cried out. "My days . . . they're nothing to write home about. Every one's a holiday, but they're empty with no one to share them. I wander around the shops. I go to the library. I've got an English friend whom I visit a couple of times a year. Nothing else. I don't do anything. I know lots of people. I'm always getting calls from people who knew Sa'id. They've recently escaped and want to meet up. I refuse. What's the point?"

And she started to cry. Adiba said nothing, leaving her to purge herself of her grief and suppressed pain.

"I don't know what to do," she continued, between her tears. "Sometimes I feel quite enthusiastic about things and make myself attend some Iraqi function. I arrive, but can't bear to remain there longer than ten minutes. I feel suffocated as soon as I enter the room. I can hardly breathe. I can't bear to see Iraqis. I regret going and swear never to return, then I break my promise and go back."

"Majda, have you ever thought of consulting a psychiatrist?" Adiba asked gently.

"Why? Am I mad?" she said mockingly, searching for a tissue to wipe away her tears.

"No, I'm sorry. But a doctor might help you understand what you're going through, your problems. I see a psychiatrist once a week."

"I know what's the matter with me," Majda said firmly, "and it's up to me to solve it, not some psychiatrist."

However, Adiba did persuade her to add a new activity to her week—water aerobics.

"I go twice a week because of my leg. If it weren't for the exercise and swimming, I would be totally disabled by now."

"I'm no good at swimming."

"It doesn't matter. I'm not much good at it either, but it's about moving and exercising in water. The water supports your muscles and does not place any strain on them."

Majda was convinced. After that, she went with Adiba to water aerobics and swimming on the women-only evening. Every Friday, from seven to eight.

All of a sudden Majda felt hungry. She noticed that it was a quarter to five, and she hadn't eaten since ten o'clock in the morning. She didn't want to go to a café or buy a sandwich. The cheapest sandwich cost one pound fifty, and it was just a piece of cheese with a slice of tomato or cucumber and a lettuce leaf.

She laughed abruptly, remembering the story of the thirty-five-dollar lettuce. During the Gulf War, the Americans had put the price of freighting a head of lettuce to the troops at thirty-five dollars. After the war, they had asked the Kuwaitis to foot the bill, and the Kuwaitis in turn had gotten the Iraqis to pay. They had paid compensation for everything—oil wells, blown-up buildings, prisoners of war, armaments, the property of the fleeing ruling family, and . . . lettuce. Majda's eyes filled with tears. A sense of longing overwhelmed her, scorching her with its pain.

"Why, why did you do this to us?" she asked out loud.

A woman on the sidewalk heard the words. She turned her head and glanced at Majda sympathetically, then carried on walking, passing her by a couple of seconds later. Majda wiped away the tears with her gloves in a matter-of-fact fashion. There was no use in crying, no point in being sad.

Her stomach rumbled. She drew a packet of medicine containing several strips of pills out of her bag. Each pill had the name of the day on it, with a picture of a sun for those to be taken in the morning and a picture of a moon for those to be taken at night. Majda realized that she'd missed the pill she was supposed to take in the morning for her stomach ulcer. She swallowed it without water. Perhaps the bus would come quickly and she wouldn't have to buy some bread and eat it before going home. She hated doing that. She hated eating between meals. Hated eating in the street and putting food into her mouth with hands that had come into contact with all the dirt outside—dirt from books, tickets, money, seats on the bus. They were all sources of germs.

She paced agitatedly up and down under the arching roof of the bus station in the square at Golders Green. The buses terminated there and also there was an Underground station and a coach station for outside London.

"Golders Green is really clean and orderly," Majda had once told the women. She thought of the conversation now.

"It's a Jewish area, that's why!" Sahira yelled. "It's so obvious. The people who live there are Jewish, aren't they? They know how to get what's owed them, and they get everything they want. They're not like us. We're like slaves. We accept anything and are satisfied with the absolute minimum."

"Sahira, how can you say we're slaves?" Adiba protested disapprovingly. "Look around you. Look at the number of Iraqis living in exile. Why are we here? Why are you here?"

Sahira muttered something incomprehensible, then added, "I didn't mean to upset anyone. I just mean that we have to learn from them."

"Learn what?" Majda demanded.

"Come on, everyone," Iqbal said. "*Salu al Nabi*, prayers be upon the Prophet."

"Praise be to Mohammed and his family," Um Mohammed intoned.

"Calm down, everyone," Iqbal said. "Just be patient with each other. I believe it is important to distinguish between Jews and Zionists. Perhaps Sahira wishes to say Zionists rather than Jews."

"Sahira's got a tongue and doesn't need an interpreter," snapped Majda.

Before Iqbal could reply, Um Mohammed intervened. Her face reddened and seemed to glow, the white gauzy scarf lending it a particular beauty.

"This is their country."

Their eyes turned toward her.

"What do you mean, Um Mohammed?" Adiba asked gently.

"I mean the Jews—the Jews living here. They are English. It's true, yes? London is their home. They are the same as everyone. But not their religion. Their religion is not . . ."

She spoke very slowly, composing and delivering as best she could a comprehensible Arabic sentence. "This means that, because this is their country, they know how to behave in it. As we knew how to behave in Iraq. Before the tyrant took power and divided us all and set us against each other."

Um Mohammed swallowed with difficulty. She wanted to stop speaking, but the others were staring at her encouragingly, so she plucked up her courage and struggled on. "Our . . . situation's different. We're foreigners. We have a different religion and come from a different race. We do not speak their language." She looked about her apologetically.

"I mean . . . I'm talking about myself. You're better than me. I don't know their language or anything about their country." Her eyes filled with tears, and she added, "By our Prophet Mohammed, I don't want to stay here."

A dark cloud of grief swirled about them. An overwhelming sense of their own alienation touched the wounds deep within them, which separated them from others. The pain of isolation and exile set them apart. Cut them off from anyone outside their circle.

Sahira wiped away the tears that sprang to her eyes as she listened to Um Mohammed. She uncoiled like a spring and bounced back. She noticed Adiba and Majda and Iqbal listening to what Um Mohammed was saying and the effect she was having on them.

"Your words are like gold, Um Mohammed," she said, quickly reverting to her previous theme. "That's what I meant to say. Exactly. It's their country and they can do whatever they want with it. What's it got to do with us?"

CHAPTER THREE

"My train goes from platform two."

"Give me a ring. We'll arrange to do something next week."

They'd stayed in the café for half an hour after Majda had gone, then walked to the Hampstead Underground station together. They separated at the station. Adiba and Um Mohammed took the Northern Line going south, while Sahira waited by herself on the platform opposite for the train going north to Colindale.

Adiba and Um Mohammed sat in silence on the train, in the tunnel, watching the rest of the passengers. Everyone sat in silence, feigning interest in the various advertisements stuck up in the slots above the windows, or glancing furtively at their chance companions on the journey. Those among them who struggled with the tedious, tiring journey on a daily basis had armed themselves with books and newspapers, like soldiers putting up their shields; they didn't look up unless it was absolutely necessary.

They sat side by side. Um Mohammed occupied the entire seat, taking over the armrests on both sides. Her short legs struggled to reach the carriage floor and she gave up. Her feet dangled in midair like a child's, peeping out from beneath the hem of her blue skirt. She wore a white blouse and a dark blue jacket. From time to time she raised her hand to check that her gauze scarf was still in place on her head.

Adiba sat upright, straight-backed like a yoga student. She wore a dark brown skirt with a blouse and jacket of the same color, but in a lighter shade. She held her handbag in one hand and leaned on her wooden stick with the other. She could see herself reflected in the dirty glass window between the passengers on the opposite side of the carriage. The breeze from outside ruffled her short gray hair. She remembered Sahira once advising her, "Dye it and you'll look ten years younger." Adiba had asked, "And will I relive those ten years?"

She concentrated on the advertisements. Among them was a poem. She moved her body slightly to get closer to it. She read it and then smiled. She settled back and took a little notebook out of her bag. She wrote:

"The Leader"

I wanna be the leader
I wanna be the leader
Can I be the leader?
Can I? I can?
Promise? Promise?
Yippee I'm the leader
I'm the leader

OK what shall we do?

Um Mohammed asked her,
"Are you all right?"
"It is a nice poem. I like it," Adiba replied.
"What does it say?"
"You know, Um Mohammed, it is difficult to translate, but I shall try. It is called 'The Leader' and it says . . ."
Um Mohammed listened attentively.
Adiba fell silent. Um Mohammed said nothing at first, then asked, "Who wrote it?"
"It's by someone called Roger McGough. His name is written under the poem. I haven't heard of him before. It says he was born in 1937."
"He's old. But he sounds like a child," said Um Mohammed, in surprise.
Adiba didn't reply immediately. She put up her hand to tuck back a wisp of hair that had escaped. She touched something strange. She pulled it out. A leaf. She stared at it in surprise. The wind outside was giving a final warning to the leaves on the trees. The trees abandoned their leaves to autumn, and autumn in turn laid down the burden of leaves and departed. It forsook them and left them behind on the pavement, in the woods, and in the gardens.
The street cleaners worked overtime to sweep up the shriveled, damp leaves. They represented a dangerous hazard to pedestrians when they were wet. In autumn, London's streets were dotted with big green plastic bags full of leaves and twigs from the trees, tied up tightly and put in specially designated places, ready for the rubbish lorries to collect.
Adiba showed the leaf to Um Mohammed.
"You know about such things. What do you think it is?"

Un Mohammed took it from her hand. She put on her spectacles, which hung over her chest, suspended on a black cord. She examined the leaf carefully, tracing its fabric with her fingers.

"It looks like the leaf of a poplar tree."

"You know, Um Mohammed," said Adiba in amazement, "I'm completely ignorant about plants. I only know what I learned parrot-fashion at school. Listen!"

She closed her eyes and recited like a pupil.

"The world of plants is divided into three categories: trees, bushes, and grasses. That's all I know. Just as all I know about motorcars is the following: the car is a metal body mounted on wheels and is powered by an engine. Though they say there are hundreds of different kinds of cars. Perhaps I don't know much about plants because I come from a city. But then why don't I know about cars, which have taken over the city?"

"In my day," Um Mohammed protested, "Baghdad was full of orchards. Houses had beautiful, big gardens. Once, I remember we were invited to the house of a friend of Abu Mohammed's. He was a judge who lived in al-Karada district. He had a huge garden that was like an orchard. There were orange, *narinj*, and apple trees, as well as four palm trees. We had lunch in the shade of a grapevine. It was like paradise. In one part of the garden, they grew damask roses, and the whole garden was full of their scent."

"I know how to tell the difference between a vine leaf and a leaf from an orange tree," Adiba said. "And between a vine leaf and a rose leaf. But when I hear about poplar trees, walnuts, almonds, castor-oil plants, and willows, I get completely muddled. I know we used to grow damask roses. Perhaps we didn't have the same rich variety that you had in Kurdistan."

"I loved the roses we saw when we went to Baghdad," Um Mohammed said. "Each one was different. It had its own special color and shape and scent. You know, Adiba, the roses you find in London, in the houses and gardens, look beautiful, but they don't smell. They're like artificial flowers. They just look like roses.

"Back then—in Baghdad, I mean—I used to say to Abu Mohammed, 'If only we had roses like that.' I've remembered those damask roses ever since because it was the first time I'd seen them. You imagine Baghdad without plants because you lived there. I had the same idea about Sulaimaniya, but Abu Mohammed taught me the importance of nature. He loved trees and green and growing things. He was on the court circuit, but while he was attending the sessions and solving people's problems, he was really looking at the ground and working out what to grow. God have mercy upon him. He wanted to retire, to settle down and relax. He used to say, 'I'm tired, Um Mohammed. I want to have a rest from traveling and meeting people.'"

Her eyes filled with tears as she thought of her husband, and Adiba squeezed her hand sympathetically.

"Um Mohammed, he is resting in peace at last. Do not upset yourself."

"'When he comes on their account, neither will they tarry for an hour, nor become old.' Allah speaks the Truth," said Um Mohammed.

After a couple of minutes, she wiped away the tears rolling down her cheeks and asked Adiba,

"Does Sahira's husband, Kadhim, work?"

"No. He's a retired journalist."

"Retired? Did he take early retirement?"

"No, he's twenty years older than Sahira."

"She's a lovely woman. Such a kindly soul. She reminds me of Fatima, my sister, bless her; my family married her off when she was fifteen, and she's looked the same ever since. She's never aged. Poor Sahira. She seems lost at the moment."

Adiba understood what she meant. Um Mohammed, she thought to herself, how easily you understand what goes on in other people!

"I know. She's got problems at home," Adiba said out loud.

"Who hasn't? Is there anything we can do to help her?"

"I think her problems are personal, and she has to help herself."

"How can she help herself?" Um Mohammed asked. "I've never heard of such a thing before. It's something we've learned in London. If a friend can't help a friend, what's the point of being friends? I would like to help her, but . . . you know, I'm not so close to her . . . I mean. Why don't you ask her? She'll listen to you. I mean, she respects you."

"I'd rather not get involved. Sahira's problems are personal; they concern her husband, children, and health. You know what I am like. If she wants to talk to me, that's fine, but I don't want to get involved without being asked."

Um Mohammed said nothing for a few moments. "Apart from her family, she obviously has a problem with Majda. She's like a thorn in Majda's side, needling her every time she opens her mouth."

Adiba laughed.

"Don't take Sahira lightly. If she'd had her way, she would have strangled Majda long ago. Anyway, Majda has her own quarrel with Sahira."

"Why is that?" asked Um Mohammed.

"Actually, I am not sure. Maybe it's political. Maybe they knew each other in Baghdad."

In spite of herself, Adiba felt tension crawl up her spine. She took a deep breath before continuing. "Um Mohammed, when it comes to friendship . . . I care for you and hold you dear. You are a friend of mine, but I cannot say the same about Sahira and Majda. They are just acquaintances."

"For political reasons as well?"

"For many reasons. They include political and personal differences."

"Sahira's a good person," Um Mohammed persisted. "It wouldn't cost us anything to help her."

Adiba realized that the train had stopped at Camden Town and, leaning on her stick, hurriedly stood up. She said good-bye to Um Mohammed and got off. Um Mohammed remained on the train, on her way to Tottenham Court Road, where she would change to the Central Line for Queensway.

CHAPTER FOUR

As she left the station, Adiba was suddenly overcome with fatigue. Physical exhaustion weighed her down so that she could barely maintain the balance between her right and left feet and her stick. She still hadn't gotten used to her "third foot," despite having depended on it for years.

Her last operation, the fourth, had been a success, although she had lost the movement in her ankle where they had fused the bones so that leg and foot were one. The pain was worse at night; the GP had first prescribed painkillers, and then sent her to an orthopedic surgeon. After examining her, he'd told her that she would have to learn to live with the pain.

"What about the pain in the other leg?" she asked him.

"Because you're walking unevenly," he said, "the nerves in your other leg have become inflamed. In time, this will also affect your back. If you use a stick, it will help ease the pain a bit." He looked at her quietly for a moment. "Luckily, you're the right weight for your age and height," he added. "Otherwise, it would have placed an extra burden on your leg."

He appeared to be in a hurry to leave the consulting room, but stopped at the signs of frustration that were clearly visible on her face. He patted her shoulder consolingly, saying in a friendly manner,

"Mrs. Baghdadi, I agree that it's a tiresome illness, but it's not fatal. The only thing you can do is adapt to it. It's the only way. Put up with it, and adapt to it."

As she limped along the long, labyrinthine corridors of the hospital on her way out, she said to herself: putting up with things and adapting to them. Isn't that the essence of my whole life?

Adiba lived near the Underground station, the bus stop, and the shops. Just minutes away from the station. She still felt indebted to her doctor. She had provided a detailed report urging the housing department to find Adiba a flat that would take into account her physical condition and, in particular, the disability, which despite successive operations, still prevented her from walking for any length of time.

She crossed the road alongside a large group of people who had been waiting for the traffic lights to change. A number of drunks and young beggars with their dogs had elected to lie out on the sidewalk, leaning their backs against the wall of the station and the bank adjoining it. People who weren't familiar with Camden Town might think they'd come upon a demonstration when they emerged from the Underground station. But they would soon realize their mistake. Camden Town was always thronged with people. Every day. It was quite normal. A crowd of youngsters stood outside the station selling, buying, eating, smoking, waiting. In a permanent state of anticipation.

What were they waiting for?

It was tiring for Adiba, edging her way cautiously between the crowds on the narrow sidewalk. But she was used to dragging herself along through streets jammed with people. Without them, the place would lose its particular character.

She went into a little shop that sold a bit of everything—remaindered books, calendars, pens and stationery, candles of all colors and shapes, compact discs, children's toys, bunches of artificial flowers, plastic flowers that never withered. Is it possible to make people who never died, she wondered?

She needed to buy a card. She preferred sending cards to her friends and family rather than writing letters. There was a restricted amount of space on a card. It limited her to the niceties. There was no room for writing screeds. It was also nice for the person receiving the card because it turned an ordinary letter into something special. She wanted a blank card. She didn't want something with "Best Wishes for a Happy Birthday" or "Good Luck on Your Driving Test" or "Good Luck in Your Retirement" or "Happy Valentine's Day."

She looked for a card that she could inscribe herself. She found a small card, decorated with a single rose. Yellow. Blank. She decided to buy it. She walked over to the assistant to pay for it. Twenty pence. Beside the shopkeeper, she noticed a new rack of beautiful designer cards. An unusual card immediately caught her attention. It impressed her. She moved away from the other customers to look at it.

The Painting

A hall divided up into little rooms that were like the cubicles in a department store or the changing rooms at swimming pools. They lay exposed, without doors or curtains to conceal them. Someone sitting on the outside could see what was going on within. In the forefront of the picture, a man sat on a low chair. He was tired and pale, with white hands, their color contrasting sharply with the general shade of blue in the background. He stared fixedly at the open rooms. There were six of them, numbered from 114 on the left to 119 on the right. Each room was a world in itself, cut off from the other worlds on either side:

1. A man stood facing a woman who had her back turned to the outside world, and who was clinging tightly to his arm.

2. A woman stood facing outward with a magazine held up to conceal her face. She was wearing smart clothes and red high heels.

3. A man stood with his back turned, propping himself against the wall of the room with one hand. In the next cubicle stood a woman; she had her back to the wall and was facing forward.

4. A man sat on a sofa in the middle of the painting wearing a hat pulled down over his face. He leaned forward dejectedly and contemplated the palms of his hands.

Their faces were ashen. Were they sick? Or were they mummies or waxwork effigies?

She turned over the card and read: *The Waiting Room*—George Tooker, 1959. She decided to go to the library as soon as possible and find out everything she could about the artist in order to understand the painting.

The painting was too gloomy to send to Iraq. It depressed the viewer. They were depressed enough. Merely glancing at it made you feel sad. Should she buy it for herself? She recalled how the doctor had advised her to avoid things that made her feel sad. She smiled bitterly. She put it back in its place.

To the right of the shop in Inverness Street was a shop that sold vegetables. Here she bought half a kilo of spinach and a single lemon for "*'ashda*," the term she used for the meal that was midway between lunch and supper. She had onions at home in the fridge.

Adiba also chose a long box of dates in which the fruit was arranged neatly in rows, like soldiers awaiting inspection. There was a small plastic fork on top of the box. She thought, have we reached the point where we eat dates with a fork? She counted the fruit. Fifteen in each row. Thirty in all. How many kilos of dates could you buy in Iraq at the moment for the same price? She sighed and told herself off. If I start thinking like this, I'll die of grief.

The box would last several "'ashdas." She smiled at the peculiar linguistic expression. She'd been looking for Arabic words for ages to describe the sequence of meals in Britain. The English had a special word for the snack between breakfast and lunch and the snack between lunch and supper, and she wanted to devise something similar in Arabic to imitate them. She had come up with the expression "al-'ashda"—('asha (supper) + ghada (lunch) = "'ashda"). Her friends used the term regularly now.

Her mother's voice echoed in her ears, "Between sunset and supper God does what he pleases." But she didn't understand why the maxim was relevant.

Adiba searched the small print on the box to find out where the dates came from. She didn't want to commit the mistake she'd made once before and buy produce from Israel. She took her reading glasses out of her handbag. She read the fine print on the box. *Country of origin: Several countries.* She was satisfied. She paid one pound to the shopkeeper, who was waiting patiently while other customers queued behind her. Most things you buy today come from more than one country, she thought. Like the people in London, they come from all over.

She started walking along Camden High Street. She preferred the main road and hated the backstreets, which had no one in them. The crowds of people pressed about her, and she felt as if they were protecting her from the unexpected, from things that only happened in deserted places.

Her friend Michael had once lived in Camden Town. "How can you live there?" he'd asked Adiba. "How can you bear the noise and the crowds and the thousands of tourists who pour into the area on the weekends? I was born there, but I couldn't stand it any longer. We reached a stage where it all became too much for us. My father and I decided to sell the family home and move to an area that was more people-friendly. Camden's changed a lot. I know it's been famous since the sixties as an island for refugees, but the market's grown so big and become so trendy it's more like an Eastern bazaar now. I can't bear it. How do you put up with it?"

She thought, I've adapted to a different country and different people. And the doctor's advised me to put up with my disability and pain. Why shouldn't I put up with Camden? "It's all right during the week," she said neutrally, in a voice from which she had sifted out all traces of mockery. "It's bearable. On the weekends I try to stay at home in the flat, or go out for the whole day."

"It must be really difficult for you, having to live amidst such terrible noise and crowds, when you come from a small, quiet town like Baghdad."

"Michael, Baghdad's not little," she said quietly, looking at him in surprise. "If you'd ever been there, you would know what noise and crowds really mean."

Adiba had gotten to know Michael six years ago, on the same day she'd met Um Mohammed. The immigration bureau at the airport had telephoned and asked her to come and interpret. It happened to be his first day on the job. "A Kurdish family has arrived at the airport seeking asylum," he told her. "A mother and son. Neither of them speaks English." "But I don't speak Kurdish," she protested. Then she quietly explained something that was always causing confusion among people working with refugees. "Kurdish is a completely different language from Arabic. I only speak Arabic." She was surprised when he said just as politely, "I know. But they also speak Arabic. That's why I called you."

She apologized and left for the airport immediately.

Adiba arrived at her flat. It was on the ground floor of a big house that was divided into three apartments. Before her last operation, she had lived on the third floor of a block of flats with no lift. The doctors' report had helped her get a more convenient flat. Her GP and her psychiatrist had written a joint statement about her condition. And she had been given a ground-floor flat.

She opened the street door and bent down to pick up the *Camden New Journal*, the local newspaper. And as she was doing so, Jim and Steve, the twins who lived on the first floor, darted in behind her. "Good evening, Mrs. Bajdadi," they chimed in unison.

She sighed. How many times had she tried to correct their pronunciation and told them it was Baghdadi? It was no use. Their tongues continued to mangle her name.

"Good evening, Jim. Good evening, Steve."

As she entered her flat, she thought how lucky she was that they were still polite and well-mannered. They were not yet teenagers. After that, who knew?

She hung her stick and coat and shawl up behind the door. She didn't need the stick in her flat. It was very small: a bedroom as big as a shoebox and a sitting room with the kitchen opening off of it in the style of a studio. The bathroom and toilet were in one room. The space was calculated in centimeters, though arranged economically. She didn't need her stick, as she could lean on the furniture.

She placed the spinach and box of dates on the counter in the kitchen. She opened the curtains to catch the last minutes of daylight, and tried to ignore the iron bars that were fixed to the windows as protection against burglars, since she was on the ground floor.

Once, when Adiba mentioned the bars, Dr. Hawkins asked her,

"Did you notice them immediately when you walked into the flat for the first time, or did you only become aware of them after you'd moved in?"

"I saw them immediately. The first time the man from the council showed me over the flat."

"What did you feel?"

"I felt stifled. I felt uneasy. Even though I knew they were there to protect me."

"Why stifled?" Dr. Hawkins asked.

"They felt like bars in a prison."

"Prison in general, or a prison in particular?"

Adiba had laughed in spite of herself. She knew where this was leading.

"It must be prison in general because the prison I was in was just a house with ordinary windows."

Television or radio?

She chose to listen to the radio because she wasn't going to sit down now and watch a television program. Television was her companion at night. She sighed, murmuring drearily to herself, "Companions, comrades, comrades of the road. Companions in life. Comrade Mukhlis." Pain took hold of her heart. "Comrade Mukhlis. Where are you, my companion, *rafiqi?*"

She put her hand over her heart. No, she would not allow depression in. There was still some daylight left. She had to get a grip on herself. Stop herself from falling into a well of despair.

She had to get supper ready. She turned on the radio. In addition to the sounds of Jim and Steve racing about on the wooden floor of the flat above, she listened to the five o'clock news. The newsreader said: "The American president Bill Clinton has signed the Iraq Liberation Act, though a new offensive against Iraq is not now expected to take place, since the American president is preoccupied with the Monica Lewinsky scandal and DNA tests on the blue dress."

In a corner of the kitchen attached to the sitting room, Adiba listened to the rest of the news as she started to prepare her supper of spinach with onions and egg.

CHAPTER FIVE

How she hated changing trains! Going from one platform to another along endless underground corridors. Um Mohammed walked slowly, keeping close to the walls, fearful of being swept away by the waves of people hurrying to get out of the station or catch a train. She was pleased when she found herself behind someone who was disabled, a woman with a pushchair, or an elderly person taking his time. She felt safe and out of the way of those in a hurry.

"People in London don't walk like human beings," she told Mohammed. "They're always in a rush, like those drivers of *nefarat* (shared taxis) in Baghdad. Don't they know that only the devil makes haste?"

She walked slowly, weighed down by her heavy body. She clasped her big black handbag to her, pressing it close against the curves of her body. She was never separated from it and took it with her wherever she went. It contained the red wallet that her sister Amina had woven for her from scraps of wool left over from a carpet she had been weaving. In its many pockets (she would not have bought a bag that didn't have copious pockets) were her official papers, four personal photographs, the keys to her flat, and her "humanitarian" travel document.

At a meeting with her lawyer, which took place several months after she and her son had requested political asylum, her interpreter had explained that the Immigration and Nationality Directorate of the Home Office had found they were eligible to receive residence permits and travel documents on humanitarian rather than political grounds.

Um Mohammed protested, "But we didn't have any problems with human beings. The problem was with the politics." Adiba translated her words to the lawyer from the Refugee Council. He smiled and said, "I understand what she's saying. But the categories are quite distinct." He proceeded to explain the law, stating at the end that it wasn't a personal issue with regard to her and her son, but a general matter that affected refugees from every corner of the globe; she shouldn't worry herself about these minor distinctions between humanitarian and political refugees, he said. She wasn't overly concerned about the distinctions and the various types of passports, and she didn't understand what the lawyer was saying when he talked about legislation relating to them in particular, but she was very distressed that their application for asylum was regarded as humanitarian rather than political. She dealt with the adjective in a literal manner.

"Madam Adiba, anyone with eyes can see that we are seeking political asylum," Um Mohammed told her repeatedly.

With great patience, the lawyer went over the distinctions between humanitarian and political refugee status, and the reasons for it, quoting the relevant legal clauses; Adiba's translation was patience itself, but Um Mohammed lost interest in the clarifications and labyrinthine clauses and conventions as they were translated into Arabic. She felt exhausted and as if the discussion that was taking place had nothing to do with her. She wanted the interview to be over as soon as possible. She turned to her son and asked him for his support. Mohammed said nothing. He was as tight-lipped as a statue in a public square. Silence was something new in him, a trait that he had adopted since they had arrived in Britain.

"Do you want to ask him anything else?" Adiba asked him in Arabic.

Mohammed replied that he did not in Kurdish, "Na sbas."

He thanked the lawyer in his few words of English and then got up, ready to leave.

When they arrived home, Um Mohammed chopped onions and cooked their evening meal. It was his favorite, *kubba* made the Kurdish way. She kneaded the meat, rice, and red lentils together. She rolled the mixture into little balls, which she dropped into the boiling lentil soup.

"Mohammed, *ibni*, my son," she said. "Adiba's a good woman and is trying her best to help us. But whenever she asks you something, you reply in Kurdish. How can the woman understand you?"

"It's nothing to do with Adiba. I know . . . I agree that Adiba is kind and considerate. But I've decided not to speak Arabic ever again. Do you understand? It's the least I can do."

"When did you make this decision?" Um Mohammed asked.

"On the day the bloody Arabs destroyed our homes."

As Um Mohammed was pulled along by the stream of passengers from the Underground, she hugged her bag tightly against her, afraid that someone would steal her official papers. These included her gas, electricity, and telephone bills. Adiba had gently pointed out that she didn't need to take all her letters and documents with her whenever she went out. They would be safe in the house and no one would rob her. In fact, it was much

34

more likely that someone would steal her bag, which was as big as a small suitcase, when she was out in the street than if she left it in the house. Um Mohammed replied, "It's not a question of someone stealing them, but . . . we have to be prepared. Who knows when we'll need our papers? We always needed documents or photographs or identity cards in the past when we went to a government office or applied for a document. Or even sent a parcel. How can I leave the house without my nationality certificate?"

"Um Mohammed, I promise you, you don't need a nationality certificate here. No one's going to ask you for it. Especially as it's written in Arabic."

"Who knows?" she persisted quietly. "It's a strange country, and I feel we should be prepared."

At last . . . Um Mohammed lowered her body onto a seat on the Central Line train, which was going to Queensway, where she lived. She drew a deep breath. She would prefer to meet the women somewhere closer. It would make things easier. But they all lived in the north of London, and Hampstead was in the middle. She'd agreed. She had given in to the majority because she wanted to carry on meeting them—Adiba in particular, who had been the one to encourage her to come and get to know the others.

"Um Mohammed, you have to get out a bit and not spend so much time on your own," Adiba told her.

"But I don't. I go to the Kufa Gallery once a week and sit there and watch the people come and go. Sometimes I listen to lectures. It's true, they're all in Arabic, and I don't always understand the poetry, and, as for the long discussions, they can be tiring . . . But I like the atmosphere there and being with people. When I listen to them talking, I remember the past."

"That's one day a week. What about all the other days?"

"I've got medical appointments. Checkups. Hundreds of them. One day it's the doctor examining my stomach, the next it's the nurse measuring my blood pressure. Or someone giving me advice on how to eat less and take more exercise. As if they don't have enough patients to deal with. Can you believe it? They even arranged for me to do an exercise class. The doctor told me, 'You're suffering from two types of illnesses: overweight and high blood pressure. And the best cure for both is exercise.' Two months ago, I started going to the gym. You wait and see;

soon I'll become a weight lifter."

They both laughed.

"Then there are the weekly appointments with the housing department and welfare," Um Mohammed went on. "They're always coming up with something new. Once, the doorbell rang at ten o'clock in the morning. I said to myself, *khair in sha' Allah*; I hope there is nothing wrong. You see, Mohammed had spent the night with his girlfriend. I looked through the peephole in the door and there was this young blonde girl there, as pretty as a picture. I opened the door and smiled at her. She began speaking and waving her hands about, but I couldn't understand a word, as she was speaking English. Finally she ran out of breath. I tried Kurdish, and then Arabic. I thought, if she doesn't speak Kurdish, then perhaps she'll understand Arabic. Finally I took her by the hand and knocked on Um Saleh's door. She's my next-door neighbor. Praise be to Allah, she was at home. Um Saleh told me the girl had come to help me clean and cook and do the shopping. Imagine! I thanked her and told her I didn't need any help. It's my place, and I'll clean it myself. I went on at Mohammed about it until he went back to the council and told them so. I'm sure there's someone else who needs help more than I do. *Al-hamdu lillah*, thank God I'm still strong enough to cook and clean and do the shopping for myself. Well, it's better than doing gymnastics . . . isn't it?

"Sometimes I watch television during the day or in the evening. I love those Arabic soaps; they're really good. Especially the historical ones, which tell stories about Islam and the Companions of the Prophet (prayers and peace be upon Him) and the Believers. And we know some people and have Kurdish friends whom we visit from time to time. Mohammed, Allah has guided him, has gotten engaged to a lovely Irish girl. She's called Mary. May Allah bless them and bring them happiness. Adiba, do you remember how he barely knew a word of English? Now, *ma sha' Allah*, he sings like an English nightingale."

Her son, Mohammed! If only he . . . She sighed, drawing up her body in an effort to prize it out of the warm comfort of the seat. She usually tried to get up at the station before her own so as to be ready to leave the train. She would stand close to the door, ready to get through it before it shut again. She lifted herself a little. She was stuck. She sat back and then prepared to repeat the procedure. This time she succeeded in freeing herself from the magnetic force that held her body transfixed to the seat. She remembered the sharp coldness with which Adiba had responded to her remarks about Sahira and her problems. And thought about Majda and Sahira, and the hatred that coursed between the two of them. Politics! Was there anything worse than politics!

Oh ... A young man hurrying past the people leaving Queensway station pushed her so hard that she almost fell down.

"Um Mohammed ... Um Mohammed."

Once outside the station, she heard someone murmuring her name. The street was always crowded with Arabs. It was an Arab neighborhood. The morning after moving into her council flat, she had gone for a walk to explore the area, but had quickly returned home.

"Are we in London?" she had asked Mohammed in surprise.

There were Arabs everywhere. Arab cafés and restaurants: Damascene, Baghdadi, and Egyptian. Bookshops. Estate agents, stores, bureaux de change, all with signs in front of their shops announcing, We Speak Arabic.

Women in 'abayas, masked ladies from the Gulf, women in long black or gray overcoats with veils covering their heads. Men in see-through dishdashas. Men in yashmaks.

Young men in elegant suits from Armani, Calvin Klein, and Yves Saint Laurent, whose clothes exuded the scent of the most expensive perfumes in the world. They held rosary beads in one hand and in the other a mobile phone that was glued to their ear, like a new organ sprouting from their bodies.

Arabic newspapers and magazines. Opposition newspapers side by side with official ones. 'Aqals and yashmaks. Corded headdresses, veils. The smell of grilled meat and shwarma. Nargileh pipes boldly dominating the cafés. Comfortable chairs packed with people smoking thronged the narrow sidewalks. Vegetables and baklava and bunches of mint, celery, and parsley. Tanour bread. Pita bread. Breadsticks. Unleavened bread with thyme, lahmacun, bread from Lebanon, bread from Iraq.

Different Arab dialects. Voices ringing out. Novelty shops. Smart boutiques. Men telling their wives to hurry up and stop their eternal shopping because their blood pressure's rising and they are going to have a nervous breakdown. Women saying in astonishment, "But we've hardly begun."

Women calling their children: "Ahmed, be reasonable." "Haidar, don't run. It's 'aib. It's naughty. Calm down and don't move." "Zahra, come here. Zahra, sit down beside your father while I try on these bras." A man asking his wife in exasperation, "Do you need all these clothes?"

His wife replying confidently, "Of course I do. Why else would I be trying them on?"

As far as she could remember, Abu Mohammed had never gone shopping with her. Not even once. Even though everyone in the *souk* in Sulaimaniya knew him. He was too busy working to pay attention to matters at home. As a high court judge, he traveled constantly, going back and forth between the cities and towns, and making endless journeys to the provinces.

His work never came to an end. When he got home, their salon was transformed into a holy shrine, where people with problems and differences congregated to plea for an end to their troubles.

Very often she refused to go away with him, using Mohammed's schooling as an excuse, but the truth was that she felt strange and sick away from home. She told him, "Abu Mohammed, solace of my eyes, I'll stay here. Go and do your work, and when you come back, you'll find me waiting for you at home, standing guard over the house."

Her son was more settled now. His love for his fiancée had helped, as had a growing sense of stability and security. In the first months after their arrival in London, he hadn't stayed with her much. He had fled the house and the area, arguing that he felt stifled in a place that was so full of Arabs. He had moved about, from one friend's house to another, saying repeatedly:

"I don't want to see Arabs; I don't want to hear Arabic spoken."

"What can we do, Mohammed? Shall we apply for a transfer?" Um Mohammed had asked.

"That's impossible. They'd never agree. It's a comfortable flat and big enough for both of us. It's in a great location. Everyone envies us. What reason can we give that'll satisfy them? That I can't bear to hear Arabic spoken! They'll grind their teeth and say with their usual coldness, 'That is not a good reason. That's racist.' They won't listen to what I say. It's best if I go away for a while. I can't stand looking at their faces and *dishdashas* and *yashmaks* and the way they sit in the cafés on the sidewalks and shout and laugh. Have you heard them laughing? It's as if the place belongs to them and their fathers own the whole of London."

"Mohammed, *baukum*, my darling, don't get so angry. Be reasonable. We shout just as much when we talk, and we walk along the streets as if they belong to us," she said, trying to calm him down.

"No, we're not like them."

"We are like them. We're from the same place, the same land. We behave in the same way; we talk in the same way. We have the same religion. But because there are fewer of us, we get lost in the London crowds," replied Um Mohammed.

"It's no use talking to you. You always defend them. Even though they killed your husband, destroyed your home, and forced you to emigrate."

"'Be sure, we shall test you with something of fear and hunger and some loss in goods, lives, and fruits, but give glad tidings to those who patiently persevere.' Allah speaks the truth."

Mohammed's anger almost blinded him.

"Oh yes, Allah tested us with fear and hunger and poverty and death!" he shouted furiously. "Allah tested *us*, but what about them? The real criminals and murderers. Why doesn't he test them?"

"I beg Allah for forgiveness . . ."

He didn't give her a chance to complete what she was about to say, but instead rushed furiously out of the flat, slamming the door violently behind him.

He abandoned her, like his father had. Left to herself, she started to cry.

A woman who was standing nearby repeated her greeting.

"Um Mohammed, how are you?"

It was Um Saleh, her Palestinian neighbor. They walked back together to the block of flats in Cavendish Street.

A week after Um Mohammed had met the group of women for the first time, she invited them to dinner. She was the last to join their little circle. She asked, "Which would you prefer—lunch or dinner?" They were sitting in a café near Swiss Cottage Underground station, in northwest London. The owner didn't mind his customers sitting over the same cup of tea or coffee for hours at a time.

"As long as it's Monday, which is my day off," said Iqbal, "I don't mind if it's lunch or dinner. Why don't we adopt Adiba's formula and have *'ashda?*"

On the day they were due to visit her, Um Mohammed climbed up and down the steps of her building four times, with an ease she hadn't felt for ages, as she went back and forth to the nearby supermarket, fetching things she had forgotten. She cooked for them as if she were back home.

They arrived at the same time. They met at Queensway Underground station and then walked to Um Mohammed's flat together, so "we won't get lost," as Sahira put it. "Don't you have an *A to Z*?" Majda sneered. Sahira retorted, "Oh, darling Majda, you know I'm not as sophisticated as you are. I can't read the maps in the *A to Z*."

Adiba inserted herself between them and pointed at a flower shop. "Just a second! I want to buy a plant for Um Mohammed."

They brought with them a box of baklava and biscuits, which they had purchased earlier, and a small plant. As she handed over the African violet, which was in flower, Adiba told Um Mohammed, "We brought you this because you love plants." Um Mohammed asked her how to propagate it, and Adiba read the instructions on a plaque stuck into the soil. "It's very easy. Just cut off a leaf and plant it in the soil, and it will grow by itself."

"Is that all? Glory be to Allah, the One, the Creator!" Um Mohammed said, raising her eyes in pious wonderment.

Sahira gave her a large blue bead, at the center of which was a white eye that in turn encircled a tiny blue eye.

"Is it from Turkey?" Um Mohammed asked in surprise.

"No, I wish it were. I'd love to go to Turkey, but Kadhim has put down his roots in London and refuses to budge. I don't want to go on my own and leave him. No, I got it from a charity shop. I thought you'd like it."

They crowded into the sitting room. It was too small for them. They distributed themselves between the sofa and the chairs. Iqbal sat on a cushion that Um Mohammed insisted on placing on the floor.

"There's not much room. I mean . . . as you know . . . this place is like a station. It's not our real home."

"Um Mohammed, it's not the place that's important, but the company and the food," joked Iqbal. "*Al-hamdu lillah*, the faces are friendly today, which just leaves the food. What are your generous hands going to give us to eat?"

Um Mohammed smiled. She liked Iqbal because she was always cracking jokes and laughing. She began to help her now in the kitchen, serving juice to the others and teasing her. As Iqbal brought in tray after tray from the kitchen and placed them on the table, she proclaimed with a smile,

"Listen, everyone! We have a real feast today. Um Mohammed has cooked everything we've ever longed for but can only have here in her flat in Singland; I mean England."

There was a chicken stuffed with rice, minced meat, onions, and cumin. It sat on a huge bed of saffron yellow rice on which she had scattered fried almonds and currants.

"It's the best chicken in the world," Iqbal announced.

There were dolmas as well. She had stuffed vegetables—onions, aubergines, carrots, courgettes, potatoes, tomatoes, and chard—with rice, meat, and dill. She had put lamb chops and broad beans at the bottom of the pot, and a layer of crossed chard sticks on top, and then covered the whole lot with tamarind juice. She had generously used more minced meat than rice.

"Is the meat *halal*?" Majda asked.

"I only buy *halal* meat," Um Mohammed said.

"I saw a program on television about the Pakistani abattoirs and the way they slaughtered and sold *halal* meat," Iqbal said. "The conditions were so dirty, and as for the germs! It made me prefer *haram*." Then she added, smiling, "But then again, they say that when something is *haram* it tastes sweet, don't they?"

Um Mohammed looked at her as she would a tiresome little girl who was saying something she didn't really mean. Iqbal reminded her of her sister Amina, who, when she had been young, had been a source of joy and merriment to everyone around her.

"We don't really need large quantities of meat at our age," Adiba said. "Once a week is enough."

"Allah wants what is easy for you and not what causes distress," said Um Mohammed. "Though . . . I do like meat."

"This is real food," said Iqbal. "It's nothing like Adiba's, which, if you'll excuse me for saying, is more like the food you get in hospitals or when you're convalescing after a serious operation. Adiba's food, with due respect, is based on the 'three revolutionary nos': no spices, no meat, no taste. Boiled vegetables with boiled rice."

They all laughed.

"'*Ashat yadaik*, Um Mohammed! This is the first time I've had stuffed cucumbers and potatoes. Is it a Sulaimaniya dish?" asked Majda.

Um Mohammed's pretty face glowed so red from her exertions and from pleasure at the praise that was being showered upon her that she looked like a round and red-cheeked Russian doll.

"No, I learned how to make it in Kirkuk. We'd gone to stay at the house of a friend of Abu Mohammed's on the Day of Arafat. And we slept there. On the morning of the first day of 'Aid, his wife gave us dolmas and chicken on rice with almonds and currants. She put the broth from the chicken aside and added chickpeas and vermicelli to it. Then she arranged the chicken breasts and legs on the rice, and left the neck and wings and guts in the broth. She and her daughter must have been up cooking the whole night. You know, it was Abu Mohammed, may Allah have mercy upon him, who taught me how to cook. He loved his food. He used to tell me how he helped his mother at home, especially with the cooking. He washed and peeled the vegetables, and cleaned and sifted the rice and lentils and peas. Every grain needed cleaning, you know. It wasn't like here. It didn't come in bags already cleaned. His mother, Allah have mercy upon her, taught him how to cook dolmas—how to roll vine leaves and stuff vegetables. He could cook better than any woman. When we got married, he taught me how to cook various dishes."

"May Allah have mercy upon him," they murmured quietly, and then set about eating the huge meal.

Several minutes later, Iqbal looked about her at the mouths that were busily chewing.

"Food makes speech redundant. I don't mean any old food, but delicious food like this," she chuckled.

"Do you know what this wonderful meal lacks?" she added after a short silence.

Their eyes were fixed on her as they awaited the answer.

"A good glass of red wine, that's what. It would make me even hungrier. Then I could eat and eat without getting full."

"May Allah come to the aid of our people . . . back home. They have nothing to eat . . ." Majda sighed wearily.

"Majda, don't start preaching," Iqbal snapped. "Um Mohammed has slaved and cooked for a whole day. Let's enjoy the food."

A tense silence settled over the table.

Sahira, who appeared to be concentrating on the aubergine in front of her, quietly began to hum an old song without raising her eyes from the plate:

> Time, just today, let my eyes sleep.
> From morning to night, I cry and weep.
> It was he who brought me misery.

Then, addressing Um Mohammed, Sahira said pointedly: "Um

Mohammed, you see how things don't last. Time has changed and will change us."

Majda's face darkened.

"What do you mean? What are you referring to?" she asked irritably.

"Don't curse time, for it comes from Allah," said Um Mohammed.

"Allah speaks the truth," Sahira quickly interjected.

"Um 'Adil, it's one of the Prophet's sayings, prayers and peace be upon him. It's not from the Qur'an," Um Mohammed reminded her quietly.

A current of tension they were unable to control swirled around the room. Majda forced herself to stay silent. Iqbal withdrew from the gloom to top up her gaiety. She stood up, and turning toward Um Mohammed, raised her glass of juice high into the air, and proclaimed,

"Your health, Um Mohammed. To Kirkuki dolmas and dishes from Sulaimaniya! Oh, it reminds me of something. Um Mohammed, with her kindness and generosity and her lovely food, which could revive the dead . . . it makes me think of an old song my mother used to sing. I don't know if any of you remember it. My mother loved it and was always singing it to us. That's why I remember it. Who sang it? It was some man, but I can't remember his name. He was a famous singer from 'Abdul Karim Qasim's time . . . could be 1959. My mother said he had a shock of white hair and didn't look like a singer. She said he played and sang like a teacher. My mother was in love with him. She used to tell my father, 'If only you had hair like . . .'. Oh, what's his name? It's on the tip of my tongue."

"Are you talking about Ahmed al-Khalil?" Adiba asked.

"Yes, yes! Ahmed al-Khalil. Can anyone remember his songs? Oh God, I've forgotten the words. What do they say? The song's about a Kurd playing a flute and an Arab playing a *rebaba* (Bedouin lute), about mountains and lakes. It's a sweet song. It pulls at the heartstrings. Oh, how can I have forgotten it?"

She sat back on the cushion. She had put her empty plate to one side and now put it back on her lap, forgetting that she'd finished eating. She sat silently, searching the empty plate for the forgotten words.

She tried to remember. For no apparent reason, the words of the old song had taken on an urgent importance. It seemed absolutely necessary to remember and repossess them, to reproduce her mother's beloved voice. The words, locked away in her memory, clamored to be let out. To be spoken. She turned to the others, looking for help. They were silent. The specter of the past appeared. It alienated them from one another. It became painful to talk. They fell silent, seeking distraction in the last morsels of food on their plates.

"My mother was always singing it," Iqbal said resignedly, her eyes fixed on her empty plate. "I don't understand! How can I have forgotten?"

Adiba sat with her head bowed. She made an attempt to spear a few grains of rice and yogurt with her fork. Absentmindedly, she pushed them around the plate she held on her lap. Quietly, sadly, painfully, she told Iqbal,

"Don't upset yourself. We've all forgotten them."

CHAPTER SIX

Her head felt as if it were about to explode with pain. Iqbal sat on her bed in the darkened room trying to remember which day of the week it was. Was it? What . . . ? How would she ever get to work? The pain blinded her. She would never be able to work for eight hours.

At least she hadn't been sick. She congratulated herself on her strong stomach. The only thing she ever suffered from after drinking vast quantities of beer and wine was a murderous headache the following morning.

What day was it? She rubbed her throbbing temples . . . Where did she go yesterday? Gradually it began to come back to her. Sunday evening . . . She'd gone out with Iyad and 'Aida, her colleagues from the office, and John and . . . She heaved a sigh of relief . . . Oh, if yesterday was Sunday, then today . . . must be Monday. Monday. Her day off.

Since there was no longer any need to hurry, she calmed down. She got up very gingerly; any sudden movement exacerbated her headache and made the nerves in her temples throb, as if someone were banging her head with a hammer.

She walked barefoot. She liked the touch of the cold wooden floor on her feet. She opened her bedroom door. The door creaked. She must oil it, she thought to herself. They were still asleep. *Al-hamdu lillah.* She didn't want them to see her like this. She made her way toward the kitchen. She drank a large glass of water. Refilled the tumbler and slunk back to her room with it in her hand.

It was five o'clock. The aftereffects of the wine had woken her up early. She drained the tumbler full of water. If she were a genuine alcoholic, like her father, she would have needed some wine now. A hair of the dog to restore the level of alcohol in her blood.

She caught sight of her reflection in the mirror hanging opposite the bed, and flinched. Face, puffy. Eyes, swollen. Two black rings encircling them, like those of a Chinese panda. Lips, chapped. Skin, dry. Short hair bristling as if she'd just emerged from a catfight.

She thought back. Had she really been involved in a fight last night, or had it been this morning? Who had she been quarreling with? A man, a woman? Had she been on her own or with someone else? When had she gotten home?

45

It had been a nice evening. After work, she and Iyad and 'Aida had gone to the World's End pub in Camden Town, where they had met up with her boyfriend, John. They were celebrating a very special occasion: their disappointment at the pay raise they had been given. The pay raise that they had been looking forward to so impatiently. The manager of the company had announced that it would be only three percent over two years. "It's like a fart in the copper market, lost before you ever get to hear it," someone said.

The proverb lost some of its impact when it was being translated, and no sooner had Iqbal finally remembered the singular of farts and arses than John began to search for a Freudian explanation.

They knocked back pint after pint of beer. 'Aida drank fruit juice. John brought up the rear. Cautiously pleading that he had to drive.

They raised their glasses. Cheers! Cheers! Cheers! They were experts in proposing toasts. They drank the first pint to failure. The second to the long wait. The third to the way they had been misled over the raise. (Three percent over two years, not one and a half percent a year.) They drank the last pint to each other. Iyad, the Palestinian, 'Aida from Syria, and Iqbal from Iraq. Fugitives from the Arab world, they had ended up working for an Arab company in Britain, as there was nothing else to do.

That evening they swigged and gobbled up the entire raise they had received, converting it into alcoholic units measured out in pints of beer, and packets of roasted peanuts and crisps. Iqbal knocked back four pints of real ale, the true English beer.

"How can you drink that stuff?" Iyad asked in disapproval. "It's warm and bitter. I like lager much better because it's cold and refreshing."

"This is proper beer. Because it's warm and bitter, it stimulates your sense of taste and revives it. I like the way it tastes. Chilled lager paralyzes your taste buds and only loosens your tongue."

Iyad didn't bother with what Iqbal was saying, because he knew what she was like when she had been drinking. She became long-winded and stubborn, doggedly sticking to whatever argument she was making. Along with the beer, they consumed packets of salt and vinegar crisps.

"Drinking is part of an odd equation," John said. "When you eat something salty, it makes you thirsty, so you have a drink of beer; but the beer makes you want something salty, which, in turn, makes you thirsty. You see, it's a perfect circle."

Iqbal teasingly raised her glass.

"To John! Creator of *djadjik* salad."

They embarked on a discussion about working in London, residence permits, and the Arab press; they heaped abuse on the leaders and heads of government in the Arab world. And then, for some reason, they became engrossed in a long and bitter argument about the difference between celery and parsley and what they were called in English, and the difference between parsley and coriander and the "celery" that was sold in British shops.

John wanted to steer the conversation away from celery and on to a discussion about how he felt betrayed by Blair and the politics of New Labour, but, as the debate over vegetables intensified, he realized that it would be futile to try such a thing. John picked up bits of the conversation that were in English, including the distinction between parsley and coriander, and the existence of an Iraqi poet, whose name Iqbal couldn't remember, but who she insisted had written a sonnet that began or ended with the poet presenting his beloved with a bunch of synthetic celery. She swore she would look into the matter, and supply them with the name of the poet and his poem the next time they had a drink.

It was a nice evening. Noisy. They laughed at themselves and their disappointment. When the pub shut at half past eleven, they stood irresolutely on the sidewalk outside, about to go their separate ways. They were overcome with a sense that the evening was not yet over; they still had plenty of time in which to enjoy the splendid state they were in. They looked at each other hesitantly. John suggested going to his flat for a drink. He hoped to tempt Iqbal in particular.

"I've got an excellent bottle of vintage wine that a girl friend of mine brought from Germany."

Iqbal was at her most intoxicated—at that moment when caution and fear evaporate and psychological taboos come crashing down, a single munificent moment in which joy and levity, courage and beauty climax.

"I don't like white wine," she said coquettishly.

"Who said it was white?"

"The best German wines are white."

"This bottle's from Spain. It's eleven years old and no one has anything like it."

"Where is she?" Iqbal asked.

"Do you mean the friend, or the bottle?"

"Both of them."

"The friend's gone back to Germany, and the bottle's hidden in my flat."

"Let's go to your flat and try and find out where it is, then," she said, continuing to flirt with him.

On the way to the flat, Iyad said that he didn't like wine and that since he had started out drinking beer, he shouldn't mix the two, but should drink beer or whisky instead. However, it was difficult to satisfy him, as most of the off-licenses were closed because it was so late.

After a long and exhausting search, Iyad finally bought a bottle of whisky from an Indian shop that had a late license. He hugged the bottle to himself as he sat in the backseat of the car beside 'Aida.

"Bastard," he said. "He charged me double. Can you believe it? He made me pay twice what the bottle's worth."

"That's what you pay for buying late at night," said John.

"Indian shops are always expensive, even during the day. Everything is past its sell-by date. They're all swindlers."

"Don't be too harsh on them," John said quietly. "Their shops are open at all hours, even at night, when it is dangerous. They work harder than many other people."

"Who's forcing them to work like that? It's their choice. They keep their shops open twenty-four hours a day so they can profit twenty-four hours a day. God, if it were up to me . . ."

Iqbal turned around from where she was sitting in the front and jeered in Arabic,

"So, His Excellency, President Iyad, may God preserve him, is going to round them up and chuck them out of the country, is he? The refugee menacing the immigrants? Thank God you're not in charge. You're as free as they are. If you're not happy with the situation, then put your freedom into practice. Don't buy anything from them and give the rest of us a bit of peace."

"I really must learn Arabic so that I can enjoy such wonderful conversations," John said, reminding them that he was there.

Iyad relapsed into silence, still smarting. He was grateful to Iqbal for switching into Arabic so as to avoid rebuking him in front of John. Deep down he felt that she was right, but he still had to get the better of his anger. Drink magnifies things and makes people exaggerate their feelings and reactions.

Once they had arrived at John's flat, their desire to continue the evening waned. They gradually came back down to earth. The atmosphere lost its frivolity and sparkle. They gloomily remembered how far the flat was from their own homes.

"John, your flat's at the end of the world," Iqbal complained. "How are we going to get home?"

"I've got enough extra mattresses and blankets. Don't worry."

'Aida protested that she had to go to work the next day, and Iqbal said that she could only sleep in her own bed.

"Let's stay awake till morning," John teased her. "Tell me one of your delightful stories and I will be your willing slave."

She didn't answer. She felt tired. The effects of the drinks were beginning to wear off. The warm glow she usually felt when she was very drunk had vanished, and with it her expansive conversation, gestures, and jokes.

"Where's the wine?" she demanded petulantly, attempting to regain her earlier mood, and bring back the brightly colored bird of joy.

"You said you would find it by yourself," John reminded her.

"For heaven's sake, John," she snapped, unable to stop herself. "That was an hour and a half ago, before Iyad set out to find his whisky and we had a discussion about the role of Indians in the British economy. Fetch the drink and let's bring the evening to an end."

He did what she asked. He didn't remind her that it was she who had quarreled with Iyad and not him. That was what she liked about him. When he saw she was in a bad mood, he treated her normally and let her fit of temper pass. With nothing to provoke her, she calmed down. He also respected her wish to keep their relationship a secret, and so he kept quiet about it and contented himself with treating her as a friend.

"How are we going to get back?" 'Aida asked.

"If you're going by train, you should leave now, or you can stay with us and we'll share a taxi," Iqbal said.

'Aida was forced to stay. She watched Iqbal, who had recovered some of her exuberance, take a cassette of Arabic songs out of her handbag. She told John that the songs were by an Egyptian singer called Amr Diab. He pronounced it Emroo. Iqbal laughed and drew him into the center of the room and began to dance. As she moved in time to the music, she sang along with the song, which she had learned by heart.

Iqbal turned up the sound, but John surreptitiously lowered it again to avoid disturbing the neighbors. It was lucky, he thought to himself, that the flat on the ground floor was empty. If it were not for that, the police would have been there by now, banging on his door because of the complaints they'd received about Iqbal dancing the *dibke* on the wooden floor.

"Come on, come on. Dancing is the nicest thing in the world," she said, when she realized he'd stopped.

"I know, but I'm feeling hungry. Who wants a cheese and cucumber or a tuna mayonnaise sandwich?" he asked everyone.

Iqbal turned down the offer. She said she preferred drinking to eating.

Iyad asked for a tuna mayonnaise sandwich, while 'Aida continued to ramble on about getting home.

"It's late. I've got to go to work tomorrow."

"Go on, then," Iqbal interrupted her.

"I can't. It's one o'clock. The Underground's stopped and I don't want to take a minicab on my own."

"Then sit down and wait, and don't spoil the evening for the rest of us."

"Don't talk to me like that," 'Aida exploded unexpectedly. "We're not children whom you can tell what to do. You're so self-centered. The only thing you're interested in is not having your precious atmosphere spoiled. The rule, Miss Iqbal, is that as we came together, we leave together."

"What rule? I've been clear from the start. I said I wanted to stay, and you agreed that we would leave together. And now here you are, whining like a baby, and going on and on about how you have to go to work."

Furiously, Iqbal spun around to the music player and angrily took out the cassette. As she thrust it into her pocket, she said to John,

"Would you be so kind as to call a cab immediately so that we can take Madam 'Aida home?"

Why had she gotten so angry?

What was it that had so inflamed her and made her act in such a hostile manner toward 'Aida? The poor woman hadn't done anything. She was right to be worried about getting home. This was the thousandth time she had ended up asking for forgiveness after sobering up and coming to her senses.

It had been a big mistake going to John's with Iyad and 'Aida. She should have ended the evening after leaving the pub and kept her relationship with her work colleagues professional. How could she have forgotten she worked in an office with other Arabs and their gossip, which might affect her reputation and her job?

Would she be so concerned about reputation and good conduct were it not for work?

In the future she really must ... She massaged her aching head, berating herself in a low voice for being such a "stupid idiot." How childishly she'd behaved. How stupidly! What should she do? Apologize to 'Aida tomorrow or pretend nothing had happened? She decided the latter proposition was a better idea, as it would protect her from 'Aida's sense of superiority, which she might use against her. Apologies sometimes had the opposite effect from the one intended, drawing attention to mistakes that had been forgotten, and causing more harm than good.

No more going out with her work colleagues and John, she decided.

Abu Samah, the office manager, was a good, pious man who allowed her to be late from time to time; he sympathized with her circumstances and didn't object to changing her hours when something came up with her son. He was an understanding man, but he wouldn't be so forgiving of her if he heard that she went out drinking and partying and was having what he would see as an illicit relationship with an English man. Hadn't he dismissed Fadil, the best translator he had, after Fadil had had half a pint on his lunch break and Abu Samah had smelled the beer on his breath?

She needed the salary. She couldn't risk losing her job now, whatever her differences with the manager.

Samer was still asleep. Sahira had started moving about in the sitting room. She could hear her mumbling to herself. Iqbal laughed. Sahira must have bumped into the bits of furniture and planks of wood piled up in there. She was planning to put some shelves up near the ceiling in the sitting room. They would do for her books and Samer's toys, which seemed to multiply like rabbits. This way, she'd be able to get rid of the relatively large bookcase and increase the amount of space in the room.

The flat, with its two bedrooms, sitting room, separate kitchen, bathroom and toilet, was becoming too small and felt as though it were shrinking around her. It was on the third floor of a well-kept building. The window in the sitting room looked out onto a large garden. When she first visited the building, in summer, she hadn't seen the garden properly, as it had been screened by the dense foliage of the tall trees. But she could see it clearly now that it was autumn, and the leaves had fallen again.

She was lucky. She'd bought it cheaply when they were selling off council flats. She had been living in it for two years and bought it for a third of the real price. But she was tied by the mortgage, and had to hold on to her job, keep healthy, and budget carefully if she was to maintain her present life.

The flat had gotten smaller as Samer had grown. His interests had developed and his games and books had crept out of his bedroom into the sitting room. She had managed to check their advance, refusing to allow them into her room. "This is my special kingdom, and you are not allowed to occupy any part of it," she had told him. She'd put their bicycles into the corridor. Had Sahira tripped over one of them? Suppose she'd hurt herself? Perhaps she'd refuse to help her with Samer in the future.

Sahira and Samer. Sin and Alif and Ra—S, A, and R. They shared the same letters in their names. She left her room to go to the bathroom. She could hear Sahira singing while she made her bed:

> I've come asking you to come back
> With your face bright as a golden lira.
> I've come asking you, from wherever you are,
> Since to me you're worth both the banks of Umara.

How nice it was not to go to work. No need to hurry, or run from the clock ticking in her head. The hours of the day vanished in front of her. Today was Monday. Her day off. A day in which she could hug the minutes to herself and stop them from moving.

In the bathroom, despite the headache, she attempted to emulate Sahira's style of singing and devise a melody that would combine Samer's and Sahira's names. How many pints had she drunk last night?

> Oh Sa . . . hira, oh Sahira!
> Sahira . . . Samer . . . Sahira
> What sweetness, sweetness, and sweetness
> Oh moon, greet our missed ones.

She almost bumped into Sahira at the door to the bathroom.

"Good morning, Sahira."

"Good morning. I'll call Samer. It's eight o'clock."

"Oh, is it? Of course. I've forgotten. I was thinking he had a day off like me."

"Samer!" Iqbal yelled. "It's eight o'clock. You'll be late."

She devoted herself to looking after him. For the next thirty minutes, she fussed around him, urging him on, prodding him to get a move on, while he played and dawdled and pretended to be tired. He wanted to take advantage of her being at home.

Usually, she left the flat at eight o'clock precisely. She woke him up before going out. Put breakfast on the table and his lunch in his lunch box. Before departing, she made sure he was up and hadn't gone back to sleep, so that he wouldn't be late for school.

At a parents' evening she had once attended, his teacher, Miss Robinson, had told her that his schoolwork was well above average, but that he talked a lot in class and was often late for school.

"Are there any problems at home?" Miss Robinson asked her.

She almost burst out laughing. Problems at home? Just at home? Or at work? In the country? The world?

"Just the usual problems," she said in a neutral voice, biting back her sarcasm. "Like all working mothers, I don't see enough of him, and I feel guilty because I don't look after him properly. But what can I do? As you know, we have to work to live."

The young teacher looked at her understandingly.

"I know what you mean."

"The most important thing, as you've said, is that he behave himself and that he keep up with his studies."

"Of course. There's no doubt about that. Samer's a popular boy with his friends and the teachers. He's clever and industrious. But there are two things that worry me. First of all, he chats so much in class, which means that he doesn't follow the lesson, and this can have an effect on the other pupils. If we could help him tackle this problem, he would do much better. The other issue is his tardiness."

"Don't worry, I'll fix the problem."

Miss Robinson considered her for a moment.

"How is your family in Iraq?" she asked gently. "Samer told me that your family is still there?"

"As well as can be expected in the circumstances. I think their plight is even worse now. In the past, they were just fighting against a dictatorial regime; now they have to fight against the regime and hunger as well."

"Because of the sanctions?"

"Yes."

"I read a long article in *The Guardian* about Saddam's regime. The problem is that Blair's government's policy on Iraq is no different from that of the Conservatives. I'm a member of a peace group. Please let me know if you're organizing any action against the sanctions."

At the door to the flat, Samer put on an impressive theatrical performance for Iqbal and Sahira. He clung to his mother's neck and kissed every inch of her face as if saying an eternal farewell to her, so that her eyes filled with tears. She pushed him away from her, though it hurt her to do so, and propelled him gently out of the flat, telling him to hurry and not . . .

After he'd gone, they sat down to breakfast. Tea with slices of toast and butter and marmalade.

"My mother used to make jam from watermelon rind," Sahira began. "I remember how, back home, we used tools and equipment that were begging to be thrown away. I think we in the third world are the ones who invented environmentalism. Imagine, we even made jam out of peel and ate it!"

"Is it because we were worried about the environment or because we were poor? In this country, they throw away gadgets and machines without bothering to repair them because they're so well-off. They chuck out clothes that are completely new and haven't been worn even once. And as for furniture! Look at this cupboard! I came across it outside a house in Kentish Town. Samer and I collected it in the car, and we've cleaned and polished it till it looks as good as new."

"Dear Iqbal, 'ashat yadaik, I really thought it was new."

She poured out another cup of tea.

"What about Samer, may Allah protect him? Does he help you at home?" Sahira asked.

"Sometimes. It depends on what mood he's in."

"How's he doing at school?"

"So-so. The problem is I don't have enough time to help him," she sighed heavily, adding, "Bringing up children in exile, on your own, is so difficult."

"That's true. But it keeps you busy and stops you from feeling lonely. It gives you a purpose in life, doesn't it?"

"I wish I could spend more time with him . . . but what can we do? Allah ghalib, as our Algerian brothers say."

"Have you lived in Algeria?"

"No, I visited Oran once on business. When we had a travel budget and our wretched office was a proper news agency."

"What do you mean? Majda said you work for a news agency!"

"That's what it's called, yes, but in fact it's nothing more than a glorified press-cutting service—what foreign newspapers write about the country.

We subscribe to English and Arab newspapers from all over the world. Every morning we divide them up among ourselves and mark up those articles that are of particular relevance. We cut them out, date them, copy them, and then arrange them in book form according to subject."

"Do you take the opposition newspapers?"

"We take every single newspaper and magazine there is, the pro-government ones and the opposition ones." Iqbal laughed. "In fact, opposition newspapers are more important than the official press. We have to create a balance between friendly and hostile sources, as we're trying to give a complete picture."

"Your work sounds enjoyable ... reading all those papers. You know, Kadhim reads a lot. He likes newspapers, especially, but I prefer television."

"It's interesting, but tiring at the same time. It would be nice to study the newspapers properly, but, actually, we barely have time to read them. We don't read them so much as scan the headlines and first paragraph of each article. It's tiring. We're cooped up in a little office, eight hours a day. Everyone says 'God bless you' when you sneeze and 'get well soon' when you cough.

"They listen to every word you say when you make a personal phone call, and offer all sorts of advice; everyone knows everyone else's problems. Then there are the long hours. I leave the house at eight, and, if things go well, I get back at six. It drives me crazy having to leave Samer all alone in the house after school."

"They say there are after-school clubs."

"I know. Samer was enrolled in one nearby, but the council closed it as part of a cost-cutting exercise, though they kept the center for younger children open. I had to give him a key to the flat so that he could let himself in. I go crazy waiting for him to phone me when he gets back home. Then I sigh with relief and say, 'That's another day gone by without mishap.'"

"When my children were small, I didn't have such problems, you see. I didn't go out to work and Kadhim worked at home. He used to write for a couple of newspapers. Iqbal, 'aini. May Allah help you! Life's difficult enough without being a young woman on her own with a child. Does Abu Samer help you? With money?" she added, looking around.

"Abu Samer lives in Moscow now. He hasn't left the city since he was sent there by the party. He phones us once a week, to make sure we're all right and to let us know he's well."

"Is this a new kind of father? A telephone father?"

Iqbal laughed, attempting to change the course of the conversation, which was slipping into dangerous waters.

"They're better than Internet fathers. At least Samer speaks to him and hears his voice."

"Frankly, I don't blame Hussein for the stand he's adopted," she added seriously. "He's never seen Samer. I left him and came to London when I was pregnant. I'm the one who made the decision, and now I have to bear the responsibility."

"What does Samer say about it all?"

Iqbal pretended to be busy preparing another pot of tea. Sahira's questions saddened her. They laid bare a wound that had still not healed completely. Why did Sahira have to pry into things that didn't concern her? When would she learn to respect other people's boundaries? If it were anyone else, she would have snapped at her by now and put a stop to the questions then and there, but Sahira was her guest and she was in her debt. Who knew when she might need her in the future? She was in a quandary. When it came to finding someone to look after Samer, she didn't have much choice.

"I've already told you," she replied, keeping her voice politely neutral. "Samer has never known his father. I mean, Samer didn't go through the pain of separation that children of divorced parents usually go through. I've brought him up by myself, and he's always understood that I am his mother and father, his entire family."

Sahira listened sadly.

"*Khatia*! That's a shame," she said.

Iqbal stood up, putting an end to the interrogation. She began to clean up. Sahira helped her clear the table and wash the dishes. She doesn't seem to want to go back home to her husband, Iqbal thought.

"What are your plans for today?" she asked her.

"Nothing much. Kadhim's staying at home. He's got one of his old friends visiting. He's doing a series of recorded interviews about Kadhim's life. Kadhim wants to publish them as a memoir. His friend has persuaded him to do so. He's told him that everyone else has—I mean, all the people who were in politics at the same time as he was. Kadhim's name has appeared in more than one of them apparently. His friend says that he should make his opinion and position clear about certain events. It isn't right to stay silent. You know, Iqbal, Kadhim was one of the most important people in the party. I've heard some people say he was the party."

She sighed wearily.

"Those days when the party was the party! You won't remember those days because you were too young. We left before al-Dharba in 1979, when Saddam put an end to the government of national unity . . . If Kadhim had wanted to, he could have held on to his official position. But he decided to leave the party so that he could follow his own ideas and do political analysis. Iqbal, *'aini*, I'll let you in on a little secret. If Kadhim does write his autobiography and gets it published, it will cause a huge stir. It'll contain secret material that's never been published before and details about the national front . . . you know."

Iqbal was forced to interrupt her.

"Sahira, I'm sorry, but I asked you what your plans were because I have a doctor's appointment at midday."

"Oh! In that case, I'll go to Kilburn. I'll wander around the shops."

Then she realized what Iqbal had just said about having an appointment with the doctor.

"Is everything all right?"

"I've got a pain low down in my tummy and a bit of a backache."

"Perhaps it's indigestion."

"No, no! I don't suffer from indigestion."

"Maybe it's an infection."

"You mean in the womb? No, I don't think so. I know what the symptoms are. Everything seems normal. Apart from the pain itself. Perhaps it's because my periods are irregular. Anyway, I want to make sure."

"Iqbal, how old are you?"

She pretended to look serious.

"A month, two weeks, and four days older than twenty-one. Talking about age, perhaps the pain's got something to do with changing the pill," she added, laughing.

Sahira looked away. The reference to the pill had taken her by surprise. Majda's hints about Iqbal were true, then. She'd heard her mention that Iqbal had had a relationship with an Arab, and more recently with an English man, but had refused to believe her. She had sprung to Iqbal's defense as fiercely as if she were defending her own daughter, Nahid. Majda had sneered, which had provoked her more than the words themselves. Um Mohammed had intervened, seeking protection from the evil Satan and asking for protection and forgiveness for all.

She stood up. Majda's dirty slander was true, then.

"I'll go now so you won't be late for your appointment," she said. "And, *'aini* Iqbal, if you need any help, give me a ring. Looking after Samer is no problem. He's a sweet and clever boy, and I really like him. He reminds me of my children when they were his age."

CHAPTER SEVEN

If she was going to Kilburn, then she should buy a bus pass, Sahira concluded. It would be cheaper than buying a day ticket and much cheaper than buying a travel card. She sighed. She'd be much better off when she reached sixty. Then, she'd be entitled to free transport all over London. Like Um Mohammed.

What about Adiba? she wondered. Did she have a free travel pass? She couldn't be sixty yet. But she'd noticed her showing the bus conductor a special ticket. How old was she? Late forties, fifty? Younger than she was, older?

Adiba acted as if she were older than the rest of them. She was quiet, composed. She didn't gossip. As for her age . . . Sahira didn't know. She was slim. It was difficult to guess someone's age when they were thin. She had been slim once. When she'd married Kadhim, the other women had been jealous of her tiny waist and beautiful body. And now, she bought size eighteen clothes; though, if she was asked what size she was, she said size sixteen, feeling embarrassed.

Walk or take the bus? Decisions . . . decisions. It's time to make up your mind, Sahira, she said to herself. If she walked, she'd get tired. It was some way off. It would take her half an hour to get from Iqbal's flat in Cricklewood to Kilburn station, and a quarter of an hour from the station to the shops in Kilburn High Road. She made the decision. It would be better to catch the bus, and walk once she was there.

"Walking's good for you," the doctor told her, when she had gone to see him.

"Walking is the best form of exercise, and remember, it's free. It won't cost you a huge fortune to get rid of your excess pounds, and at the same time, you'll be improving your overall state of health."

"Thank you, doctor," she shrugged unenthusiastically at his comments. "But I lack the willpower. Where can I get the willpower?"

He placed the prescription he had written out to one side and looked at her with concern.

"Mrs. Zubeidi, you're still young, and let me say that you are still a pretty woman. So pull yourself together, pull your socks up, and look after yourself. Otherwise, Mr. Zubeidi will find himself another wife," he added jokingly.

If only Allah would hear you, she thought to herself now. If only you could make something happen just by saying it. Let's see who would be prepared to live with him!

Did she need anything in Kilburn? No. It was a means of passing the time. Pushing it away. She had been counting on spending half the day with Iqbal, not leaving at ten o'clock. Having a nice time with her, killing time. She smiled. Her smile broadened. She chuckled out loud at the literal translation of the English phrase into Arabic and its reverse. She found such phrases funnier and more amusing than jokes.

One day, Adiba had noticed her amusement at the differences in translation and since then had taken to passing examples on to her.

Sahira liked the doctor's phrase about pulling her socks up. She guessed its meaning and repeated it to herself. And here she was now. She'd "pulled her socks up" and was preparing to "kill time," as the English said. She'd be "getting rid" of it. Her laughter vanished. She sadly recalled what had happened when she told Kadhim the joke.

"Is it time we get rid of our lives?" he said.

What life? She stared at her reflection in the window of the bus. She saw a fat woman of forty-six. "You're not fat but you're overweight," the doctor told her politely. That was the difference between the English and the Arabs. The Arabs would say to your face, "You're fat" or "You're short and ugly," but the English would say, "You're overweight." If they were put on the spot, they'd content themselves by saying something like, "Well, let's say that you're different . . . You're attractive."

From the dark confines of her memory, she dredged up a forgotten image. Herself and some other girls from year three eagerly, gleefully chasing one of their classmates across the school playground, chanting in their high-pitched voices: "Samina . . . samina . . . dabba . . . samina . . . dabba . . . hamisa . . . Fat . . . ty, fat . . . ty, roly . . . poly." Poor kid!

How lucky we are, she thought. We live in a country where people don't look at each other and hassle them and find fault with what they look like. Now, what was that fat girl called?

She touched her hair. She had fine hair, too fine perhaps, pressed close to her scalp. Recently, though, she'd noticed that it had started to fall out more than usual.

When she had asked her hairdresser what was wrong, the Iranian woman first gave her a long lecture on the correct way of looking after her hair, and then asked,

"Do you use the right kind of shampoo?"

"Yes."

"Do you wash it properly and rinse it well?"

"Yes."

"Then it must be your diet. Are you eating enough fruits and vegetables?"

She could feel herself getting irritated. She kept a grip on herself and managed a yes, but decided that this was the last time she would visit this salon/clinic.

The hairdresser didn't give up. She was silent for a moment, and then announced triumphantly, "It must be hormonal."

Sahira sighed. Hormones were the latest fad. She had been plagued by her size, but now it was hormones. Stupid hormones!

Last Thursday evening she had decided that what she desperately needed to dispel the cloud of depression and sadness that was hanging over her was a fresh look. She told herself to follow the doctor's advice and take care of herself. The roots of her hair were beginning to lose their color and the dye was fading elsewhere as well. How many different shades could she see? Three, four! And those were just the colors that were visible at the front. God knows what it looked like at the back.

She soaked some henna that she had bought from an Indian shop in Southall. She added some coffee and drops of lemon juice. Two hours later she applied it to her hair, combing each lock through separately. The following morning she washed and styled it.

"What do you think?" she asked Kadhim.

"Are you going out in the street like that?" he asked irritably.

It had been different from other mornings.

Her mornings were usually gray. Routinely dominated by scraps of bad news of one kind or another. She might hear from one of her sons, who lived elsewhere in Britain, or from what remained of her family in Iraq. Sometimes a misunderstanding flared up between Kadhim and herself, an instance of rancor, an outbreak of bickering. They always made up, to preserve their sanity, accepting that their relationship would continue, though time gnawed at it from within. They each kept to their particular part of the house. Kadhim read or pretended to write, while Sahira invented tasks outside the house that required her immediate attention. She left him alone, returning a couple of hours later with bags full of shopping that she didn't need.

But Friday had been worse than these other mornings. She had been exhausted when she got out of bed, angry with herself and with the world. She hadn't slept well. She had wrapped her head in a plastic bag the night before and tied a piece of cotton cloth around it before going to bed.

Every time she turned over during the night, the bag rustled as the henna dried inside. Finally, at dawn, against her will, her heavy body fell asleep, and she had a nightmare that the family home in Baghdad had burned down.

She got up, the dream weighing heavily upon her, making her head buzz with a sound that was louder than the rustling caused by the granules of dried henna. She wanted to talk about it, to shake it off. But there was no one to talk to.

Kadhim had been awake since five o'clock, walking about the house, enveloped in his own bad dreams.

There was silence while they ate breakfast in the kitchen. They avoided looking at each other. Sahira glanced out at the neglected garden through the glass kitchen door. It reminded her of herself.

At the start, Kadhim had been so enthusiastic about tending the garden, digging, planting, weeding, and pruning; he put in bulbs, rose cuttings, and vines, but, bit by bit, he had neglected it. Harmful weeds sprouted and gobbled up the plants. She pointed it out to him several times. She reminded him of all the effort he had put into it. But he had lost interest. He neglected the garden, he neglected her, and he neglected himself.

He sat opposite her in his white *dishdasha*, turning over the pages of an Arab newspaper. He had on a pair of glasses; one of the arms was broken and he had fixed it up with Sellotape. His face was dotted with tufts of cotton wool where he had cut himself with his razor blade, and there were patches of bristles he had missed while shaving.

The telephone rang. She rushed to answer it, desperate to speak to someone. It was her daughter, Nahid, phoning from Cardiff to say that she would not be coming home that weekend. She said she had an important assignment that had to be handed in on Monday, and that if she came up to London, she wouldn't finish it in time. She would try to come the following week. But she would call them again to tell them definitely. The conversation ended abruptly because she had no more ten-pence pieces left for the pay phone.

Sahira's spirits sank even further. She had been looking forward to

Nahid's visit. Her sons were far away. 'Adil, the engineer, was settled in Scotland. He only came to see them twice a year, saying it was too far and he had too much work to do. Shakir was a junior doctor in a hospital in Surrey, near London, but his grueling hours made it virtually impossible for him to visit them on a regular basis.

Was it really work that kept the boys away, or did they use it as an excuse to escape from the family and from Kadhim's overbearing personality and depression, his neglect of their mother and his frustration at himself and his sons?

And Nahid! She could have finished her studies in London. She had been accepted by two excellent universities, but she chose Cardiff instead, which was far away from home and from her mother. To begin with, she had visited them regularly, every two weeks, but as time passed, her visits became less frequent. She would say she was coming, and then phone to apologize. Hurriedly, quickly. Nahid did everything in a hurry. In haste. Her mother was unable to keep pace with her. Her father doted on her from a distance.

She hadn't seen Nahid for two months. In spite of their differences, and the occasional arguments, Sahira yearned for the noise and bustle Nahid brought with her: the loud music, the sarcasm, and the way she imitated others for her own amusement. She longed to have the family around her, to have youth and change—to have life.

She resentfully returned to her chair.

"Nahid has to study and won't be coming," she said, hoping to drag some words out of Kadhim.

"I heard."

Then he stood up. He left everything on the table, just as it was: the plate he had used for breakfast, the empty *istikana*, the tea glass, the bread crumbs, the milk bottle without its top, the butter, with the lid off and thrown down beside it, and the knife, smeared with traces of grease, sitting on top of the butter. He picked up his newspaper and headed for the sink. He placed the folded newspaper under his arm. Then he rinsed his hands under the water, gargled, and spat in the sink. She looked away so she wouldn't have to see him or hear the disgusting noise. There was no point in admonishing him. It would only provoke a quarrel that neither of them needed.

Yawning, she rose and began to clear the table. As she put the things back in their places, she sang to herself:

Where are you going, where to?
What of our pledge?
Night and day, my eyes weep for you.
Where are you going, where to?

Cease tormenting my soul,
It isn't to blame.
After all that comfort and care
You cast her in shame.
Where are you going, where to?

She washed the plates slowly, dawdling over the teacups, spoons, and knives. The song soothed her. As she sang, she gazed at the garden through the window. She finished washing up and opened the door of the fridge, musing on the contents.

What should she cook? Stuffed aubergines, or okra with rice? There was no point in asking Kadhim, because he no longer cared what he ate. The Kadhim who used to love choosing his food, and was forever praising its infinite variety, now ate anything she put in front of him. Should she clean the house? There was no need. Her head itched. She raised her hand to her hair and felt the cloth. She remembered the henna and went to the bathroom.

As she passed through the sitting room, she heard the presenter mentioning Iraq. She went to the radio to concentrate on the news.

The newsreader was saying, "Iraq is threatening to expel the UN inspectors, and the United States and Britain are warning that they will take action against Iraq if it does not comply with the UN resolution . . ." Then he gave further details that she couldn't understand, though she caught references to the oil-for-food program and Iraq being a danger to the rest of the world and several mentions of Clinton.

Threats and menace, she thought. That's everything that our great leader, may God save him, is capable of. He threatens, he creates a crisis, then he retreats.

Every retreat caused more damage. It was like the Arab war to free Palestine. In the beginning, they were going to liberate Palestine, but now, they'd forgotten about Palestine and were calling for the liberation of occupied Arab territory instead. And what did the people do? They sang and danced for His Excellency, the President, chanting their support for his victories and achievements.

She turned off the radio angrily. Kadhim did not protest.

She was thinking about phoning Adiba, to talk over her fears for Iraq and her family and to tell her about her nightmare, when she suddenly felt something warm dripping down her legs. She returned to the bathroom and found drops of blood smearing her knickers. Damn it, she swore to herself. That's the third time this month.

She sat on the edge of the bath, overcome with despair. What was the matter with her? She was fed up with everything—the bad news from Iraq, the way her hair fell out, her bloated stomach, and the unexpected changes that were affecting her body and personality. She was upset by her husband and her children, the kilograms that kept on accumulating, even though she ate nothing but air, and her moods, which seemed to be out of control. Upset by her stress and anger at the whole wide world and the frustration she felt at Kadhim's despair, which infected her like the plague.

It was true that she could still attract admiring glances, with her rose pink complexion, pretty face, and bewitching smile. Others might admire the clever way in which she put on her makeup and the elegant clothes she wore, but it was the way that Kadhim looked at her that reflected the way she looked at herself.

Throughout her youth, Kadhim had been like a mirror in a fairy tale, telling her over and over again, "You are the loveliest, prettiest woman in the world."

Now, the mirror had cracked, and she had come to see herself as misshapen.

She pulled herself together. She cleaned herself, then washed her hair. It took her half an hour, squatting on the bathroom floor with her head held over the bath as she sprayed it with water. Her back ached from sitting in such an uncomfortable position. It was a complex operation. It was not surprising that women now used chemical hair dyes instead of natural henna. It was not easy ridding her hair of all traces of the red paste.

Who else, apart from us, she wondered, would waste their mornings and evenings washing gluelike henna out of their hair?

She combed her hair. It was as smooth as silk, and an attractive fiery red. She was delighted by her success. Her spirits rose. She dried it. She arranged it, and then called Kadhim to ask him what he thought. His words, matchlike, set fire to her anger and loathing. Her patience and silence exploded.

"Are you going out into the street looking like that?" he asked irritably.

"Yes. What's your problem?"

"I don't have a problem; you're the one who does," he snorted derisively. "People are going to laugh at your orange scalp."

"People? What people? In this country, people don't laugh at what other people are wearing, or what they look like, or the color of their hair. What are you talking about?"

"People are the same the world over. They laugh at what's funny. Supposing you bump into your friends or meet someone from Iraq?"

"My friends have nothing to do with my hair color. As for other Iraqis, if they are anything like you, they should be thinking about their own problems rather than making remarks on my hair. Why don't you say what you're really thinking? That you're the one who's changed, that you want to laugh."

"Why should I want to laugh at you, Sahira?" He shrugged his shoulders disdainfully. "If I had the energy and was in the mood, I'd laugh at myself."

"Well, I've got the energy, and I'm in the mood to laugh at you!" she screamed.

She burst out in hysterical laughter. The fit continued. Tears of laughter, mingled with black kohl and pink foundation powder, streamed down her cheeks until her face turned cyanide blue and Kadhim was forced to rush to the kitchen and fetch a jug of cold water. He splashed it over her face until she calmed down, and started to cry instead.

She got off before the bus reached the area where the main shops were, at the stop closest to her favorite Oxfam shop. She definitely preferred the branch in Kilburn, because it was cheaper than the other branches she had seen. Certainly cheaper than the branch in Colindale, where she lived. The director of the shop had somehow managed to fix a new form of pricing. Whether it was a dress, a skirt, or a winter coat, nothing cost more than two pounds fifty. Small household goods and accessories were fifty-nine pence, books were twenty-nine pence, shoes, hats, and bags were ninety-nine pence.

There were only two things she didn't buy at Oxfam—secondhand shoes and books. Shoes, because she was afraid of catching athlete's foot. And books, because they reminded her of Kadhim. Every book she set eyes on had come to symbolize her husband. He had put a stop to any fondness she might have had for books. It was true that she had never been an avid reader, like her brothers, but, before getting married, she used to read her schoolbooks and any magazines she came across, as well as the occasional adventure story or novel. She had particularly squabbled over the magazines with her brothers. If she had finished secondary school and gone on to university and graduated, like her brothers had, she would have worked as a teacher, or at least as a teaching assistant, who knows? If, if . . . ! But her life had changed direction the day she met Kadhim again, when he returned after a long absence.

She was still in her teens. It was a boiling hot day in June. She had left school early. The heat had made it difficult for her to breathe, and she had asked the teacher if she could go home. As she neared her house in al-'Aywadhiyya, she saw Kadhim.

'ABED KADHIM AL-ZUBEIDI

"Uncle! '*Amu!*"

He swiveled around. He was almost at Comrade Jalil's house. It had been years since he had visited his comrade and friend at home. This was partly due to the pressures of his work for the opposition and the demands made by having to work in secret, and partly because he was always away, representing the Communist Party at international conferences and acting as the party representative in Prague.

He was tired. The fierce heat of the midday sun was unbearable and had exhausted him; he was desperate to reach his friend's house as soon as possible. To cool down. To relax.

"'*Amu*, welcome, '*amu*," the girl panted, her chest wheezing between each strangled cry.

She was a pretty, young girl, he noticed. Her face glowed red; she was fair-skinned, with wide black eyes and a large mouth that would have been out of balance with her other features were it not for her beautiful, luscious, and tempting lips. She was happy to see him. Such a smile lit up her face, that on seeing it, he was powerless to do anything but smile in return. She brought delight to his heart. Breathlessly, he gazed his fill at her.

"It's impossible! Is it really you, Sahira?"

His astonishment delighted her. She was pleased by his reaction because she understood what it meant. Recently, she had grown used to hearing such comments as "*Ma sha' Allah*, how big you've become. You've grown up! You've become a woman! How lovely you are! Are the young men blind? My God, Sahira, what a pretty girl you are. You deserve the best wedding Baghdad has ever seen."

When was the last time he had seen her? He couldn't remember exactly. Four, five years ago? Was it in '67 or '68?

She had been a skinny, awkward girl then, her hair set in pigtails, her face covered in pimples. She had helped her mother serve the food, and, when they had paid attention to her, she had read a composition to them, which she had written at school and which the teacher had praised. When she was younger still, she had sat on his lap, hiding away from her brothers when they chased her or from her father's anger.

He let out a breath. After having three boys, her parents had spoiled her and now here she was. A young woman! She stood in front of him, her beauty enhanced by her dark blue school uniform; she clutched her school bag to her chest as if to conceal the secret of her new charms, which she was not yet accustomed to. She turned her face away in embarrassment. She found it hard to withstand the scrutiny of his eyes, which thirstily drank in her appearance.

They were only a few meters away from her house in al-'Aywadhiyya. He slowed down intentionally to prolong the moment, and give himself a chance to comprehend and enjoy the new situation. As if he were meeting a girl he hadn't met before.

"How's school?" he asked, trying to get to know her.

"Fine."

"What class are you in now?"

"Year four, secondary."

"Which school?"

"Al-'Adadiya al-Markaziya."

"What a coincidence. I went there as well. To the boys' school, of course," he added with a laugh. "What time do classes finish?"

"Three o'clock, but I left early."

"Why?"

"I have asthma, and sometimes I can't breathe properly and have to rest."

"I hope you'll feel better. *Salimtik.*"

She answered his questions concisely. Where was the little Sahira who never stopped talking? She would talk and talk, until he had a headache and had to beg her to keep some of her words back for the following day.

He had intended to spend a week at their house—as a friend. He wanted to get far away from the arguments and disputes and the threat of more dissent, which hung over the Communist Party. He wanted to stay somewhere where he felt safe, somewhere that would make him feel that any divisions in the party were extrinsic and did not represent a major danger to its existence; he needed reassurance that the party was still deeply rooted in people's lives and would continue to have far-reaching influence over the lives of the masses. Comrade Jalil exemplified this notion. He was a trade unionist who had inherited communism from his father and would hand it on to his sons before he died. Jalil was a good man, a friend, and a refuge. He was always ready for the struggle and to sacrifice himself. He was known as the "dove of peace" among his friends because of his marked composure, though those who differed with his opinions and despised him called him "the pawn" instead. "You are the only dove of peace left in our fragmenting party," Kadhim told him sadly one day.

Kadhim had been looking forward to the peace and tranquility of Jalil's house, but, when he saw Sahira, he decided not to stay longer than one night. His hopes were confounded, his aim frustrated. He was attracted to this girl with the wide smile. Overwhelmed by the sense of youthful freedom that surrounded her.

He continued to look at her. Her body was blooming. Lush. Untasted. Her face was as smooth as silk, unmarked by the sadness of life. Sahira—girl-woman. How should he behave toward her? Should he avoid looking at her now, though in the past he had joked and played with her? Should he tease her? His words might seem out of place today, unsuited to her sudden leap from childhood to maturity, which had distanced her from the girl he had known in the past? How could he look at her and not alert the others to this new emotion that made him long to gaze at her and feast his eyes on her youth? How could he conceal it from her, and from her father, mother, and brothers, who were so close to him?

He fled the next morning before she got up to go to school, running away from feelings that in his mind had assumed the tinge of a forbidden craving. Feelings that were like the slow ascent of desire, leaving in their wake a constant warmth and heat. A rapacious desire that fixed itself on a particular woman. Nothing else would satisfy him now except the embrace of the young girl.

He thought back to how he remembered her. He recalled how she would take refuge in his lap from her father's wrath, and how she would race toward him every time he came to visit them. He wished she would do the same now. He imagined her sitting in his lap, clinging on to his knees. He shook the image out of his head and decided to leave the house. No, he would not remain another night. They were surprised. They asked him, "What's the matter?" He told them confusedly that he had remembered an important appointment. "I must go. I'll visit you soon," he said.

He dashed out, like someone who had just been set at liberty after being arrested for committing incest.

That evening, he ventured to attend a performance of *Hamlet* at the National Theatre in Salahiya, in west Baghdad. He didn't particularly enjoy the theatre or the acting, but he had a pressing need to see Amal. He knew that she would be there, as she was playing the part of the young Prince of Denmark's mother. He warily chose a seat in the back row, near the door, so he could easily get away if someone recognized him.

When the play ended, he breathed a sigh of relief. He preferred the restful world of books, even those that were full of shouts and tears, screams and lamentations. He stood outside the theatre smoking a cigarette while he waited for Amal to emerge. She came out with a group of youngsters. He called to her. Her face lit up with unexpected joy. She excused herself from the group and ran over to him. Her joy was quickly replaced by her concern for him. "Kadhim, when did you return?" she whispered, turning her eyes toward him in the darkness, aware of the risk he had taken in coming to see her. "Today," he lied. "Shall we go to the house?" "No, it's not possible," she said. "Father and mother are there. They've come to visit me." "Shall we go to the flat, then?" "What about your brother Suheil?" "He's away in Basra on some party business."

He spent that night with her in the flat, which for some time had witnessed the warmth of their physical encounters. He recognized then that the image of Sahira—the young girl teetering between childhood and womanhood—would pursue him forever. He realized that what he felt for her wasn't mere lust, or the desire to possess something *muharam* (forbidden), or even the pangs of middle age. It was a combination of all three. If not that, then why did he fail to quench his desire for her as he flooded Amal's eager body with his heated emotions?

While he was on top/beside/under/with Amal, he was dreaming of Sahira and thinking, how can I have her?

He was the same age as her father. She was the youngest child in a family in which none of the children were married yet. She was sixteen, and he was forty. In his mind, he went over and over the difficult issue of the gap in their ages to persuade himself so that he could persuade others. She was young enough to be his daughter. Had he gotten married at the same time as Jalil and settled down and had a family, he would now have children the same age as Sahira. The maddening thing was that he had lived with Jalil and Sahira's mother when she was growing up. He had spent the first year of her life living with the family in what had once been the party house in Ali Salih district. He could remember her first steps, their joy when her first teeth appeared, her lisping speech, which no one apart from her mother could understand, the way she danced whenever she heard music, and then, at later intervals, her screams and tears of pain when she was suffering from measles, chicken pox, and a chronic eye infection from trachoma.

Where had this insane passion come from? He had been happy without her. It was not mere lust. He knew how to deal with that. How to cure it. There were women whose bodies he briefly visited to rid himself of pent up feelings of lust, and whom he forgot immediately afterward. What he felt now was completely different.

The feelings were ten years late in reaching him. He had briefly encountered them in his twenties but had distanced himself from them, afraid that they would distract him from his primary purpose in life: The Communist Party. The political struggle. The people and the unity of workers.

The years passed. They brought with them prison, flight, clandestine work, travel, conferences, and meetings. He shifted from one party house to another, and from one city to another. He slowly advanced up the party ladder, moving on from being a member of the party to being a member of the bureau, until he assumed that he was more suited than the rest to become leader of the party.

He became aware of extraordinary emotions that he couldn't express in words. He was like someone trying to describe the colors of the rainbow to a man who only knew the muddy color of clay. How could he describe them?

He gradually dismissed the reasons that would prevent a union with Sahira from his mind. He conveniently pushed the objections aside, to the darkness beyond. In their place, the reasons that made such a union necessary began to hold sway, and made him go forward to ask for her hand.

SAHIRA JALIL

She stared at his confusion in amazement. When she had been walking behind him in the street, she had been following a tall, thin, tired man. He had black hair. His temples were tinged with shining silver. He held a paper bag in his hand, which looked as if it contained books. From time to time, he glanced cautiously around him.

After getting up from his siesta, he spent the evening with her father in the salon. She made a point of popping in now and then to ask innocently, "Would you like some tea? Juice, perhaps?" She picked up a couple of small objects from the room and replaced them. During these snatched moments, she heard familiar phrases: "ideological dissent," "exaggeration of minor mistakes," "spirit of despair and defeat," "fear for the safety of the party from internal dissent," "plan for uniting the national forces," and "the non-capitalist model of development."

For the first time, she observed how softly he spoke, and how he played with the tones of his voice, whispering to cajole and invite attention. He leaned his head forward, murmuring the words as if confiding a very important secret or command known only to him. In particular, she liked the way he showed his interest in her without saying a word. He raised his head and gazed at her as he had done while they were standing in the street. He looked straight at her and she felt important.

For some reason, her father appeared unnaturally silent at times, though he appeared to agree at the end of Kadhim's remarks with successive nods of his head and his habitual "yes, yes," said quickly, like someone hurriedly pulling on a rope, hoping to find something valuable at the end of it.

They talked for a long time. The four hours of discussions were permeated with her father's arguments and Kadhim's patience and constant cigarettes. They drank five lots of tea and four lots of iced water. The smell of cigarette smoke pervaded the room. Kadhim was the only person smoking. He smoked one cigarette after another without pause. Her father had given it up after suffering acute chest pains. Her mother sent her to tell them that supper was ready. She stopped at the door, listening to their final words.

"As far as I'm concerned, I am completely satisfied with the decisions made by the party," said her father, in the voice of someone capitulating to reality. "I've been a member of the party all my life, and the party always takes precedence. But I have to tell you what our comrades in the rural areas outside Baghdad are saying. Our comrades are saying that we should have nothing to do with the Baʿath Party. They are completely against it. How will you persuade Comrades Sabr and ʿAdnan, for example? They are high-ranking and command a lot of respect. An old comrade in al-Kut told me, 'Comrade Jalil, the Baʿath Party is like a snake. It's quiet at the moment but when it grows strong, it will bite.' Someone else said, 'They'll take our flesh and leave our bones.' In other words, they'll use us, then get rid of us when they no longer need us. Our rank and file regard them as murderers, Comrade Kadhim. People still remember the names of those who were imprisoned, tortured, and murdered after the Baʿath coup d'etat in 1963. Tragically, they are still carrying out such practices. Yesterday, for example, I heard of a university lecturer who had been arrested. We don't know his name yet. Try and understand ... in such circumstances, how can we convince the comrades?"

"It depends on whether you're persuaded yourself that the party's doing the right thing. You must be convinced. As for everyone else, tell them that the party leadership thinks that the interests of the party and the people, at this crucial time, demand that we cooperate with the ruling Baʿath Party, and take part in the national front. Are you convinced? Then convince everyone else."

She coughed.

"Mama says supper's ready," she said.

They spread out a thick plastic sheet, and sat around it cross-legged on the ground.

"Damn politics," Kadhim said jokingly. "Let's hear your news."

Her mother was in the kitchen dishing up the food, and Sahira came and went helping her.

He was relaxed with them, as if the burden of the years had slid off his shoulders. He laughed and recounted funny stories and took turns with her father in telling jokes. They competed with each other in making fun of their comrades. They transformed the suffering into funny anecdotes that recalled their comrades who were far away, in prison or abroad, the separatists, those who had quit the party, and those who had returned to the fold. He told them about Prague. "It's a beautiful city," he said. "The people are very good, and the comrades there are amazed at the enormous sacrifices made by the Iraqi people." "When you were in exile, did you miss Iraq and your family?" Sahira asked. "No, I was among family and comrades," he said. He grew in stature in their eyes. Their admiration for him deepened. She and her brothers regarded him as a great leader, willing to sacrifice his home and family for the sake of the masses. Her mother came and sat with them. She joined in the laughter and gaiety of her family with its friend in its midst.

Sahira asked him what his real name was, and he said it was 'Abed Kadhim. "I mean, the name that's on your birth certificate and certificate of nationality," she said. "Sometimes 'Abed and sometimes Kadhim," he replied quietly. "That's impossible," she said. "Everyone who visits us has a party name such as Abu so-and-so or Um so-and-so, some special name they've adopted." "That's what I thought," he said. "I won't change my name because everyone else does. My party name is my real name."

She had liked him as a child. She continued to like him as a young woman. Now, as well as being attracted to him personally, she was swept along by her father and brothers' admiration of him. She saw him as a charismatic politician. Detained, imprisoned, struggling in secret to improve the lives of the masses.

She painted a romantic picture of him in her mind befitting a dreamy girl of sixteen. On his subsequent visits, her feelings toward him fluctuated—sometimes they were those of a young girl who wanted to be looked after and sometimes those of a mother who wanted to look after him.

Over time, her desire to play the mother triumphed. She wanted to kiss away the dark circles under his eyes. To put her arms around him when his voice wavered and give him back his strength. Whenever anyone mentioned that he had left it too late to get married and was now old, she would justify his position and leap to his defense so fiercely that tears came to her eyes. And if anyone hinted that it was mere ambition rather than genuine feelings or the interests of the workers, as he claimed, which had provided the incentive for his political work, or that his tireless calls for the party to work with the current government and overlook the nature of the regime were at the expense of the victims among his comrades, she would let fly at them, saying they did not understand the nature of political work as well as he did.

Kadhim was a living embodiment of her dream man, and Sahira was preparing herself physically and psychologically to take him to her.

When he asked her father for her hand in marriage, Jalil paled in bewilderment. He was unwilling to show his friend and comrade how he felt, so he said quietly, without looking at Kadhim, "Sahira has been raised in the same way as my other children, so it is up to her and her mother to decide whether she agrees."

"I agree," she told her father.

Her mother, who was usually so quiet, bitterly opposed her decision.

"He's old enough to be your father," she said. "And he's part of an important party cadre. His life is in constant danger, and he has no home of his own."

"I've grown up in a party house," Sahira said. "My father's been a member of the party all his life, and you married him and brought us up in party houses."

"That's why I'm advising you not to marry him. I don't want you to go through what I've suffered. Why are you in such a hurry? Wait. Finish your studies and marry a boy your own age. Men won't fly away. You'll always find someone."

After thinking about it, her father complied with Sahira's wishes.

"At least she is not marrying a stranger about whom we know nothing," he told his wife, trying to convince them both. "He knows her well and will look after her. As he's so often away, I'm sure that if we broach the question of her studies with him, he can easily arrange for her to obtain a grant so that she can continue them in Prague or Moscow. There's something else, and this must remain a secret. Kadhim's told me that although the party said that it would support 'Aziz Sharif as minister of justice three weeks ago, this does not mean that it is ready to form a coalition government or national front. Nevertheless, the signs are that the party will soon announce that a national front is close to being realized. This will mean that he no longer has to work in secret; perhaps they will go abroad. There'll be a greater need for Kadhim to represent the party abroad than to stay here. I could suggest to Kadhim that, as Sahira is still young, they should wait and finalize the marriage once the front is announced."

Sahira and Kadhim had to wait three years, five months, and twenty-six days for their wedding to come to pass. It finally took place on the day on which 'Aziz Mohammed, first secretary of the Communist Party, and President Ahmed Hassan al-Bakr signed a national action charter.

The splendid wedding of Kadhim Zubeidi and Sahira Jalil also signaled the end of his having to work in secret and the impending announcement of the formation of a national front.

Sahira picked out a white shirt with a Jonelle label. She turned it over. She examined it for stains and looked at the buttons. It was in good condition but there were two buttons missing. She put it back. It was not worth buying it and then having to mend it. The two buttons would cost the same as the shirt.

She searched the secondhand clothing shops for designer clothes or particular labels. When people admired her taste, she pretended that she had bought the clothes new.

Neither her sons nor their father interfered in what she bought or wore. In fact, sometimes she wished they would interfere a bit more and pretend to show some interest. But Nahid was a different matter. She meddled and pried, poking her nose into everything she did, whether it was household matters or her mother's private affairs. Sahira dubbed her "the inspector." In revenge, she called her mother "the bag lady," since she never came home without a bag full of secondhand clothes and cheap accessories.

No one, especially not her mother, escaped Nahid's sharp probing eyes and malicious tongue. Sahira sighed audibly. Who said that bringing up boys was more difficult than girls? Nahid was much more of a problem than her brothers. She recalled 'Adil and Shakir with longing. How handsome they were! How well-behaved! They were obedient and heeded her advice. It was true that they had a tense relationship with their father, but she didn't blame them for that. It was Kadhim's fault. He behaved like an autocrat, expecting his orders to be carried out the moment he gave them. He was stern and demanded the most from them, without spending a single day trying to get to know them. On their arrival in Britain, the situation had worsened as Shakir and 'Adil gradually grew more independent and spent less time at home, while Kadhim aged and grew more tired and frustrated.

So when they chose to study and live in a manner that differed from his expectations, he reacted violently; a wall of disappointment grew so high between them that neither side was able to surmount it.

His relationship with Nahid was different. She was his darling girl, his little Sahira. He spoiled her as a grandfather would spoil his granddaughter, so she stopped listening to her mother. She spent most of her time outside the house, having a good time, enjoying herself, paying no attention to her studies apart from during the final examinations.

In her heart of hearts, Sahira recognized that Nahid was very similar to her. She reminded her of herself. Of her snobbishness, insolence, and frivolity. She was, therefore, particularly afraid that Nahid would do what she had not done as a young woman, overprotected as she was by her family and society. She feared that Nahid would commit a foolish mistake that would damage her and result in God knows what. She disclosed her fears to Kadhim and asked him to have a word with her. He admonished Sahira. He said Nahid was an intelligent girl, and she shouldn't worry about her. He said she had been learning about sex and how to protect herself since she was ten years old. What more could they teach her?

The relationship between Nahid and her mother had deteriorated in the days before her departure for Wales. They were no longer able to carry on the simplest type of conversation without becoming irritated with each other. She was now thoroughly immersed in playing the role of a young woman who knew everything and who was most capable of changing her mother, if not the world.

The day before Nahid left for school, Sahira had shown her a silk suit made up of a jacket and a skirt.

"Guess how much I paid for this smart suit?" she asked proudly.

Nahid responded angrily,

"Mama, when are you going to stop buying other people's rags and rubbish?"

"What's wrong with it? It's beautiful, cheap, and has a designer label," Sahira responded.

"Instead of buying ten rags, why don't you buy one new thing?"

"First, they are not rags. Second, I don't want to wear the same clothes every day. Third, I enjoy browsing around the shops, and last but not least, they are cheap. If I don't like something after a couple of days, I can wash it, put it in a plastic bag, and take it back to the place I bought it from. Then I can buy something else and so on, again and again and again." She finally laughed. "From dust we come and unto dust we shall return."

She chortled, pleased to have roused her daughter, who was eyeing her sharply, and then asked more seriously,

"Nahid, what have you got against those shops? Are you worried that one of your friends will see me and tease you because your mother buys her clothes from Oxfam?"

"The smell of secondhand clothes and shops makes me sick. I hate it. Think of the people who owned the clothes before you! They're either dead or suffering from some sort of skin disease."

The anger spread to Sahira, making her jerk involuntarily.

"Wash them, sterilize them, then! They'll be as good as new!" she yelled.

She went into another charity shop. It was more expensive than Oxfam, but she had come across things there in the past that were of good quality and cheap. She bought a blue jacket with a Wallis label. She had five jackets already but she loved blue. She paid three pounds seventy-five pence for it. Then she bought some Dove toilet soap from a basket outside a shop that sold odds and ends cheaply. She preferred this make of soap because it made her skin soft, and she desperately needed something these days to soften her dry skin.

She brought her shopping trip to an end by going into an underwear shop. She hesitated a bit before buying anything. She had at least thirty pairs of underwear at home, half of which were new and had never been worn. Once, when Kadhim was searching the wardrobe for the mate to one of his socks, he had turned on her.

"For God's sake, how many pairs of underwear do you wear a day?" he shouted at her angrily.

"One pair, like everyone else."

He had become infuriated and started tearing the carefully folded clothes off the shelves of the wardrobe, and flinging them about the room.

"So why have you got hundreds of pairs of underwear and bras and stockings, then?"

"I liked them, so I bought them."

"But you can't wear all of them. Do you intend to take them with you when you die?"

"I didn't think you believed in the afterlife," she retorted coldly.

"Sahira, anyone who lived with you would believe in nothing but the afterlife."

He slammed the door of the wardrobe so violently that it almost split apart, and left the room, carrying two different colored socks. She laughed, and screamed after him,

"Ya Kadhim, ya Zubeidi, at last you're going to be fashionable! You'll be wearing socks of different colors!"

To irritate him, she bought two pairs of high-legged black and red satin knickers. And two lace bras, which were black and red as well. For an instant, she thought he might be right about her piles of underwear.

Why did she continue throwing her money away on things she didn't wear and which no one would see her wearing?

Kadhim was no longer interested in having sex with her, or with anyone else for that matter. He had become impotent. She'd once told him that other men slept with their wives into their eighties. He hadn't replied, reproaching her with his silence.

For years now they had been sleeping in separate beds. Before they got separate beds, he would excuse himself on the grounds that he was reading late or couldn't sleep or was watching a television program and would sleep on the sofa in the sitting room.

Nevertheless, when buying her clothes, she still persisted with an unwavering obstinacy in choosing the colors in which he used to like her.

She thought back to the years in which they were first married. How he had loved her then! His eyes would follow her as she moved around the house. He was amazed and proud of her, and would boast about the smallest thing she did. It filled her with self-confidence. His great love was broad enough to contain her faults and errors.

Their nights were a continuous feast of embraces, kisses, and lovemaking. Night after night. And if it happened that he went away on party business for one or more days, he would return to her ardent and demanding, charged with passion. She would flirt with him. She would say, "Relax, you must be tired from all that traveling and those meetings and discussions." But he wouldn't listen to her.

He was compelled by the extraordinary attraction her body and youth and the softness of her touch held for him. She had the power to dispel his weariness and the pressures of work and to chase away his concerns and preoccupations. His vitality was renewed, and his intellectual vigor returned. Who said that he could not be as vital now as when he was young? He had regained his youth through being with her. For the first time in his life, politics took a backseat. Pride of place went to their physicality, their lusty, fleshy union, with all the fever and sweat and heaving it entailed.

One night, after having extinguished the flames of his desire inside her for a second time, and as he greedily drew on a cigarette in the same way that he sucked the nectar from her day after day, he told her,

"Sahira, you're like a magnet in the way you attract elements."

"And you? What are you?" she asked.

"I'm the poor element! Once I come within your magnetic field, I lose all sense of equilibrium."

"Does this mean that you are only attracted to me when you are close to me?"

"No, I would be drawn to you even if you were at the North Pole."

And he'd nestled against her breast like a little child.

She reached her hand into the bag and touched the bras. She felt a warmth course through her body. She wanted him. How he used to love red and black, especially in her underwear. He would grow excited just by touching the silky bras, and when in the evening she wore a see-through black nightdress with a red bra and panties underneath, he would go crazy with desire and lust, and launch himself at her.

She had been sure of herself then. Of her youth and love and flirtatious ways, and her ability to please him sexually. However tired and exhausted he was during his brief visits home, she was always able to make him desire her—a quality that led to her having three children and four miscarriages.

And now?

She was afraid of returning home. She fled from the house—from him. She avoided looking at him, as the sight of him kindled despair in her. She found it difficult to accept his rapid decline. His air of exhaustion and age. The waxy sheen on his skin. The wrinkles massing around his neck. The spindly legs. The desolate eyes. The tufts of hair sprouting out of his ears, trailing like plants dangling from a hanging basket. The suit he used to wear that now wore him. His isolation.

Friends/comrades deserted him.

Their belief died. The bonds that had tied them together withered. Faded. The comrades withdrew from each other even as they bore the coffin of their belief on their shoulders. They buried it. Recited elegies and poems over it, then separated. Each one searching for his own route. His resting place.

What should she do with the rest of the day? She phoned her old neighbor Jean, but she wasn't at home. She phoned Adiba. "You're welcome to come here," Adiba said. "Come over immediately and we'll think of something to do together." At the warm sound of her voice, which asked for no explanation, Sahira was filled with a deep sense of gratitude.

CHAPTER EIGHT

Adiba noticed the heavy bag that Sahira was carrying. She invited her to sit down, then asked,"What have you bought?"

"A jacket and some underwear."

"What's the weather like? Is it cold?"

"No. It's all right. The sun makes me forget the cold."

Adiba was quiet for a moment. She studied Sahira closely. She seemed tired.

"How's Kadhim?" she asked.

"He's well. He's been better recently. A young man who's studying for his PhD at London University has been in contact with him. He got our phone number from Abu Salim. He wants some information about the history of the party and some documents. For the first time in months, Kadhim seems interested in something."

"That's wonderful. The research will keep him busy and lift his spirits."

"I hope so. Since 'Adil and Shakir have left home and Nahid's gone to Cardiff, he's been more and more depressed, especially in winter."

"I read an article in a newspaper about depression in winter. The scientific experts say that it is due to a lack of sun," Adiba said.

"If that's true, then everyone back home should be happy all the time, because there's so much sun."

"That's a different matter. The suffering of our people in Iraq has nothing to do with nature."

"How do you cure such depression?" Sahira asked.

"The scientists say exposure for half an hour a day to benign rays that have similar properties to those of the sun will help raise your spirits and get rid of your depression."

"Well, I think they're completely right. Look around you. The moment the sun starts to shine, people's moods change; they relax and rush off to parks, where they lie around half naked. They even smile on the Underground instead of looking like gray moles."

She was silent for a moment, and then asked,

"Do you think we're made differently from the English?"

"Whatever do you mean?"

"I mean ... well, we long for sun and light more than the English do. We need it because we're used to it; we were brought up in a country that was made up of sun and light. Well, I mean … are our bodies fundamentally different from theirs?"

"Do you mean genetically? It's possible, Sahira. If you'd said that several years ago, I would have accused you of racism, because the politically correct social position was very clear on the matter. It said that we were all exactly the same physiologically, apart from having different colored skin and differently shaped features. Any allusion to physical difference meant superiority or inferiority. But now the general view has changed. They have begun to attribute many positive and negative qualities and diseases to genetic causes. It's therefore possible that what you're saying is true. Perhaps we have a gene that is related to the sun's rays."

"If there are genes that make certain people love the sun, then Kadhim definitely has a special gene connected to the party," Sahira said, in a tone of false jollity.

Adiba ignored her remarks. She didn't want to get drawn into a tortuous, emotional, and endless discussion about Kadhim. Sahira always went around and around a subject, then brought it back to Kadhim.

"Sahira, would you like tea or coffee, or shall we eat, as it is one o'clock?"

"Coffee, please. I feel a little light-headed because I haven't had any coffee this morning. I was wandering around the shops and forgot. I hope I'm not disturbing your work?"

"No, no. I was going to the housing department with some clients, as I'd received a letter saying the appointment was for two o'clock on October 19th, but they phoned this morning and apologized and said there had been a clerical error. They are fixing up another time."

"Were the clients from Iraq?"

"Yes. Most of my work is with Iraqis. They have asked me to translate for other people a couple of times."

Adiba began to prepare the coffee. As she ground the roasted beans in a small electric grinder, the smell of coffee diffused throughout the flat. She spooned it into a special jug and it percolated slowly. She paid particular attention to each step of the process, as if preparing a cup of coffee for Sahira was one of the most important tasks of her life. Every movement revealed her concern over detail. Like the simple arrangement of her flat, the classical style of her dress, with its neutral design and colors. Beige, brown, and white. Sahira glanced about her, examining the simple furnishings and the large number of bookshelves.

She inhaled deeply, breathing in the aroma of the coffee.

"Allah! That's a smell that would wake the dead. I don't know what I do wrong. Whenever I make coffee at home, it never turns out like yours. Where do you buy it?"

"Nowhere in particular. But I only buy roasted beans, not powder or granules. And I always get coffee from Latin America or one of the third world countries." She laughed uncertainly. "A holdover from my revolutionary days, I suppose. Just grind the amount you are going to use, and you will see the difference," she added.

She served *klaicha*, a pasty stuffed with dates, with the coffee. She watched the way Sahira gobbled it up in three bites, then wiped away the crumbs that had fallen onto her blouse. Adiba looked at her out of the corner of her eye to avoid embarrassing her.

"How good that was, Adiba! *'Ashat yadaik*! You must give me the recipe."

"May you enjoy good health! You will have to ask Um Mohammed, as she is the one who made them. I will put the rest in a bag for you."

"No, no thanks. I've cut down on sweet things and cakes. The doctor's told me to lose weight. My knee hurts and he says I'm like someone carrying a bag of stones down the street. To be honest, I don't know how to lose any more weight. I only eat one meal a day, and we eat healthy food . . . well, like you. You look after yourself. I've noticed that you don't like sweet things."

"No, I prefer savory dishes. I have to be careful about my weight so as not to put any more pressure on my leg."

"I thought the operation had cured the pain."

"It is a lot better than before."

She fell silent.

"Oh, speaking of Um Mohammed, how is she?" Sahira asked.

"Well, I saw her yesterday, and she gave me the *klaicha*. She called to ask about the latest news from Iraq. She said she had seen pictures of Baghdad and the UN inspectors and Tariq Aziz on the English news, and she was worried about a new offensive. The satellite channels were not working, and her son had gone to Ireland with his girlfriend. She could not find anyone to explain what was happening. She phoned me because she was shy about asking the neighbors."

"I wanted to phone you, too. Then I thought you might be busy, and I didn't want to disturb you."

"Phone me whenever you need to," Adiba offered. "If I'm busy, I shall tell you. Generally, it is the same news. But every couple of months a storm breaks over the heads of the besieged."

"The news from Iraq is all doom and gloom. Our friend Saddam is full of air and stubbornness. He blows up and retreats. Takes one step forward and a hundred steps back. If only he had some self-respect and listened to what others were saying . . ."

"Um Mohammed is worried about her relatives in Baghdad," Adiba interrupted.

"I am worried about my family as well. I don't sleep a wink at night. I have horrible nightmares. Shall I tell you about them?"

Adiba nodded.

"I dreamed last night that Nahid and I were walking home along the street. I mean our family home in al-'Aywadhiyya."

"Decades after leaving, we still call it home," Adiba murmured.

"There was a pile of leather suitcases in a dark corner of the street under the electricity pylons, near the dustbins. They were very smart. I opened one of them and took out several dresses. Long evening dresses decorated with sparkling stars. They were lovely. One of them was like my wedding dress. I held it up to show Nahid, but she sneered. She said it was old and secondhand. I told her it just needed a simple cleaning, and it would be as good as new. I squatted down on the pavement and opened the other suitcases. One of them had trinkets and fabulous old jewelry in it. Some of it was broken. I picked things up and put them down. Another case contained belts and watchstraps. I remember thinking, I have to take Kadhim's watch to be mended. He hasn't been able to do anything since the strap broke; he's thrown it away, arguing that he doesn't know what the time is. In another bag, there were pictures and letters. I wondered if the cases belonged to a woman who'd died. Perhaps her relatives had decided to get rid of the things because they reminded them of her.

"The last bag was full of children's clothes. I'd never seen anything like them in my life. They were so beautifully made and designed. I turned to Nahid and said, 'They'll be just right for a girl about eighteen months old. Do we know anyone like that?' But Nahid wasn't there.

"A few minutes later, I was standing on the spot near our house where I'd met 'Abed all those years ago. Through the windows I could see my mother sitting silently on a wooden bench like she always did; my father was sitting nearby reading a newspaper.

"The house was starting to burn. There was smoke. I tried to warn my mother. I banged on the window. I held up the child's dress, so I could ask her about it. I shouted, 'I can only find this dress. All the clothes are for some eighteen-month-old child.' She said, 'I know. The child hasn't grown.' I called out to them. I said, 'Move, come outside. The house is on fire. I'll help you.' I realized they couldn't hear what I was shouting. My voice stuck in my throat. I stood there yelling and screaming, but no one would listen to me."

"You must have been worried about your family and your home," Adiba concluded. "Too much fear can drive people mad. And being on your own makes it worse. At least your children are well, and you have Kadhim with you. Think of Um Mohammed."

"Kadhim!" Sahira protested. "What are you talking about? Kadhim, with me? Kadhim is an absent presence. Adiba, 'aini, believe me. I feel as if I'm living on my own. If you saw . . ."

"Sahira, I do not want to delve into matters that do not concern me. However, as you have brought the subject up . . . I believe that if you got out of the house more, you might feel less depressed. Why do you not enroll in a course, for example? Learn a language, pottery, cookery, something that interests you that you would like to learn."

"Go to school, at my age? What about the house and Kadhim? Who's going to look after them?"

"I am not suggesting that you attend a full-time course, but that you enroll in a class once or twice a week so that the house and Kadhim do not get you down. Um Mohammed is twenty years older than you, and she attends an English class. Have you noticed how persistent she is? Why not visit Um Mohammed and ask her?"

"It's a little difficult because she lives a long way away."

"Phone her. Come to some agreement. Perhaps you can meet her halfway."

At night the pain spread throughout her body and her soul. Darkness. Fear. Insomnia. Sweats. Adiba stretched, got up. Walked about. Drank chamomile tea. They said it was good for the nerves. Went back to bed. Slept. Woke up an hour later. A voice droned in her head, preventing her from sleeping for any length of time. She repeated the cycle of the hours in its nightly rotation. She was in a maze of time; she knew how she had gotten into it but was absolutely unable to leave. Where was the exit to the outside world? She turned over the pages of a newspaper or read a book. The sleeplessness worsened. She watched a television program. She felt tired. The news was tiring enough for someone who was physically and mentally strong, so what about for someone in her position?

She was restless. She limped from the bedroom to the sitting room. She returned to the bedroom. When was the last time she had had a full night's sleep? She couldn't remember. There were many things she couldn't remember. She looked at the clock beside her bed. She checked the time although she knew what it was. An hour had passed since she last checked. She thought back to Sahira's nightmare. What was it she had said about Kadhim's watch? Had Kadhim lost his sense of time or had he lost the watch itself?

For months Michael had been urging her to go back to the psychiatrist. He told her that what she was going through wasn't normal and that she was clearly exhausted.

"It's the situation in Iraq. Every time the crisis gets worse, I feel like I did before—afraid, tense. I get less and less sleep. I had those ten sessions with Dr. Stewart, but they didn't help much."

"When was that?" Michael asked.

"A few months after I arrived in London."

"They must have been slightly useful. From what you've told me, you were very introverted at that stage. You didn't want to see or talk to anyone. You're different now. You've gotten better. I've seen a huge change in you in the time I've known you. You're stronger now, much stronger than you were even a year ago. You're more confident, more at peace. I think it might be the right time to return to therapy. You've overcome the first crisis, but what you have to do now is face up to what happened and come to terms with it."

"If anyone hears you talking to me like this, they will think you are some kind of psychiatrist," she said. Then she added quietly, "It will be like picking open a scab that has already healed."

"You've recovered by forgetting and burying it in a way that can be damaging. You are like your broken leg—healed wrongly. The wound is still there, buried inside. The only solution is to open it up. You'll be imprisoned throughout your life in the nightmare of the past. It'll drag you down into the darkness."

"I cannot bear the thought of sitting opposite a doctor and answering a series of questions. Just the thought makes me feel tired and depressed."

"Would you prefer to go on being punished every night and suffering from mental exhaustion for the rest of your life?"

Adiba was persuaded.

She phoned the hospital and asked for an appointment with Dr. Stewart, whom she had seen before. She said she had been ill in the past, and wanted to make another appointment with him. The woman responsible for arranging appointments laughed and told her that Dr. Stewart had retired years ago.

"Have you got a letter from your GP?" she asked.

"No, but I have an old appointment card from you. Dr. Stewart told me that I could return whenever I wished."

They made an appointment for her to see a Dr. Hawkins.

"I am very sorry, Mrs. Baghdadi, but I haven't been able to track down your file," Dr. Hawkins told her, when she first visited her. "I've written to Dr. Stewart asking him for information, but until I hear from him, I will have to go back to the beginning with you. What do you think?"

Anguish flooded through her. She regretted having come.

"Wouldn't it be better to wait until you receive his report," she asked in despair. "It will save a lot of time."

"You're right. But you arranged the appointment and have come. Why don't we talk a little? Tell me what the matter is."

"Now, or in the past?"

"Now, please."

Adiba felt depressed. Her gentle face tightened as if she had been struck with a sudden sense of pain. She felt a strong compulsion to get up and leave the room. She wanted to run away, but she couldn't. She felt paralyzed. She reminded herself of her condition and her promise to Michael.

"I suffer from continual insomnia," she said briefly.

"Can you describe it?"

"I sleep for an hour, then I wake up. I check that everything around me is secure, then I try to go back to sleep for another hour, and so on."

"How long did you see Dr. Stewart for?"

"Two and a half years."

"Then?"

"I stopped coming."

"Why?"

"I did not see any point in carrying on."

"Because you had been cured to some extent or because you hadn't been helped at all?"

"I felt that I had improved sufficiently to get on with my life and did not need any more sessions."

"Did Dr. Stewart agree with you?"

"Yes and no. No, he wanted to carry on seeing me, and yes, because, just as I have explained, he could not do so without my agreement and against my personal wishes."

"You said you set your mind at rest about your surroundings. Is there an obvious danger that poses a threat to you or your security?"

"I don't think so."

"What are you afraid of?"

"I don't know. I wake up terrified. I look around. I can see everything is where it should be. But I feel something is eluding me. It is taking place in my absence. When I am asleep. When I am not awake."

"Do you feel the same if you sleep during the day?"

"No."

"Do you sleep during the day?"

"Sometimes."

"If I say the word 'night' to you, what comes into your mind?"

"Darkness."

"Do you think that what makes you wake up at night is different from what might make you wake up in the day?"

"The day is different. I am not afraid during the day."

"Because there are other people about?"

"Perhaps, but I don't feel afraid even when I'm on my own."

"Is it because you're busy during the day, occupied with your daily routine?"

"I don't know, but I . . . During the day I don't feel afraid."

"I'll arrange an appointment for you in two weeks' time. I can't see you more than that because there are so many refugees and too few resources. The center is a charity and depends on donations and a small grant from the government. I hope by your next visit that we will have tracked down your file."

Two weeks later Adiba returned to the clinic.

"I am very sorry," Dr. Hawkins said. "We haven't been able to trace your file. Dr. Stewart has been in touch, and in his reply to my letter told me that you were referred by Amnesty International and suggested I write to them to get a copy of your report. I've done this. I'm expecting to get it in the next couple of days."

Then she looked at Adiba sympathetically.

"Shall we go on?" she said.

Adiba nodded.

"When I asked you to tell me about yourself last time, you asked me whether I was asking about now or the past. What do you mean by the past?"

"The time following my release from prison."

"What sort of state were you in?"

"I don't remember much. My brother told me that in the first weeks, while I was awake, I would stare at him and my mother and smile. I smiled a lot. My brother said he thought it was a vacant, meaningless smile. As if I couldn't recognize anything around me. Then, gradually, I began to remember everything that had happened in prison apart from a few days, which remained a blank."

Dr. Hawkins noted that Adiba's voice was shaking and her body trembling. She had changed the way she was sitting. She looked sideways, leaning slightly forward. She put her head into her hands as if by holding on to it, she could lessen the pain. The pain arising out of dark memories. Dr. Hawkins decided to change the course of the discussion and return to the present. They were quiet. The clock ticked. Tick, tock. Tick, tock. Sufficient time passed for Adiba to recover her poise. Very slowly, she lifted her bowed head. She removed her hands and looked dry-eyed at Dr. Hawkins.

"How are you feeling? Shall we continue?"

"Yes."

"If you leave the lights on, are things any different?"

"A little."

"Supposing there were someone else with you at home, would you be less afraid?"

"A little."

"Would your sleep be more relaxed, for example?"

"No, I would just feel slightly more secure."

"Is there an ideal situation in which you can sleep properly?"

Adiba laughed irritably.

"After exhaustive tests, I have come up with the following formula: I have someone I trust in the house, I leave the lights on, and I do not close the curtains in the bedroom."

"Does that enable you to sleep through?"

"Almost. The main thing is that I don't feel afraid."

"What things usually make you afraid?"

"At night, or during the day?"

"In general."

Silence.

"Don't rush into an answer. Take your time."

"Not knowing. Something happening unexpectedly. Something I can't see. I can be asleep and feel two eyes watching me. I try and stay awake so that they will go away."

"These eyes? Do they belong to a man or a woman?"

"A man."

"Do you know him, or is he a stranger?"

"I don't know."

"Is it always the same man, or does he change each time?"

"The features are familiar, but I cannot identify the individual."

"Is it an Iraqi or English face?"

"Iraqi."

MEDICAL REPORT

Dr. Hawkins, the psychiatrist at the clinic for the victims of torture, in London, received a copy of the medical report on Mrs. Adiba Baghdadi from Amnesty International, and, like all the cases that preceded it and succeeded it, it was printed on a form.

She read:

Case No. 7

Personal details	Female, 32 years old
State of health before arrest	Good
Length of stay in prison	She spent 45 days in a secret place in Baghdad, at the security headquarters.
Place of torture	Secret place in Baghdad
Length of time torture lasted	7 days in the final quarter of 1979
Any medical treatment during incarceration	Nonexistent
Methods of torture	Beaten and kicked in all parts of her body. In the first days, blows to the head, face, and temples. Kicked particularly in lower abdomen. Undressed three times, and made to stand naked once in the interrogation room in the presence of interrogators and twice in the courtyard of the center. During the night was put in a room next to torture chamber. She was left there from midnight till eight o'clock in the morning, with the changeover of the *shebab* shift (name given to the interrogators). Sleep deprivation during her initial period of interrogation. Sudden beatings on her legs with rubber tubes, into which metal rods had been introduced, every time sleep overcame her. Not allowed any contact with anyone apart from the guards and her interrogators. There were four interrogators (*shebab*). She didn't meet anyone throughout her time of imprisonment apart from her husband. Remembers seeing him at the end of the first week. He was bruised. Collapsed in a chair. Blindfolded. Only recognized him because of his voice, when he denied that she had been interested in, participated in, or had any knowledge of any political activity.

	Never saw him again. She has never discovered what happened to him.
Short-term symptoms	Bruising on the skin and bleeding from blows to face, chest, and womb. Hemorrhaging in the womb. Loss of memory after the second week. Loss of appetite and weight loss (15 kilos). Breaking of right anklebone. Suicidal.
Long-term symptoms	Partial memory loss. Persistent lameness in left leg.
Physical examination	Introverted, complains of depression, fear, insomnia, interrupted sleep, and nightmares. Some weakness found in the muscles of the lower part of her abdomen, womb, loss of control of bladder. Irregular periods. 15 by 15 mm long scar on her right anklebone and another under the left side, 10 by 10 mm long, resulting from blows from a solid instrument such as a truncheon.

Conclusions: The examining doctors found, from the information presented, the symptoms and distinguishing marks were consistent with torture.

CHAPTER NINE

Iqbal canceled her appointment with the doctor. She felt the pain was passing and would go away of its own accord. She ran a hot bath. She filled the tub with water and left it to steam for a while. She added some drops of oil of lavender to the water and dissolved pineapple-scented bath salts.

Naked, she stood in the bathroom while the scented mist rose around her. She gazed admiringly at her body in the large mirror, which hung the length of the wall parallel to the bath. Heavy-breasted. Round, beautiful shoulders, small-waisted. She stood sideways to get a closer look. Her stomach clung to her back. There were no stretch marks. She had been careful. While she was pregnant, she had massaged her belly with refreshing oils and enriched creams, to avoid getting stretch marks. She turned around and inspected her back. A fold of skin hung down a bit between the lower part of her shoulders and her waist. She felt uneasy. It was the first time she'd noticed it. She would have to exercise or walk more.

Since buying the car, she'd turned into an invalid. She no longer walked anywhere. She patted her flat stomach in delight. At least her belly wasn't showing signs of the large amounts of beer she'd been drinking. She turned to the right and the left. She cupped her breasts in both hands. She wished they were a bit smaller—a size B bra rather than a size C. Then she recalled how Hussein had loved to hold them, like a baby suckling at his mother's breast. John, too, never tired of fondling and looking at them, treating them as if they were pieces of rare artwork. She sighed contentedly as she stretched out in the steaming, scented water. Not a bad body at all, she thought, despite its thirty-six years!

It was her day off and she had a right to pamper herself before Samer got back from school, and she had to busy herself with him. She had arranged for them to go out to the cinema in the evening with John, but Samer had been invited to his friend's birthday party and was now going to spend the night at his house. She'd changed her program. She'd take him to his friend's first, then drive to Camden Town, where she'd meet John after work. Then they'd decide what to do. They'd no longer have to go and see Walt Disney's *The Lion King*, but could choose an adult film, as Samer wouldn't be with them. She veiled her eyes and yielded completely to the sense of relaxation. To the idea of the coming sensuous night with John.

"John, you look tired. We can cancel the date, if you want."

"No, no. Cancel our date? Are you crazy? However, what do you think about putting off the film tonight and going back to my flat instead?"

"Your flat's so far away."

"Let's go out to dinner. It'll be my treat. Where would you like to go? Greek, English, fish and chips, or that French restaurant we went to last time."

"I don't want anything at the moment. I had a late lunch. If you're hungry, let's go to the café. Or, if you can wait, we'll go to my flat, and I'll make us something light."

He smiled happily.

"When you speak in such a soothing voice, I feel my tiredness slip away," he said. "I'm ready to go to the ends of the earth with you."

As they went toward where she had parked her car, he said,

"By the way . . . did you know that Camden Town is midway between my flat and yours?"

"That's impossible. Your flat is miles away."

"Numerically speaking, the distance between the two is almost equal, but it's a different matter if you look at it from the point of view of emotions and feelings. The way you feel is directly related to the fact that you know the road to your flat better, and, therefore, it seems closer. As you refuse to come to my flat so often, it seems further away. Generally, I don't mind giving in and going to your flat instead of mine because, like you, I feel more comfortable in it."

"I thought you were tired," Iqbal reminded him.

"What do you mean?"

"Since we met, you haven't stopped talking and analyzing."

John laughed out loud.

He explained, "You must love the sound of your own voice if you are going to work as a teacher. How can you teach if you enjoy silence?"

They reached the car. She'd parked it on one of the backstreets in Camden. She pointed out a three-story building on the right of the street and said,

"I've got a friend who lives on the ground floor."

"Who is she?"

"Adiba. I'll introduce you to her sometime."

"Adiba. Not Um so-and-so, or mother of so-and-so? Strange."

"She hasn't got any children ... so we can't call her Um so ... Her husband was arrested and disappeared. She's heard nothing about him for hundreds of years."

John seized on her exaggeration.

"You mean several years?"

"No, twenty years, I think."

"Has she tried Amnesty International and the human rights organizations?"

She turned the steering wheel blindly from right to left, finding it difficult to rescue her car from the narrow parking space into which she had tucked it.

"No, she's been at home waiting for some sympathetic humanitarian organization to find her husband," she snapped. "Of course she's contacted all the organizations. What do you think she's been doing? Sitting back and relaxing? Do you know what you remind me of when you ask me something like that?" She didn't wait for his answer, but carried on angrily.

"You remind me of that story about an Iraqi man who spent hours explaining how bad the political situation was in Iraq to his English neighbor. At the end of it, she advised him, quite seriously, not to vote for the same president in the next elections."

"Ha, ha, ha!" John snorted derisively.

"She's still trying to get information from international organizations," Iqbal said seriously. "She contacts Arab officials, asking them to intervene, and writes to newspapers from time to time. It's as if he disappeared yesterday. She still hopes to find him."

"What do you think?" John asked.

She finally managed to get out of the parking space.

"About what?"

"Do you think there's any chance she'll find him?"

"Knowing what we do about the regime, I should say it's impossible. If someone disappears and there's no trace of him after a few days, it means he's dead."

"I wouldn't want to be in her shoes at all. It must be difficult and frightening. I think it would be easier to know that he was dead, so that she could come to terms with his death. But like this, she's trapped between life and death. It must be a continuous nightmare for her," John said.

She didn't say anything. He noticed her turning off the main road.

"I used to think that it was easier and quicker to go in a straight line," he said.

"Well, that theory doesn't apply to Swiss Cottage. That road's crowded and busy. Even though it's the most direct route, it takes longer; it's quicker to go through the backstreets."

She turned in to West End Lane and drove toward West Hampstead. It was a narrow road with cars parked along both sides.

"This reminds me of *Sirat al-Mustaqim* (the Straight Path)," she said in Arabic.

"Sorry?"

"Nothing."

She didn't want to explain. She was tired of driving.

They reached the flat. To get into it, they had to sidle along the corridor.

"Have you bought some new furniture?" he teased.

"No, it's Samer's new bicycle. He's put it behind the door. His old bike was stolen from the ground-floor landing. So we decided to bring it into the flat."

"And your bike?"

"I've moved it into the bathroom."

"How do you use the bathroom now?" he laughed.

"It's easy. I pull the bike outside, then I go in."

"What about guests?"

"I tell them to feel at home, so they do the same as me."

"Some flats are provided with a small shed outside. Have you got one?"

"Yes, and it's full of things. Most of them Samer's. He's very attached to his old games and books. And I don't want him to feel that he has to get rid of them."

"Do you know that my mother still keeps my old things in the attic? I've told her to get rid of them. She says, 'You'll need them someday for your own children.'"

Iqbal ignored this last sentence. He watched her as she quickly tidied up the sitting room. She piled the newspapers and magazines in a corner. She pushed the planks under the sofa. She took out a damp cloth and wiped the low tea table. Finally, pleased with her accomplishments, she said contentedly,

"We'll sit down in a clean and tidy sitting room. Who says that cleaning the house is hard work?"

"Iqbal, have you been listening to a word I've said, or are you pretending to be deaf?" he asked, watching her attentively.

"What . . . what did you say? I'm all ears." She chuckled. "I must remember that expression for Sahira. She'll like it a lot. She's obsessed with English expressions.'I'm all ears.' I'm listening to what you're saying. I wonder . . . would you be so devoted to me if I really were all ears, and had them growing out of every corner of my body?"

"Iqbal, I'm going to repeat what I've said a dozen times before. I want us to live together. I want us to settle down. I'm not bothered about what form our relationship takes. I'll do what you want. If you want to live together, that's fine. If you're worried about people gossiping, or going against your culture, and want to get married, that's fine, too. The important thing is that you make up your mind and choose what you want."

"I read somewhere—I don't remember where—that a lover who's satisfied does not need much. He's replete. Happy with the situation as it is. Aren't we happy enough as we are? We see each other at least once a week. What more do you want?"

"I want us to live together every day."

"Why do you have to be different from other men? I'm sure other men would be pleased with our current arrangement. Meet a woman. Have something to eat. Sleep with her. And bid her good-bye. Adieu and farewell. No responsibility. No obligations. No being the breadwinner. No paying off mounting debts and loans. No miserable, bad-tempered faces to wake up to in the morning. We meet when we're ready. I'm bathed and scented, and you're clean and yearning for me. It seems like the best arrangement in the world. Why do you have to be different?"

"Are you being serious or joking? Could you love me if I was not different?"

"John . . . my beloved, dearest John. Because of you, I spent over half an hour in the bath today, soaking and dozing in the scented water and dreaming about our date; I was so wrapped up in my thoughts that I almost drowned. As you see, I've cleaned the flat for you and am about to prepare one of your favorite *mezzes*. If you look around, you'll see that Samer's not here to pester you with his questions and remarks and those awful television serials he loves watching. Why do you want to ruin this wonderful atmosphere and drag me into a long discussion which I'm not prepared for?"

He withdrew. It was futile. He got up from his seat. He approached her. He hugged her tightly, then pushed her away from him with a sigh.

"I'll help you prepare the *mezze*."

He washed several plates and cups. He searched for a clean tea towel to dry them with.

"Leave them where they are," she told him. "We don't dry the dishes."

He didn't ask her, "Who do you mean by 'we'?" because he already knew the answer. She would laugh, and say, "There is only one cultural difference between the great British and Iraqi people, and that is that, unlike you, we don't dry our plates after washing them!"

When he had first met her, her malicious, whiplashlike taunts had sometimes hurt him. She would seize on the tiniest mistake to draw comparisons between them and make fun of him. As he grew closer to her, he recognized that she wasn't poking fun at him personally, but rather at the deep-seated differences between her previous life and her current one. Between her first country and her second. Between her first marriage and her uncertain secret relationship with him. Between her defiance of her traditions and her covert wish to practice them.

He tidied things in the little kitchen. Warmed some pita bread, cut it up, and placed it in a small basket. Covered the table with a paper sheet and helped her carry the dishes of sunflower seeds, humus, yogurt mixed with cucumbers and chopped up mint, white cheese, and sliced tomatoes.

"And now, poor worn-out teacher, what are you going to drink?" Iqbal asked.

"What have you got?"

"Beer and wine. I've got a bottle of whiskey. Kept for special occasions."

"Whiskey, please. Have you got any soda?"

"No, I'll add some water."

"No thanks. I'll just have it with two ice cubes."

She laughed.

"What sin have I committed now?"

"Why do you persist in calling them ice cubes when they're shaped like bananas, strawberries, or pigs?"

"In that case, let me extend my apologies to Iqbal for committing such a linguistic heresy and say I'll have my whiskey with two ice bananas, please."

She sat beside him on the floor. They leaned back against the sofa. Their legs touched as they stretched them out under the low table. In front of them was the blank, silent television screen. They enjoyed a moment of silence. She closed her eyes and sighed with pleasure. She leaned toward him. She felt the embrace of his blue eyes. She put up her hand and turned it sideways to shield herself from his gaze.

"Why are you staring at me?"

"I'm not staring. I'm enjoying myself, looking at you."

She lifted her glass to change the subject of conversation. His romantic words confused her, and he liked embarrassing her.

"Cheers," she said.

"Cheers."

"Shall we listen to some music?"

"If you like."

"I've bought a cassette of Um Kulthoum that you haven't heard yet. I think you'll like it."

He nodded.

"It begins with a musical introduction," she said.

"I know."

She didn't comment. She thought of the many times he had listened to Arabic music with her, especially that of Um Kulthoum; he had begun to recognize the style of her songs.

"Iqbal, how's your group of Iraqi friends?" John asked.

"They met last week, and Sahira told me they've decided to meet regularly. Once a month."

"Do you like the idea?"

"I don't really know. We used to meet up when we felt like it, either individually or in a group. I'd phone Adiba and meet her, and she'd phone Um Mohammed, and we'd share the invitation. Now, I don't know. I feel reluctant about such a commitment. I don't like strict rules. It reminds me of being in a political party."

"I know how you feel."

"Really?" she queried coldly.

He detected a patronizing note in her voice, a vibrating undertone that he had often heard and which said, "I belong to a people who are politically aware. We're not like you. You don't know what's happening in other countries. You don't even know the difference between Iraq and Iran."

"That's true," he replied quietly. "That was my problem with the

Socialist Workers Party."

She gulped down a mouthful of red wine, then scooped up a handful of sunflower seeds, which she ate one at a time. He pointed to the seeds and said,

"But I'll be the first to admit that you've got me beaten when it comes to eating sunflower seeds. You're definitely the champion in the way you're able to get the seed out and separate the kernel from the husk."

She threw a handful of seeds at him.

"Don't provoke me," she said, pretending to be irritated, "or . . ."

"Or what?"

"Nothing. Do you want an ice pig?"

"No thanks."

He sipped his whiskey slowly, contentedly.

He chewed on a piece of bread that had been dipped in yogurt and olive oil.

"How did you meet the group? I don't think you've ever told me."

"First of all, I don't tell you everything I do. And second, I don't know why you call them 'the group.' We're five women who met by chance and decided to carry on meeting. However, I'll answer your strange question to satisfy your curiosity. I met Adiba, Sahira, and Majda at a vigil outside No. 10 Downing Street, the house of your prime minister, which was being held to show solidarity with the Iraqi people."

"He's not *my* prime minister," he protested. "I voted for the Loonies."

Iqbal ignored his remark and went on with what she was saying.

"I remember telling you about it."

"That's true. It was the day I had the flu."

"Exactly. I went with Samer. We were standing among a crowd of British demonstrators of all ages, who were shouting against Blair, America, and the bombing. I was holding a placard and so was Samer. I felt a bit like an orphan. I looked around for someone else from Iraq, then I heard a woman with an Iraqi accent abusing Clinton and saying he should be tried. I said hello to her, and she started with fright. She was wearing dark glasses and a black hat. I asked her if she was from Iraq. She said, 'How did you know?' I smiled. 'The spirit, and traces of Baghdad boil.'

"At first she was upset and afraid of me; she was one of those Iraqis who feels constantly threatened and hounded. However, when she saw poor Samer shivering with cold and carrying a placard, she started to trust me."

"Was that Adiba?" John asked.

"No, Majda. Adiba, on the contrary, limped up to us, leaning on her stick. She introduced herself. She said she'd heard us talking and wanted to get to know us. We were the only Iraqis at the demonstration. We stayed like that, standing side by side, in keeping with our Iraqi identity. We exchanged telephone numbers and agreed to contact each other if there was another such demonstration."

"Sahira told me she took part in the demonstration without her husband knowing," John said.

"I know. Kadhim believes such demonstrations only benefit the regime. He says they prolong its existence and, therefore, the suffering of the people."

"It's a difficult question. We faced something similar when we held demonstrations and continuous vigils outside the South African embassy. The sanctions were double-edged," John said.

"I believe that lifting the sanctions is vital—to enable people to think and act. How can you think if you're hungry, sick, and poor?"

She sighed heavily.

"Anyway, since then I've felt a sort of responsibility toward them."

"But you told me that they were the ones who usually took the initiative!"

"I know. But I still feel responsible . . . deep inside."

"It's clear they feel responsible for you. Iqbal, why don't you let me shoulder all your responsibilities, including those of your friends, so you can sit back and relax?" he added jokingly.

"And you'll start behaving like Hussein, my ex-husband!"

"Do I resemble your ex-husband in any way?"

She examined him closely.

"To look at, no! But inside, God knows!"

"Are you trying to tell me that you still don't know me properly? After two years?"

"I was a comrade of Hussein's, and then engaged to him for a whole year. We got married and lived for a year in al-Kut. Then we escaped and fled to Kurdistan and from there to Moscow. I suppose I'm saying that I'd shared a whole life with him before I got to know him without his mask and he showed me his real face."

John felt he was about to lose the argument again.

"Speaking of him, where is he now?"

"A friend told me that he's gone back to Kurdistan."

"Why?"

"They say he's joined the military wing of one of the opposition parties whose members are training in Iraqi Kurdistan."

"He's very brave to leave his settled life in Europe and risk his life in such a dangerous and uncertain venture."

"I wasn't very surprised when I heard. He's political by nature."

As was her habit, she avoided talking about Hussein. She became aware that Um Kulthoum had stopped singing. She got up slowly, leaning on the edge of the low table so as not to lose her balance. She had drunk about three-quarters of a bottle of wine on an empty stomach. John urged her to eat something.

"There's no point in drinking if I eat and don't get drunk," she said.

She put on a record—Iranian *tar* music.

"What a fool I am! I've forgotten to light the candles!" she exclaimed.

Iqbal rushed off to the kitchen and grabbed a handful of differently sized candles. She lit them and placed them about the room.

She lit a stick of incense and turned off the light. She sat beside him. John reached out a hand and pushed away a lock of hair that had fallen down over her face. He held her chin gently, then bent forward and kissed her shuttered eyes. He kissed her quietly, softly, as if he were getting to know her features and the softness of her skin. He drank in the fragrance of the oil and perfume that her smooth skin emitted.

In a hoarse whisper that marked time with her aroused body, the sound of string music, the shadowy candlelight, and the spicy scent of incense, she murmured,

"I must get you that supper I promised you."

He wasn't listening. He reached out his hand to her blouse and undid the buttons. He unzipped her skirt. The touch of the youthful, bare skin underneath aroused him. She felt the tremor of his hand. Her body responded. His warmth coursed into her. He lightly touched the side of her left breast. His fingers inched up the mound. They stopped at the peak. A luscious, deep cherry red fruit, surrounded by a lighter aureole ring. He moved his fingers in a circular fashion about the nipple. It became erect. He watched it swell with pleasure. As his fingers encircled it, he whispered, "Round and round I go." With his other hand, he drew up her skirt. About her right nipple, he whispered humbly, supplicatingly, "Round and round I go." Before touching the tip of her nipple, his breath coming in hot pants, his voice like liquid in her ears, he asked in a whisper,

"Where now?"

She wasn't listening.

She had slipped far away to a steamy, misty, sensuous world, where she lay as if in a bath of aromatic incense. She was deaf and blind to everything beyond it. She heard and saw nothing, feeling only his touch. She undid his trousers. They sloughed off their outer garments. She took his hand. She steered it, like she would a blind man, to her belly, to the gate of her absolute delight. She drew it down gradually. She guided it to the core of her feelings. With her other hand, she took him very slowly into her world.

CHAPTER TEN

She neither looked nor behaved like her mother. She took after her father. Tall and soft-featured. With small sharp eyes. Like his, they shifted nervously from right to left as she talked, so that her sense of anxiety and perturbation transferred itself to the person she was addressing.

When she was a child, her mother used to yell at her,

"Majda, look at me when I'm speaking to you! Concentrate!"

She also differed from her mother in the way she felt about children. She hadn't tried to start a family when she got married to Sa'id for the simple reason that she didn't like children. She didn't like looking after them. She didn't like the way they screamed and carried on. She abhorred their monkeylike antics when guests were present. She was nauseated by the love, affection, and adulation showered upon them. Under no circumstances was she going to allow them to upset her comfortable life and indolent daily routine.

How many women in the world would be prepared to acknowledge such a shortcoming? Her mother, for example, had been prepared to spend her entire life getting pregnant and giving birth, waiting on the house during the day and lying recumbent under her husband at night. Through the mercy of God, the Great and Exalted, she had been released from her marriage early on, and left as an estate a hovel in Souk Hamada, one of the poorest areas of Baghdad, and four children, the eldest of whom was Tahsin and the youngest Majda.

Majda's days followed an exemplary pattern. She woke at about ten o'clock. Sa'id had already left the house at seven. Na'ima prepared tea for her. She ate a freshly baked piece of bread spread with qaimara, and then had her first cigarette. She took her time getting ready for work. Dawdled. Carefully chose what she was going to wear. Combed her hair and made herself up adroitly. First the skin moisturizer, then the foundation cream, and finally the blusher, the shades of color blending harmoniously into one.

On one of her rare visits to Majda's house, her mother had watched in exasperation as her daughter unhurriedly put on her clothes, applied her makeup, and smoked one cigarette after another, while all the time

Sa'id stood outside waiting for her. "Well, well, well, may God have mercy on us! See how quickly you've forgotten Souk Hamada!" her mother had grumbled in dismay.

She walked to work. The school was close to her home in Hayy al-Mansour. They had chosen to live there because it was the most affluent area in Baghdad. She held the post of deputy headmistress at Saddam Central Secondary School. She was really just a primary school teacher, but when she had gotten married to Sa'id and joined the Ba'ath Party, she had been quickly promoted to secondary level; and she could have, if she'd wished, gotten a much more influential job in the ministry, but she was lazy and lacked ambition.

Her work was just a formality. She arrived late and left early. She rarely worked the hours she was supposed to. Who was going to complain? The opposite was true. The teachers as a whole, whatever their political beliefs and affiliations, were glad when she didn't turn up. Some meekly carried out her work, hoping that she would repay the favor one day by acting as an intermediary on their behalf. Others relaxed when she was away, glad to be rid of a party official whose eye was trained on them like a video camera. She was worse, in fact, because she was not content with keeping an eye on them and observing their behavior, but would sometimes write detailed reports about them.

Because of her rank in the party, Majda was entitled to be promoted to headmistress if she wanted to, but she preferred to remain as deputy. She was very content with her position. Miss Munira, the current headmistress, was a member of the old guard. She carried out her duties punctiliously and was said not to have married so that she could devote herself to teaching and her students. A worthy woman. Concerned about education and maintaining standards. Or, as Majda told Sa'id, "She works like the proverbial donkey, and I earn twice as much as she does."

Why should she give up her comfort and happiness just to be called headmistress?

She felt the same about having children as she did about work and teaching. She was happy without them. Why should she make herself sick giving birth? Her friends asked her whether she would think the same if Sa'id, in common with other men, wanted to preserve the family line. She answered carelessly, "Who knows?"

Apart from the two hours she spent at work, the party meetings on Sundays and Thursdays for the teachers, and the weekly visit to the General Federation of Iraqi Women, the day belonged to her. Na'ima did the housework. (They had changed her title from servant to employee following a decree by the Revolutionary Command Council, and they had allocated her a salary and a pension.) Her duties entailed preparing the food and looking after the house, assisted by Mushatat, guard/gardener/chauffeur and employee.

A great life. Many people envied her it. What would be the point of changing it all just to have children?

"Aren't you afraid that he will abandon you?" asked her friends, when they advised her to start a family. "Tie him down with children, and he'll stay with you forever." Majda shrieked with laughter. "He knows and I know that we're bound together by something much stronger than a child," she said and winked, alluding to the strongest ties of all: her affiliation with the party, the sacrifice of her brother, who had been a martyr to the cause, and her personal acquaintance with His Excellency, the President.

How many times had she told the story of the time she met His Excellency, the President?

Dozens of times, hundreds, perhaps.

She'd told the girls in her class. Her teachers. Her friends. Her neighbors. Her relatives. She told the story at a time in the past when it was a mark of great honor to have met the President, and not something shameful to be hushed up. Each time she recounted the story, she altered and modified it, added to it and subtracted from it, deleting some parts or subtly stressing others, according to how old she was or the mood she was in, or the circumstances and importance of the audience.

She had gotten to know Sa'id during a party conference. Once, after they had announced their engagement, he'd asked her, with an apparent show of disinterest,

"Is it true that Saddam Hussein hid in your house for several months?"

"No, he stayed with us for two weeks."

She knew how much to reveal to her future husband and how much to conceal.

"I was in the third year at secondary school," she went on, with a similar semblance of indifference. "I was lazy, just like I am now, and hated school, but I adored Tahsin, may God have mercy on him! He was totally committed to the party, and I wanted to be just like him. He told me that the party was going through an extremely difficult time; it wasn't safe for him to go out often and that's why he had to send me to the comrades with messages and instructions. I owe my political awareness to Tahsin. He was like a father to me at that time, and from him I learned the meaning of Ba'athism and the dream of a single Arab nation. He taught me how to distinguish between the Ba'athists, those people who were proud of their national identity, and the Communists, who were lackeys of a foreign power.

"We lived in al-Karkh district. Its maze of little alleyways made it a no-go area for the outsider, and our house became a safe house for the party. Well . . . surely you know that already. To get to the point . . . one night, during that difficult time, Tahsin brought one of his comrades to the house, a tall, serious-looking young man, who kept his eyes modestly lowered. He greeted my mother and me politely and went up with Tahsin to his room on the first floor.

"Tahsin warned us not to tell anyone he was in the house, because he was a wanted man.

"My mother said, 'There's no need to put us on our guard. We're used to misfortunes.'

"I didn't see him after that," said Majda, shrugging to show how little the incident had meant to her. "He stayed with us for two weeks, but it was more like having a ghost in the house. He came in late, while we were asleep, and left early, before we awoke."

She looked him straight in the eye.

"I didn't even know his name at the time," she added.

And what Majda told Sa'id was true, apart from two things, which she considered too intimate and unsuitable for the ears of a future husband, and kept to herself.

The first thing she failed to mention was that Tahsin's friend, the young Ba'athist, had looked at her so boldly the moment he walked into the house that he had made her blush. His penetrating eyes had pierced her young teenage body and awoken feelings that confused her. After that, she had secretly watched his comings and goings from the window in the sitting room, which looked down onto the courtyard, for the entire two weeks he was in the house. Once, she had plucked up her courage and emerged from the sitting room into the courtyard when she heard his steps on the stairs, pretending that she was going to the toilet.

She had planned the meeting in her mind in detail, imagining the questions she would ask about the party and his activism, and the words she would exchange with him; she had practiced her gestures and smiles for ages in front of the mirror. But when she came face to face with him, she was overcome by trepidation. She stood there unable to move, looking at him as if he were the first man she had ever seen in her life.

He looked steadily at her and greeted her in a slightly strange accent, which was not from Baghdad.

"What's your name?" he asked.

"Majda," she stammered, as if she were choking.

He repeated it very slowly after her, as if he were savoring an appetizing dish.

"Majda. Ha! Majda the Glorious. What a lovely name! It's a fitting name for a Ba'athi girl and the sister of a Ba'athist."

He thought for a moment, and then said:

"What a sweet name! In fact, it should apply to all Ba'athi women. Majda in the singular, Majdat in the plural. I swear by God, Majda," he added resolutely, "we'll make all Iraqi women Majdat."

After that extraordinary meeting, she didn't see him again. He slipped away from the house without saying good-bye.

Once she'd gotten married, Majda no longer fantasized about that meeting, until something happened which brought the picture she had locked away in her memory vividly to mind. Something totally unexpected befell her. Or more correctly, befell her and Sa'id, and made them submit, in spite of themselves, and agree to have children as quickly as possible.

It was a Thursday evening. She and Sa'id had gone to Nadi al-Sayd, an exclusive club in al-Mansour. She liked the place and the youthful music and meeting up with comrades and their wives. Her friend Samira, in particular—'Izat's wife—never missed a Thursday without visiting Nadi al-Sayd. Majda would arrange to meet her friends at the club and invite her guests there, saying over and over again: "There's good food, a good atmosphere, and nice music. Why should we pine away at home when God, *Subhana wa Ta'ali*, has given us enough money to enjoy ourselves?"

Majda was wearing a gray dress with a red collar, and matching shoes and handbag. She'd bought them, together with a quantity of underwear, from a *dalala*, one of the women traders who brought back merchandise from Beirut and Kuwait and sold it from their homes. Majda was pleased with her tall, slender figure and her sense of style. Sa'id had told her that he didn't like her wearing high heels, because he wasn't very tall. He'd warned her jokingly that anyone who saw them together might get the wrong impression. "They might think you have the whip hand over me," he'd said.

She could still remember that evening in detail. How can we remember things that happened decades ago as clearly as if they happened the day before, but forget things which have just happened?

It was on one of those days in July that followed the celebrations marking the Blessed 17th–30th July Revolution. In a surprise ministerial reshuffle, Sa'id had been appointed minister of information and culture, in addition to the posts he already held as a member of the Regional and National Command Council of the Ba'ath Party. A month before, in the final days of the school year, and despite her protests, she had been promoted as well: to the position of headmistress of Saddam Model Secondary School. She had been unable to refuse. She had received the letter of promotion at a "meeting of allegiance" held especially to honor women from the Ba'ath Party who had played a significant role in the struggle leading up to the glorious revolution of 17th–30th July.

The comrade minister of education had attended the meeting and read a speech from His Excellency, the President in which he said:

> Women of the Ba'ath Party should not only be praised for the role they played in, and their contribution to, the underground struggle, but also for the increasing part they are continuing to play in the battle today, particularly on the current stage, which demands resistance of a different nature. This is a struggle that establishes different meanings, understandings, and values for the party, in a more comprehensive and broader fashion than in previous years.

She had been forced to change her routine. During the period of festivities, which coincided with the beginning of the summer holidays and the unbearable, impossible heat of July, when tempers blazed and nerves were stretched to the breaking point, constant demands were made on her. She was in charge of mobilizing the teachers, cadres, and students, spurring them on to celebrate the revolution, decorate the school, take part in the demonstrations and marches of the masses, and, finally, participate in a large party at school that was attended by important officials, as well as local people.

Her promotion had brought additional headaches. She had to compose and deliver the opening address, but didn't know how to write a speech. She asked Sa'id to help her. He interrupted his hectic schedule to fetch a number of copies of *al-Thawra* and *al-Jumhouria* newspapers for her, which he threw onto the table. He pointed at the many party pamphlets scattered around the house and said, "Take what you want. You'll find everything you need to say in there."

Sa'id was exhausted. He was under great pressure. He'd grown pale and started to suffer from dizziness and nausea. As part of the National Dieting Program—enforced by a presidential decree—which directed officials to lose weight, he had stopped eating anything apart from bits of salad and taken to smoking immoderately and drinking vast quantities of tea and whiskey. In one week alone, he had lost five kilos, due in part to his heavy workload and in part to the fervor with which he carried out the presidential decree.

He worked on ten tasks at a time. He told her bitterly that he felt like someone trying to hold ten pomegranates in one hand. She consoled him, "If you and I, who have been rewarded so generously by the Leader, don't celebrate the anniversary of the revolution and Comrade President's achievements, who will?"

His work engrossed him completely. He had to supervise the media—newspapers and magazines, radio and television—as well as organize a march of intellectuals and writers and popular poets. As particular associations, general unions, and other local committees and organizations tried to outdo each other in their zeal and expressions of support for the revolution and the Leader, the situation became more complicated.

The popular poets, for example, demanded to march on their own, to show their gratitude for the generosity extended to them by His Excellency, the President.

And Sa'id was forced to implement what they wanted because he didn't dare to question the idea, let alone dismiss it.

He was also busy welcoming official delegations from the Arab world, well-known Arab thinkers, poets, and artists, who would be taking part in various events; he had to reply to an endless stream of congratulatory telegrams from organizations and Arab and foreign governments, write an editorial for *al-Thawra* newspaper, and, finally, take part in a seminar about the reasons they had lost power in October 1963, which would be published in *al-Jumhouria* newspaper.

Majda asked him to spend Thursday evening with her at the club, where they would find some respite from the frenzy of public celebrations. He protested and said he had an appointment with two Arab poets. She suggested he meet them at the club. He agreed.

They made their way to their usual table, which was some way away from the band. Sa'id was suffering from high blood pressure and couldn't stand the noise. He wished the management of the club would change the program and play traditional *maqam*, and *chalgi* music from Baghdad instead of the Western dance music that was on offer.

As they walked between the tables, they stopped to greet acquaintances and friends. They were kissed and congratulated on their promotions. They invited Sa'id to come and sit with them for a little while, but he excused himself, saying they were expecting guests. Mihyar Ikhlasi and Mi'ad al-Salim arrived shortly after they had sat down. The two famous poets were in Baghdad at the special invitation of Sa'id to celebrate the anniversary of the revolution.

Sa'id had had his reasons for selecting them from among the hundreds of poets who wanted to take part. The Leader had indicated his special interest in the poetess Mi'ad al-Salim at an important poetry festival, which he had attended at the beginning of the year. Mi'ad had recited a poem in which she had woven together her love for Iraq and its people, embodying that love in their Leader—the symbol that represented them. The poem was written in a lucid and magical language, very different from the traditional turn of phrase used in the classical *madih*, or adulatory poems. At the end of the *qasida*, she had apostrophized them with words that were no less passionate than those in her poem. She declaimed:

> All of you
> You, Mr. President, you, his people
> You are the image of what we dream of
> We might not follow in your footsteps
> But I/we
> In the depths of my heart as a human being
> I wish I were like you
> Because I see you as my role model.

Turning toward the place where His Excellency, the President was sitting, she had raised her arms high into the air in a gesture midway between a salute and an embrace, and extemporized these additional lines:

> I have come to Baghdad
> Blind

In despair,
At the capitulation of the Arabs, and their humiliation,
At the total darkness that engulfs me,
And behold
Saddam Hussein
Trickles sun into my eyes,
He casts out my grief
He brings back migrating birds
To my forest.

The whole hall had risen and clapped with an enthusiasm that they rarely showed to other poets. The standing ovation had gone on for several minutes as they demanded an encore.

Mi'ad had stepped down from the dais that had been erected on the stage. She stood on the edge of the stage, right in front of His Excellency, the President. She thanked the audience, bowing humbly before them. And she bowed again to the President and her long jet-black hair hung down, swathing her face like a veil. Every time she raised her head to acknowledge the President, in particular, it was as if she were seeking his permission to rip apart her black veil of hair, in an action that would defy tradition and enable her to preserve his image in her eyes.

From where he was sitting, His Excellency, the President favored her with a rare smile.

She held up her hand, indicating that she would accede to demands for an encore, and returned to the dais, the gold embroidered skirts of her Hashemite dress trailing behind her. She stood behind the microphone and in a hoarse voice, roughened by emotion, recited the final lines a second time.

"Mi'ad is not Iraqi, but she deserves to be known just like Iraqi women as al-Majda the Glorious," His Excellency, the President had said to the people around him, of whom Sa'id was one. "She is one of the greatest Arab women."

Sa'id had invited Mihyar Ikhlasi to participate in the celebrations for a number of reasons. Not only was he hugely popular in the Arab world, where his poems were frequently recited, but he had also promised to compose a new poem especially for the occasion, which he would dedicate to His Excellency, the President.

Sa'id introduced them to Majda. She greeted Mi'ad warmly, then reached out her left hand to Mihyar. He took it caressingly between his own and bent his head and kissed it. Majda blushed.

"This is the first time someone's shaken hands with me like that," she murmured, stammering slightly.

Mi'ad looked at Mihyar fondly.

"That's because it's the first time you've met a poet like Mihyar. That's how a great poet cherishes and salutes women."

They roared with laughter.

The club was noisier than usual. The sound of music and laughter penetrated every nook and cranny. Everyone wanted to display their joy at having gotten through the strenuous program of official and popular celebrations. The simplest words and movements resulted in noisy outbursts of communal laughter, as if all the comrades there were congratulating themselves on reaching the end of the race and crossing the finish line.

Sa'id asked the waiter to bring whiskey for himself and Mihyar. Mi'ad asked Majda,

"What are you ordering?"

"I'd like some Farida beer," she said shyly.

"I'll try that, then."

"Farida beer?" asked Mihyar in surprise. "A beer named after a woman. And they say the Iraqis lack delicacy!"

"Rumors," said Sa'id. "My God, rumors. As you can see, we are so gentle and refined."

They hooted with laughter. Sa'id asked,

"I hope the hotel's comfortable."

Mihyar assured him that they were comfortable.

"I asked the manager of the hotel to reserve two of the best rooms overlooking the Tigris, so that you would enjoy the scenery."

"You're a thoughtful person," Mihyar said.

"And what about the car and the driver?"

"Everything's fine."

With the arrival of the drinks, Sa'id and Mihyar began a discussion from which Majda could only glean occasional sentences. She heard Sa'id whisper,

"Absolutely untrue. There aren't any Communist prisoners. She is imagining things."

"She came to see me in the hotel a few hours ago. She said that her husband, a university lecturer, had disappeared some months ago. She was also a university lecturer."

"Oh, yes, I remember," said Sa'id, in a voice tinged with alarm. "I know who you mean. I remember. I know him. Dr. Mukhlis. He's a Communist who renounced the party and opposed the national front. He worked against his party and against the front. As far as I know, he resigned from the party and the university, and left the country."

Sa'id laughed shrilly to conceal his embarrassment.

"Just between the two of us, he seems to have gone the whole hog and resigned from the marriage as well." He added firmly, emphasizing every word, "I assure you, my dear Mihyar, there are no political prisoners in Iraq, a country you know well."

She sighed, hoping that the mention of Communists would not disturb the evening. The sound of music drowned out the rest of their whispered conversation. Mi'ad wasn't paying attention. She was busy looking about her. There was a pause as the band came to the end of a tune. Majda heard Sa'id say,

"The President has insisted on this meaning more than once. He is driven by his belief that Islam is a revolution, and a great revolution at that. It's not logical to witness revolutions rising out of moribund societies or weak and dying nations. Therefore, the Arab nation is a great nation. What we want to prove is that a national identity is part of a wider and more comprehensive Arab identity. And this stage is not a mere phase of history."

Mihyar replied quietly,

"I've come here to learn. Because of my concern for a national ideology."

Concern. Jealousy. *Ghaira.* One word, two meanings. Majda lit another cigarette. As she stole surreptitious glances at Mi'ad, she could feel the jealousy eating away at her. She thought, so this is Mi'ad, the famous poetess. How often have I seen her photographs in magazines and newspapers? She was much more beautiful in real life than she had seemed in the photographs. Brown-skinned, captivating. Wide eyes ringed with kohl, and jet-black hair gleaming and smooth, hanging down to her shoulders.

She was elegant in an understated way. She moved and spoke and gesticulated with an attractive femininity. Her jewelry was expensive, but simply designed: a diamond necklace, a pair of diamond earrings, with stones fashioned like droplets of water, and a diamond bracelet around her wrist. She wore little makeup, but the kohl emphasized the lure of the whites of her eyes. The glitter of the candles was minutely reflected in her gleaming red lips.

Majda was plunged into a deep well of despair as jealousy took hold. Painful reminders came back to haunt her as she recalled the care Saʿid had taken over Miʿad's invitation and the importance he had attached to her attending the anniversary celebrations. She remembered how impressed he had been by her poem and the way she had stood in front of the President and the loud whispers her poems had provoked.

Was she jealous of Miʿad and Saʿid, or Miʿad and His Excellency, the President?

Majda pushed the jumble of thoughts away; she turned around, afraid that someone would read her thoughts.

She made an effort to attend to what was being said around her. Miʿad had the self-confidence that came with her personality, her beauty, and the status of her family. She could talk skillfully about any subject they touched upon. Saʿid spoke in the style he used in writing his editorial for *al-Thawra*.

"The party leadership had failed to put into place a comprehensive program, so the subsequent revolution had to take into consideration the achievement of a true balance between goals and aspirations."

"You needed an experienced, inspiring leader who had an overall view and deep insight," Mihyar interjected suavely.

Saʿid nibbled on a lettuce leaf, then changed the subject of conversation. He asked Miʿad if she was ready for the following day. Many journalists wanted to interview her, including the editor in chief of *al-Jumhouria*, who would be among the first to meet her. Then there would be interviews for radio and television, as well as for the Iraqi News Agency and the newspaper *The Baghdad Observer*.

"Are you prepared for such a media marathon?" he asked politely.

"Yes, as long as Mihyar is alongside me."

"Of course he will be. The journalists long to meet him as well, especially as we are going to publish his new poem tomorrow."

"Do you know, I haven't heard it yet?" Miʿad said.

"Neither have I," Saʿid said. "Our media and our hearts are completely open to a poet like Mihyar and won't scrutinize him in advance."

"I have some conditions," said Mihyar, taking a sip of whiskey.

"That's fine. Tell us what they are."

"First of all, I won't talk about poetry. You know very well that I don't like talking about poetry."

"My dear man, you're free to choose what you talk about."

"I warn you that my opinions might be provocative and are not flattering."

"That's fine. Provoke as much as you like. Release poetry into the open air. Push it to escape. Don't play the hypocrite and don't pay attention to anything but your true feelings. As far as I'm concerned, the most important thing is that you're here celebrating the revolution and its leaders with us. That's the main thing."

"I have another condition."

"Go ahead."

"That you publish my poem in my own handwriting."

"Are you sure? Why tire yourself out, when we can typeset it and print it?"

"No, no, I want it to be in my own handwriting. To give the reader a sense of genuine warmth. To allow him to see that it is not like so many other poems, which start with a dedication but could apply to anyone. I mean the type of doggerel that's produced for such occasions. I don't write poetry for occasions."

"God forbid," Sa'id interrupted him enthusiastically. "Who told you that?"

Mihyar ignored the question.

"I want the reader ... I want him, Sa'id, to feel ... to know with absolute certainty that the poem is dedicated to Saddam Hussein personally, because I've written it out *personally*."

Mihyar uttered this last sentence with such emotion that it brought tears to his eyes, a feeling that was made more intense by the amount of neat whiskey he had imbibed.

Mi'ad was also feeling slightly drunk. Her cheeks reddened, and as Sa'id and Mihyar started a heated discussion on prose poetry and modern Arab poetry and the noise around them grew even louder, she insisted on reading out verses from one of her latest poems. Majda felt embarrassed because she was the only non-poet among them.

"But, Miss Mi'ad."

"Call me Mi'ad," she interrupted Majda politely. "There's no need to address me like that when we're like sisters."

"I wanted to ask you to forgive me, because I don't understand poetry like the rest of you."

"My dear, poetry's not about understanding but about feelings, and, Majda, you're a sensitive woman who has taken part in the struggle. I'm very interested to hear what you think."

Majda glowed at Mi'ad's praise and ventured to ask what the poem was called.

"It's called 'Saddam, the Shining Moon of the Arabs.'"

She launched into the first line:

> Deep into our palm trees,
> Our blood,
> And our eyes,
> Into the waters of the Tigris and Euphrates,
> Assyria, Babel, and Sumer,
> To the furthest reaches of the ancient texts,
> I descend
> There I find
> Saddam
> Saddam, the essence of our homeland.
> Our great and ancient Iraq.

Suddenly, the band stopped playing. The noise died down. A wave of silence rolled over the room. Heads turned toward the band. They saw the musicians looking toward the entrance. In unison, the crowd swiveled around to stare in that direction. Their eyes encountered a man in a white suit, surrounded by a posse of uniformed guards.

The whole room leaped to its feet as His Excellency, the President unexpectedly, and without fanfare, entered the hall. They were frozen in their places—standing at attention like a squadron of soldiers waiting to be inspected. Majda clung to Sa'id, seeking refuge from the rapid thudding of her heart and a desperate urge to gaze her fill at the Leader. It was the first time she had seen him in person since that one meeting in the courtyard of her house all those years ago.

She wanted to savor the sight of him from a distance.

She wanted to feast her eyes on his radiant face, his handsome features, and his dignified figure, and to bask in the charisma that emanated from him. She embraced the way his presence dominated the room. She would hold him in her heart forever. Save him deep within her, like a talisman that would protect her from the evils of the world—from its dangers.

Her throat felt dry. A sense of yearning and desire, tinged with fear, rose within her. Her legs trembled. She was face to face with the object of her dreams.

She watched, with eyes that were filmed with tears, as he drew nearer to them—to her—in his rapid tour of the room. She thought, he's much more mature and distinguished than he was before.

"Kuwaitis, Syrians, and Iraqis together—now that's Arab unity," His Excellency, the President joked, as he gestured to their various nationalities. "Arabs everywhere will say this model of ours is essential."

He was thoughtful for a moment, and then turned to Mi'ad.

"Al-Majda Mi'ad, we want our people to be seen by others through your lovely poems."

Mi'ad answered with drunken sweetness.

"Mr. President. My poems are all dedicated to Iraq, even if I don't mention it within them. May I appear before the altar of Iraq as a Sumerian servant and a princess from Babylon! As a servant, I shall serve Iraq, and as a princess, be cosseted by it."

"Blessings upon you. May we continue to see you! And what about you, Mihyar? We haven't seen you for a long time. I hope you haven't encountered any problems in coming to Iraq."

"Mr. President, such obstacles are insignificant. I am a believer; Iraq is the country of Adam and Noah and Abraham. No other country on the globe can compare to it. It is the cradle of civilization—the birthplace of the first prophets, the first alphabets, and the first laws. As it is like that . . . so are you. A great leader rises from within his people, and a great people rise from within a nation, and a nation rises and advances for the sake of humanity."

The President laughed boisterously and clapped the poet on the shoulder.

"This is what we hope for you."

Then he turned toward Sa'id.

"And Comrade Sa'id. What do you say?"

"Sir, when we see you, we are filled with a sense of certainty, assuredness, and calm."

"You are giving your utmost," His Excellency said.

The President's eyes moved from Sa'id and settled on Majda's face. The moment felt as long as a century. She swallowed and looked down, as frightened and overawed as she had been at fifteen years old when he had looked straight at her. She prayed that he wouldn't ask her anything, as she felt unable to put her feelings into words. What had the poets left for her to say?

Her feelings intensified. Too overwhelming to express, to articulate. She wanted desperately to be near him, to touch him. She was reminded of how she had felt as a child when she visited the holy places with her mother. She had gone into the shrine, which was shrouded in a green cloth, and the sanctity of the place had overcome her; she had clung to the iron grill that encircled it and wept with the others, without knowing why.

She felt enormous pride that she'd known this great man. She had known him in secret, when he was just a comrade and before he became president and leader, and the sense of superiority and honor she felt was sufficient reward for her. She had shared moments with him that no one else in the room had been afforded. She and her family had offered him sanctuary.

A tear rolled down her cheek. She quickly wiped it away before anyone could see it. She was face to face with a legend incarnate and a moment in history that epitomized the fulfillment of centuries of mankind. His manhood. His magnificence. His trimmed mustache. The smile that touched the hearts of those who were favored with it. The towering stature that made Sa'id appear tiny beside him.

She crooned to herself: What a marvelous man our Leader is . . . What a marvelous man!

A strange warmth coursed through her. Her eyes sparkled. He said in a low voice, "Ah, Majda, *bint al-'am*, cousin."

Her body quivered. Her soul lit up at his words. She thought, oh, the wonder of the man! He remembered her. Remembered her name. He'd called her Majda, not al-Majda like the rest of the women, because he knew she deserved something special now that her name was used as an epithet for others.

Could she believe what she had just heard? Had he really called her *bint al-'am*? That special Bedouin term of respect and protection. If he continued to stand so close to her, *to her* alone (she was no longer aware of anyone else in the room), then she would kiss his feet.

The sound of his voice brought her back to her senses. Affection was combined with an undertone of menace as he addressed them both. "Comrade Majda, Comrade Sa'id! We have learned that you don't intend to add to our young people." His shoulders shook with laughter. "Don't you know that the revolution can't continue without new recruits to its ranks?"

"*Hayakum Allah*, may God grant you life!" he added, as he was about to leave. "We're relying on you."

The following morning, which was Friday, and an official holiday, Majda went to see a doctor acquaintance of hers who specialized in gynecology. She phoned and arranged for the doctor to open the clinic especially for her. After examining her, the doctor told her that what she was suffering from was a simple and common problem: a narrowing of the neck of the uterus, which prevented the sperm from reaching the egg. She assured Majda that it would take no more than half an hour to rectify the problem. Sa'id noticed her hesitation and suggested that she should get a second opinion. Just to be sure. The specialist confirmed the doctor's diagnosis, but Majda pretended to be nervous.

"I don't have much confidence in doctors in Baghdad," she said. "Samira says the best doctors in the world are in London. We could go to London . . ."

"Impossible," Sa'id responded.

"It would only be for a matter of days. Two weeks at the most."

"If the situation were normal, then I'd agree with you, but it's the wrong time. I'm expecting there to be party changes in the near future."

"You're always expecting changes. Everyone else goes abroad and enjoys themselves, while you just sit in Baghdad. As if you're afraid that, if you go away, you'll come back to find they've appointed someone in your place."

"That has happened to other comrades and ministers, hasn't it?"

"To others, yes. And why? Because they're traitors. Conspirators. Spies. They're a danger to the security of the nation and the party. You're not like them, so why are you so afraid? No one gets reshuffled or kicked out without a reason. The party was built on the backs and sacrifices of people like you. You're honest and pure, and as long as you stay like that, you're in no danger."

"Majda," he sighed. "Believe me, I really must stay here."

She sensed she was about to lose the argument.

"What about my treatment?" she demanded tearfully. "How can I get pregnant without being treated?"

"You can get the help you need in Baghdad, and you won't be put to any inconvenience. Stop nagging me."

"Do you think I would have begged or even thought about going abroad to get treatment had the President not asked for it?"

Sa'id considered her through the smoke of his cigarette. Was there a hint of menace there, or was he just tired and imagining things?

He decided it was just his imagination. He drew deeply on his cigarette to calm his nerves.

"Majda," he said, "I'll take you to a specialist who qualified in London. What do you think? It'll mean you'll get the same doctor and treatment you would get in London, but here in Baghdad. And you'll have your friends and family with you as well. I'll reserve a room for you in the Ibn al-Baitar Hospital."

He'd scored a point. She changed her tack.

"Sa'id, my darling," she coaxed. "We need a holiday to relax. We haven't been abroad for years. We only go to the north. We spend the summer in resorts like Shaqlawa and Salah al-Din. Every year it's the same thing. And there's everyone else, going off to Switzerland one day, and London and Paris the next. Do you know the wife of Dr. 'Isam? She goes to Switzerland every day."

He was close to losing his temper.

"Don't exaggerate. It's impossible to go to Switzerland every day. She probably went once and is still boasting about it to the women she knows. Her husband only travels on business. He was head of a medical delegation and got permission from His Excellency, the President to take his wife with him."

"Well, what about Samira, 'Izat's wife? How many times has she gone to London? Do you know why she went the last time, and at the country's expense? To have a breast enlargement. Can you believe that? She told me that 'Izat was always complaining that her breasts were too small, and forever asking whether he lived with a woman or a young boy."

"Majda," he objected sharply. "That's an exception. Comrade 'Izat's decision to send his wife for treatment was personal. It's up to him whether he wants her to get her breasts enlarged or her arse made smaller. As far as I'm concerned, going abroad at the moment is out of the question. Do you understand?" In an attempt to lighten the atmosphere, he leered at her jutting breasts and added, "Let's praise Allah and thank him that we don't suffer from the same complaint as Comrade 'Izat."

Despite her efforts, she failed to persuade him.

"We're not going," he told her. "The subject's closed. Contact the doctor and arrange a date for the operation."

But then, much to her surprise, he changed his mind the day before her operation. He came home at midday, in a departure from his usual custom. He was frowning.

"You look like Burt Lancaster in *Trapeze*," she teased him. "Particularly in that scene when he's walking along the tightrope stretched out across the top of the tent, and is afraid he's going to fall."

He didn't smile. She didn't know whether he had heard her or not.

She tried to draw him out over lunch.

"Sa'id, is everything OK?"

"I've been given permission. We can go away next week."

She leaped up and threw her arms around his neck, raining kisses on his furrowed brow and cheek. She wanted to kiss his lips, but he turned his head away and wearily freed himself from her embrace. She was shocked by his coldness and went back to her chair on the other side of the table. She couldn't understand why he was so downcast, and then something else occurred to her.

"But Sa'id, I didn't know you had put in a request to go. You were so adamantly opposed to it that I accepted your decision and thought the matter was at an end."

"I wanted to surprise you," he said, with great sadness.

But she was ebullient. She put his frowns down to stress and the strict diet he was on and the demands of his job and his never-ending meetings.

"My darling," she told him. "Aren't I always telling you how tired you look? You need to relax and have a change of scene. Too much work can wear down even a rock."

It was their first trip to London. At the beginning they went out together. They consulted a gynecologist in Harley Street who carried out all sorts of tests on her. He sent her the results a few days later and told her the method of treatment. "It's a simple matter," he explained to her. "A narrowing at the neck of the womb is a physiological condition which can correct itself spontaneously over time, but it persists in some women as a consequence of a growing urge to have children."

She laughed to herself. Who said she'd been thinking about having children? She wanted to protest but restrained herself. No one would believe her. In her culture, all women wanted to have children. And if the words of the consultant were anything to go by, British women were no different. Up to now, she had been happy with her married life. She'd had an uninhibited sex life, secure in the knowledge that she wouldn't get pregnant. There were no prophylactics, no precautions to take away from the pleasure.

She sighed. Things were going to change from now on.

Once she had finished her business in Harley Street, she went shopping in Oxford Street every day. Sa'id went with her once, and then said that he was too busy with the ambassador or had meetings with Iraqis living in London. She didn't argue. She actually preferred wandering around the shops on her own, and felt constrained by his presence. She liked taking her time, selecting what she was going to buy quietly and without being rushed. The one time they had gone shopping together, he had trailed along behind her, dragging his feet and grumbling constantly. "Don't you want to go home yet?" he kept on asking, looking sideways at her. "Aren't you tired? Haven't you had enough?"

"You behave as if I am taking you to the gallows," she snapped at him. "How can I see where I am going if you're standing in my way, sighing and moaning?"

Majda shopped prodigiously. She spent ten days in Oxford Street, applying herself assiduously to the task. She got up early. She entered her first shop at nine o'clock precisely and left the last at five o'clock in the evening. She considered it one of the finest times in her life. She went from shop to shop, from one department to another, like a butterfly, indefatigable and unwearied. She bought everything she had ever dreamed of—suits and dresses, makeup and beauty products, and five pairs of shoes with matching handbags, whose unusual colors would make her friends sigh with envy. She bought swaths of beautiful material and copies of *Burda* magazine so that her seamstress in Baghdad could make similar clothes from its patterns.

Bahija, the wife of the ambassador, took her to Carnaby Street. She told her it was a street of weirdos, wonders, and hippies. Majda bought knickknacks and novelties in its carnival-like shops. T-shirts with pictures of big red London buses on them, Buckingham Palace guards, caricatures of politicians and singers, and rude messages. They could be made up and printed on the spot at the request of the customer. The owner of the shop told her, "You can write or draw anything you want on them, except you can't attack the Queen."

"And they say they are a free and democratic country!" she later told Sa'id sarcastically.

In the evening they met up at the ambassador's residence. She asked him where he had spent the day. "I went to a museum and the Iraqi cultural center, and met several people," he answered tersely. "Were they Iraqis?" she asked him. "Arabs and Iraqis," he said. "What kind of Iraqis? Communists? Dissident Ba'athists?" She wagged her finger at him. "Comrade Saʿid. You're meeting up with conspirators and agents of imperialism."

He pretended not to hear and changed the subject. He asked her about her day and what she had bought. He stumbled over the shopping bags. They were now so numerous that they had spilled out of the wardrobes and were taking over the whole room. "I'm sorry," he said. "I don't need to ask you how you spent your day. It's patently obvious." She giggled happily.

She was pleased with herself, exultant, living in a dream from which she never wanted to wake. "Why don't we visit the British Museum together, for a change?" he suggested.

She was trying on a long evening dress.

"But you said you'd visited the British Museum," she said warily.

"I've visited some of it. The British Museum is so huge that it would take days to visit every gallery. I want to visit the Assyrian Gallery."

"But I'm sure I remember you saying that you'd visited the Assyrian Gallery."

Her reply angered him, catching her by surprise.

"I want to visit it again. These antiquities belong to us. And I want you to see them with me."

She sensed he was concealing something from her. Details about his day, perhaps. The people whom he'd met, and whom he refused to name or even talk about. But she was too absorbed in her shopping to give him much thought, and was happy to abandon him during the day.

They did go out to dinner together in response to official and semiofficial invitations.

One evening, one of Saʿid's old acquaintances invited them to his house. When Saʿid introduced her to him, he said, "This is Hamoudi. He uprooted himself from Haditha and planted himself in London." Hamoudi said, "I come from a family of plants with aerial roots. They grow anywhere and thrive as long as the air is free." "Take no notice of him," Saʿid said. "He's a poet." She pretended to be exasperated. "May God help us all! You're all poets and artists."

They spent several hours there, reliving old memories and gossiping about friends and colleagues. She was vaguely aware that they lowered their voices from time to time, but she didn't pay them much attention, because she was watching a program on television and then concentrating on the news.

While they were having supper, she remarked that she found English television strange.

"What do you mean?" Hamoudi sounded interested.

"I've been watching television, and especially the news, but I haven't seen a single item about the British leaders with their people. Neither the Queen nor the prime minister. I've been thinking of how our Comrade Leader visits the cities and the people and is so compassionate to everyone, young and old."

"Not everyone's as lucky as we are in Iraq, Mrs. Majda!" the poet said sadly.

When it was time to leave, Hamoudi put his arms around Sa'id and hugged him tightly. She stood uncertainly on the doorstep, waiting for them to finish their conversation, which sounded as if it had just started again.

"How can he bear to live outside Iraq all these years?" she asked Sa'id in heartfelt tones, when they left his house. "By God, even if the streets of London were paved with gold, I could not leave Iraq."

Another evening they went to see the musical *Cats*. Sa'id told her that it was adapted from poems by the American-English poet T.S. Eliot. They enjoyed the musical, the songs and dances, the wonderfully colored costumes, and the amazingly swift changes in scenery and decor.

"Do you know what the difference is between our theatre and theirs?" she asked on the way home. "In Iraq, even the comedies are full of people weeping, moaning, and wailing. The Communists have appropriated the Shi'ite ritual of al-'Azza al-Husseini [trans. note: Shi'ite ritual weeping and flagellation to commemorate the murder of Hussein] and transferred it from the streets of al-Husseiniya to the theatre. Between Hana and Mana, he lost his beard. You can't satisfy everyone." [trans. note: A man had two wives, Hana and Mana. Hana plucked out the black hairs from his beard, and Mana the gray ones, so that between the two of them, he had no beard left.]

"Our theatre's still young compared to English theatre," Sa'id said.

"My God, even after a thousand years we're not going to learn. Have you seen who's in charge of our theatres? The same faces and the same plays. We need . . ." He let her carry on talking.

"Were it not for the efforts made by our Leader, and his guidance, and his relentless revival of our history, and our great civilization . . ."

He nodded, but his mind was elsewhere.

They got back to find the ambassador's residence in a state of turmoil. It reminded them of similar occasions in Baghdad that had had the same sense of fearful expectancy. The ambassador, ashen-faced and alarmed, was making phone calls to Baghdad. His wife was giving special orders to the staff (two servants, the housekeeper, and the cook). Rooms were to be readied immediately and additional security taken on from a private security firm.

Sa'id asked what was happening. The ambassador lowered his voice to a whisper and looked about, as if fearful that someone would overhear him. He told Sa'id that he had received special orders from Baghdad to prepare for an extremely— "extremely" emerged from his lips as a long-drawn-out moan—important guest, who was coming on a sudden visit.

"Who is it?"

"I don't know."

"Have you asked?"

"Of course I have. But all they said was: 'You'll know when you see him.'"

They lay stretched out on their bed. He, staring up at the ceiling. She, looking at the magnificent wallpaper. They called it paper, but it was made of flock velvet. Decorated in an amazing color that combined purple and gold. If only their bedroom in Baghdad were as magnificent as this, she thought. She would ask Sa'id to buy something similar and have it shipped to Baghdad. It wouldn't be difficult. All they'd need would be a couple of rolls. They could carry it back on the plane with them. They were traveling first class, and no one was going to risk gainsaying the order of a minister if he wanted to take back some wallpaper. She would find a way of clearing the excess baggage. How many kilos had she bought so far?

She sighed contentedly. Weight wasn't a problem. No, the problem would be Sa'id. Persuading him to buy and carry the paper. He couldn't bear owing anyone any favors. But the bedroom … there would be nothing like it! It would amaze everyone. She began to picture it with its new decor. She could almost hear the jealous comments of her friends and see Samira, 'Izat's wife, go green with envy as she touched the paper. She would die of jealousy.

"Sa'id," she murmured caressingly.

"Yes."

"What do you think about the wallpaper?"

"Er … what did you say?" he asked.

"Don't you think the wallpaper's really lovely?"

"Yes."

"What's the matter with you? Have you got a headache? Have you taken one of your blood pressure pills?" Majda asked.

"No."

"Where are they? I'll fetch them for you."

"What?"

"The blood pressure pills."

"Who said I needed a blood pressure pill?"

"You did! I asked you whether you had taken one and you said no."

"Oh, I was talking about something else."

"What's the matter? Tell me, darling, what's worrying you?"

"It's this sudden visit."

"Why are you worrying about that?" Majda asked. "It's nothing to do with us. Let whoever it is come. It's up to the ambassador to deal with him. It's his job and his house. Isn't that so? We're going back to Baghdad in two days' time."

"That's the problem. The ambassador's told me that he's been told I have to stay on."

"What? But we're going back in two days' time," Majda protested.

"I know. But orders are orders. That's what's worrying me. Who's coming? The vice president? I can't see him leaving Iraq like this. One of the ministers? I wouldn't have to remain if that was the case. The ambassador, as you mentioned, can look after ministers. Why is the visit surrounded by such secrecy and caution? There's something strange going on here, something out of the ordinary."

"Don't exaggerate. You're always exaggerating and making things more complicated than need be."

"Majda, I exaggerate? Well, perhaps I do, but isn't that better than being taken by surprise and not knowing how to respond? You can't deny that everything's in a constant state of flux. Have you noticed how quickly things change? You can meet a director one day who's minister the next, or who has been sent off to work in the provinces. We balance precariously between promotion and demotion. We go to sleep at night in a particular job and position and wake up in the morning to find we've been given quite another post. You tell me not to exaggerate. Am I exaggerating?"

"Sa'id, my dear. Come on, Sa'id, calm down. Remember your blood pressure. Why do you compare yourself to the others? What's happened to you? Why are you so frightened? It's so unlike you. You never used to talk like this. This is the first time I've heard you being so critical. How can you say your position's precarious? You were appointed minister because you deserved to be a minister and because the party and the revolution and the Leader needed you."

"Majda, I have a strange feeling . . . No, perhaps I'm imagining things. That's all it is."

"They've probably asked you to stay on because they need your assistance. They respect and value you. Why do you always have to be so negative? Maybe it's because you can speak English. Or because you've got many good contacts among the Iraqis and Arabs living in London. Or because you're known and respected by Arab intellectuals."

"I know, I know. Everything you say is possible. I don't know what's been the matter with me recently. I feel as if there's a lump in my chest. My heart feels heavy. It's probably just the tension and strain." She reached her hand out to his face. She stroked his brow. She turned on her side and drew a soft paper tissue out of the box (she must remember to take a dozen different colored boxes like this back with her to Baghdad). She wiped away the beads of sweat from his forehead. She ran her fingertips gently over his face. She began to stroke the thick hair on his chest, noticing as she did so the growing number of gray hairs. Her movements aroused her, and she murmured throatily,

"Darling."

He pushed her hand away from his chest, as if her smooth touch were hurting him. Then he clasped her fingers, and looking straight at her, he whispered tentatively,

"Majda . . ."

She was quiet, so he pressed her further.

"Yes, darling!" she responded.

"Majda, I want to ask you something. It's a question based on an imaginary premise. Consider it hypothetically."

"There is no power and no strength save in God. Please ask me before you lose me."

"This isn't a time to joke. Suppose, just suppose that like the former minister of culture and Comrade Adnan and Comrade Hardan and comrade so-and-so, etc. . . . I don't really want to go through the whole list. The names aren't important. Just suppose that I were accused of working against the Leader, against the revolution. Remember, this is an imaginary hypothesis. But I want to know. Tell me truthfully. What would be your position? What would you do?"

She wrenched her wrists out of his grasp and drew away from him.

She was almost hysterical.

"It's nonsense to talk like that. It's meaningless," she hissed.

"We're only supposing. I said it was hypothetical."

"Are you mad? Why do you insist on disturbing the evening?"

"I said 'suppose.' It's not forbidden to imagine."

"What are you saying? Sa'id, what's happened to you? Do you want to destroy our life? Have you gone mad? A few weeks ago you were given the highest position an artist or writer or poet could wish for. The revolution has promoted you from being headmaster in a provincial secondary school to a minister. Arab and Iraqi intellectuals kowtow to you." She gaped at him, her eyes starting out of her head. "You're a minister," she reiterated. "Do you know what you're saying? Where have these stupid ideas come from?"

She drew a deep breath and forced herself to calm down.

"Listen, my dear," she went on in a whisper. "Get rid of all these suspicions. Put such evil thoughts out of your head. I don't know who's been putting such ideas into your mind, or how they got there; but there's one thing I'm sure of, and that's that all the ministers and comrades who've been removed, all the people who've been executed, have been properly guilty, not just suspects. No, my dear, and I am one hundred percent sure of this—they've all been agents and traitors who have conspired against the security of the revolution and the Leader."

He tried to calm her down. He moved nearer and held her hand, hoping to quiet her voice and stop her body from trembling.

"Majda, may God grant you a long life. I said 'suppose,' 'imagine.' I'm not suspicious about the authorities and the changes. All I'm doing is asking whose side you'd be on."

He awaited her reply, as if he were the accused before a court, waiting for sentence to be handed down.

Immobile. Mute. Unable to think. Disregarding the legal arguments. She rubbed her hands violently and quickly. It was an anxious movement that betrayed her fear and hesitation. Consoling herself with the thought that it was just make-believe, she agreed to play the game. Her eyes glittered with unshed tears, and she sighed, as if she had decided on a course of action, whatever pain it might cause.

"Sa'id, you're my husband and my comrade, and you know how dear and important you are to me. And may God bear witness to my love and devotion to you! But as Tahsin, my brother the martyr, and you have both taught me to do, I'll answer you in the same way you'd answer me if I were asking you the same question. You ask whose side I'm on. I can only reply that I'm like you, Sa'id. My life is his to do with as he pleases."

Majda's explanation as to why their departure had been postponed proved to be correct, as did what Sa'id had told her. It turned out not to be hypothetical or imaginary, suspicion or fantasy. Sa'id and the ambassador and their respective wives discovered that the hush-hush visitor was none other than Mrs. Sajida, the wife of the President. She had come to London for two reasons: to do some shopping and to take her daughter Hala to the doctors in Harley Street.

And the reasons behind Sa'id and Majda remaining were twofold as well. They were to accompany Mrs. Sajida and translate for her. Despite her weak grasp of English, Majda had to accompany Hala, the President's daughter, together with her governess, Um Kemal, and two personal bodyguards, to see a consultant with whom an appointment had been arranged from Baghdad. Majda spent several days coming and going while the specialist diagnosed what was causing the girl to lose consciousness repeatedly. Apparently, she had mild epilepsy, and the doctor prescribed the necessary drugs for her.

At the same time, Mrs. Sajida took Sa'id with her on her daily shopping expeditions. On the first day he attempted to change places with Majda, but Sajida insisted that he accompany her, remarking that she had received her orders directly from Abu Hala, His Excellency, the President. He had advised her not to leave the ambassador's residence unless she was accompanied by and under the protection of the minister of culture, Comrade Sa'id.

With some satisfaction, Majda listened to his complaints when, at the end of the day, he told her about the interminable trips to Harrods and Marks & Spencer and the countless heavy bags he had to carry.

"You refused to spend even an hour with me. Verily, Allah takes his time and does not forget."

Sa'id's fears were realized two months after they returned to Baghdad. Majda was in her first weeks of pregnancy. Sa'id was summoned to an extraordinary meeting with His Excellency, the President's chef du cabinet. He didn't come home. Majda looked for him in all his usual haunts. She phoned his colleagues and the Bureau of Ministers and high-up officials. She phoned his family. Her family.

She was met with silence.

The evening following his disappearance, his colleague 'Izat came to visit her. She received him hospitably, taking heart at the visit and expecting good news.

Refusing her invitation to sit down and drink a glass of grape juice, he stood in the sitting room and informed her gravely, and without mincing his words, that her husband, Sa'id, had been arrested and tried by a special court of the party. She stood there dumbfounded, unable to take in what he was saying. Without looking at her, he concluded,

"And . . . he's been sentenced to death."

Once he had uttered the awful words, he made a move toward the door. He wanted to get out of there as quickly as possible. Majda stood motionless, as if she'd been struck dead. Her face was warm, but the spark of life within had been extinguished and would not return. She stood in his way, like a stone blocking his path, ice cold, staring into space, unable to believe what she had heard.

"Majda," he said, trying to move her out of his way. "I'm in a hurry. I've got work to do."

She didn't hear him.

Then, slowly, the inert muscles of her face twitched. Her dry lips moved. She squeezed the words out, letter by letter.

"I want to see him. Make an appointment for me. I want to speak to him."

"Comrade Majda, try to understand how I feel. It's impossible. You can't see him. Sa'id's been my comrade and friend since before he got married, but he's become involved in a conspiracy to harm the Leader and the revolution, and the special court has found him guilty. It's impossible."

"No, no. You don't understand. I don't mean Sa'id. I want to see His Excellency, the President. Make an appointment for me with him immediately."

"Oh, I see. But Comrade Majda. His Excellency, the President is very busy at present and has ordered us not to disturb him. It's therefore impossible for you to see him now. We'll try and organize an appointment soon. Tell me what you want."

Majda was beginning to return to her senses, and her voice rose shrilly.

"I told you to arrange an appointment with him immediately. I have to talk to him. To tell him what's happening around him. I am sure that he doesn't know about Saʿid's imprisonment. If he did, he would not have consented. How can they risk imprisoning such a good and loyal friend of the President? Who's got the power? It must be someone conspiring against him. I must tell him. I'm Majda, sister of Tahsin who died for the party. Don't you remember him? And Saʿid. Have you forgotten who Saʿid is? Saʿid is Comrade President's favorite poet, his friend . . ."

ʿIzat tried to calm her down. He was exhausted from the many sleepless nights he had spent during the long official interrogations. He desperately wanted to go home and lie down and sleep. He felt dizzy. He was pale. He made an effort to control his irritation. Majda's a vulgar woman, he thought to himself. She'll soon begin to scream and howl. If she were a man, I'd know how to deal with her, but she's a woman. To make matters worse, he had received clear and unambiguous instructions to treat her gently and not to harm her in any way.

"Comrade Majda. Listen to me. Listen to what I'm saying. His Excellency, the President himself gave the orders for an inquiry to be set up to look into the allegations against Saʿid. The committee of inquiry and the court established that Saʿid had been in contact with and had met with other traitors who had previously been imprisoned."

"That's impossible. I tell you it's impossible. It's a conspiracy against the President, against Saʿid. He's my husband, and I know him."

"Comrade Majda, since you're such a dear friend to all of us, I'll go further than I am supposed to and tell you that the charges state that Saʿid has been disclosing information, and planning and plotting to cause damage to the revolution and its symbol, the Leader. He was an agent who received a monthly salary from a foreign power."

Hysteria swept through her. Her body quivered and shook. She laughed. She wept. She screamed. Her voice grew hoarse as she clamored to meet the Leader. Begged to know where Saʿid was.

"It's impossible. I tell you it's impossible that Saʿid conspired against the President. I want to see the President to tell him so . . . Saʿid . . . he can't be a traitor. He's like me . . . He loves and serves him. We adore our Leader. Tell him . . . let him know . . . tell him Majda says you're our Leader and comrade. Tell him . . . remind him how we protected him during the difficult days . . . No, no, don't tell him. Don't remind him . . . It's wrong to talk like that. He's the Leader and the Leader doesn't forget . . . Tell him he's our Leader and our friend and not to listen to what the enemies are saying . . . Tell him that Saʿid and I, we've sacrificed our lives to protect him . . ."

Adiba tried to prop her stick against the edge of the chair, but she couldn't find a suitable place for it, and it fell to the floor. It made a loud clatter in the quiet office. She picked it up, smiling cautiously to hide her embarrassment, and finally succeeded in leaning it against the side of the desk.

They sat facing each other in two armchairs, with a low tea table between them. Dr. Hawkins raised her eyes from her notebook and asked,

"Why didn't you come to the previous session?"

"I did come. I got as far as the door to the clinic, then I changed my mind."

"Fine. I wanted to let you know that I have received and read the report made by Amnesty International."

Adiba took refuge in silence and examined the office/clinic for the first time. A large room with two windows that looked out onto the hospital courtyard. Two large trees. Two willow trees towering like twins.

There was a wooden desk and two chairs. A filing cabinet. A small plant placed on the wide windowsill in a corner facing the desk. There were no curtains on the windows. The monotonous tick of the clock on the wall broke the silence.

"Has there been any news of your husband?" Dr. Hawkins asked.

"No."

"Why did you run away last time?"

"I don't know."

In a quiet voice, and in a manner that combined gentleness, understanding, and respect for the person facing her, Dr. Hawkins explained:

"Mrs. Baghdadi, Adiba, I will speak frankly and explain certain things to you, because I think that you would prefer me to be honest with you. I don't think that answering with a 'yes' or 'no' or 'I don't know' is going to get us anywhere. You're an intelligent, educated woman who has gone through a traumatic experience; to a certain extent, you have succeeded in overcoming the difficult stages. I specialize in treating people who have been through traumatic crises, in particular, people who have been subjected to torture. Our experiences of working with victims of torture show that in most cases the initial symptoms return and affect the victim at different periods in his or her life. It can be months or even years after the trauma. The victim suffers from the same symptoms he suffered at the time of the trauma or when he was exposed to the crisis. There are many reasons for that, and we will talk about them in more detail at a later stage."

She paused for a second, as if waiting for some kind of reaction.

"Forgive me if this sounds like a lecture. The important thing now is that we must work together if you wish to come to terms with the remaining symptoms. Your problem is complex, but it is not impossible.

"I am not promising you a miracle. You are suffering from something that happened twenty years ago. You have neutralized it to a certain extent and learned to live with it. I am sure that talking about it will be extremely painful for you. You will find it particularly upsetting when we come to those issues with which you are still struggling psychologically. Issues that remain very hard for you because you have not yet faced them and accepted that they occurred.

"In other words, this is the start of a long journey that we will make together. I cannot draw up a simple list of issues that you must talk about, or make out a list of symptoms that you are suffering from. The question is much more complex than that. I will not be able to help you until you have decided to trust me. In order to achieve that, we will need to meet for more than a few sessions."

Adiba looked Dr. Hawkins in the eye for the first time, as if asking, "What do you mean?"

"It will be very useful for both of us if I explain how I work. I will tell you how I will proceed. First, we'll work on getting rid of the physical symptoms by learning some exercises. Second, I will squeeze the budget and arrange to see you once a week over the next six months. Then, we'll organize a session once every two weeks, depending on how the therapy is going and how successful it is. What do you think? Are you ready for that?"

Adiba remained silent, though she slowly accepted what Dr. Hawkins had said. For some reason, the distress she usually experienced when being interrogated in an office had vanished. Dr. Hawkins had succeeded in instilling in her a sense of confidence. Why? Was it because she had explained the situation? Or because she had spoken in a rational and balanced manner? Was it because she hadn't promise her miracles, or because she had turned things on their head and asked for her help?

Silence.

"Mrs. Baghdadi!" she chided her gently.

"What is your first name?" Adiba asked.

"Catherine."

"Can I call you Catherine?"

Dr. Hawkins laughed and pushed up her reading glasses, placing them on top of her head.

"Of course. I'm sorry I didn't raise the matter with you, even though I've been calling you by your first name. What do you think? Will you agree to continue coming to therapy?"

"Yes."

"Then let us start with why you didn't attend the last session."

Adiba went red. She felt a blast of searing heat scorch her face. She bowed her head in silence. She ran her hand repeatedly over her gray skirt, smoothing down the material before answering.

"I don't know exactly. I was scared," she said hesitantly, searching for the appropriate words.

She was silent.

"Of what?" Catherine prompted her.

"Of the idea of being questioned. Of being interrogated. I also felt ashamed. Ashamed of myself. I was partly thinking about my husband. I don't know what's happened to him. I don't know what he has to go through every day. Whether he is alive or dead. I was also thinking about my country, which is facing a new attack. My people are hungry and under siege. And the regime is still clinging on to power. My case is not unique among Iraqis. Every refugee has been imprisoned and tortured, or forced to flee their country. Many of them have suffered much worse than I have. So what am I hoping to achieve? What am I doing here? Consulting a psychiatrist because I am suffering from insomnia and a couple of nightmares?"

"But you changed your mind and attended this session. Let's leave the reasons why you decided to attend therapy aside. We'll talk about them a bit later. I want to emphasize certain points that you have mentioned and to talk in greater detail about what you have just said. Let us start with your attitude toward interrogation. Does any question addressed to you assume the form of an interrogation, or is it just questions that are put in a certain manner?"

"It is questions that are put in a certain manner."

"Do you think it's the question itself or the milieu in which the questioning takes place? For example, does it become an interrogation when there is a desk between you and the questioner that appears to give the questioner a certain power over you?"

She reflected carefully.

"It is a mixture of all these things."

"Therefore, it becomes an interrogation when the questioner is a person who possesses the authority to make you feel that you must answer whatever he asks you."

"Yes."

"A person in authority who, in particular circumstances, can completely deprive you of your will. Your terror paralyzes you; you miss appointments because you think they're going to be like that. You run away."

"Yes."

"This must mean that you've missed countless important appointments with doctors, lawyers, and social workers," Catherine added, laughing.

"Particularly with people working in the passport and immigration office," Adiba added with a smile.

Silence.

For a second Adiba's eyes challenged Catherine, as if asking, "Well, I have told you about the problem. What are you going to do about it?"

Catherine was busy jotting down her comments.

"Perhaps you would like to ask what steps you can take to get rid of this confusion. Frankly, I don't have an immediate solution, or any clear guidelines for you to follow that will instantaneously relieve you of your fear. What I can promise you is that I will help you to confront head-on those problems that your symptoms reveal. Remember that my role is to help you change the things which you can change, and to face the things which you are unable to change."

"You have said several times that you are ashamed of yourself. Do you mean that you feel guilty?"

"Both."

"Why?"

"I feel ashamed because I am not strong enough to overcome my problems by myself. Because I am weak. People have always seen me as a strong person. My compatriots in particular. I was regarded as a heroine in my country, for example, but inside myself I have never lived up to those expectations. When I look at myself, I am struck with disappointment at the huge contradiction that exists between what I had once hoped for and the sleepless woman I have become, who is even afraid of the night. I am also ashamed of the way I have begun to inflate my own problems, which I didn't see as particularly important in the past. I mean, I didn't worry about them before. You mentioned feelings of guilt. Not a day passes when I don't feel guilty."

"Adiba, you will forgive me if I look at things differently. First, deciding to have psychotherapy is a plea for help and not a sign of weakness. In fact, it requires great courage to make such a decision. Second, with regard to your expectations of yourself in the past and the subsequent frustration of your hopes, don't you believe that this is a natural result of what you have gone through? You were an active member of the opposition under a repressive regime. You suffered persecution. Your husband was imprisoned. You were detained and tortured, dismissed from work, and, finally, forced into exile. Haven't you struggled enough?"

"No. If I had fought back, if I had resisted like the others did, then I would not have stayed alive."

"Do you measure the extent of your struggle by whether you die or not?"

"In my country? Yes, we do. The living are accused; the dead are pure, innocent. Death liberates them from accusations, accountability, and self-doubt."

"What about the struggle to survive? To carry on the fight? Don't you find that life is much more difficult than death? More complex and more dynamic? Don't the living deserve to be congratulated because they have faced their problems, and worked and achieved something?"

"Death is the passport to eternal life, or at least that is what we believe back there."

"Is that what you believe now?"

A look of bewilderment flashed across her face. She shrugged her shoulders submissively.

"I don't know."

"Don't you think that this way of thinking is more suitable to the torturer than to the victim?"

"What do you mean?"

"You make light of the dreadful experience you have gone through. You berate yourself for having allowed your past experiences to dictate your life. You minimize them because you did not die, because you were not cut to pieces. You feel guilty, lack self-confidence, are permanently weak, because you are alive. It is a very deliberate process that makes torture an acceptable form of social behavior, a normal condition of life. This process transforms something unacceptable into something mundane to make it acceptable."

Dr. Hawkins fell silent while Adiba looked through the window at the two trees standing on their own.

She thought, how many years have I been silent? If minutes in this room are so painful, how have I borne the years? The painful silence of years has become familiar. We can tell the age of a tree by counting the rings on its trunk. How can we calculate the years of humiliation, silence, shame, self-blame, and weakness; how do we quantify the sense of being crushed and marginalized? It's like a heavy corpse, whose weight increases with the passing of the years. We carry its load internally wherever we go.

"Are you involved in any form of political work now?"

"Not really. I take part in a few minor activities."

"Such as?"

"Demonstrations against the sanctions and the airstrikes and in support of the Iraqi and Palestinian people. Occasionally, I attend various Arab activities. I am also still busy following up on my husband's disappearance."

"Why don't you continue to be a political activist?"

"I don't think I have the energy to take part any longer."

"Physical or mental energy?"

Adiba hesitated a little.

"Perhaps energy is the wrong word to use. The truth is that I no longer possess the strength of belief that I used to be so proud of having."

"That's a completely different matter. Do you feel that you were misled previously, that the political leadership duped you? Have you changed your political ideas?"

"Um . . . yes, to some extent. But I need to think about this."

"Let's leave it till the following session."

Then Catherine remembered something.

"Do you like writing?"

"I love reading."

"You're like me, then, but our choices are limited. One of us shall begin writing. I have a suggestion. Why don't you write down the details of your nightmares immediately after you wake up? Put a pen and notepad beside your bed. Write down anything you remember. Don't worry about the style. Just write for five minutes, and then shut the book without reading what you have written. When you come to the next session, we'll read it together.

"The other thing you should do is deep breathing exercises. When you wake up in a panic, leave the bedroom. Sit down on a chair in the sitting room and take ten deep breaths. Open the window if it's not too cold and won't affect your chest, and breathe in deeply as well. Repeat this exercise whenever you feel afraid or find it hard to breathe. Using exercise to overcome the physical symptoms generally helps to overcome the thoughts which are causing the turmoil."

It was a fine day. Summer in London was beautiful. Days that were longer than usual promised hours that stretched far ahead. The sun never set. It seemed never to leave the city, only sinking into the night at eleven o'clock in the evening.

Adiba's appointment with Dr. Hawkins was not till ten o'clock that morning, but she left the house early, rejoicing in the bright light. She decided to walk to the clinic in Kentish Town; it was a slow journey. What would take others ten minutes, took her closer to forty.

The office appeared different in the bright light. Dr. Hawkins was wearing a yellow cotton blouse and a linen skirt. Adiba threw herself onto the chair wearily and didn't bother to pick up her stick. She left it on the floor, lying beside her handbag like a faithful dog. They chatted happily about the weather and the way that people felt relaxed and contented when the weather changed.

Then Adiba presented a small notebook, saying,

"My book of nightmares. Here is the tenth installment."

Then, very hesitantly, she asked,

"Catherine, do you think it's too early for me to ask what you think about my case?"

"I can tell you what I think about our sessions up to now, but I . . . When did we begin meeting?"

Catherine leafed through her notebook.

"Oh . . . in February. Isn't that so?"

"February 15th, 1998," Adiba clarified.

"Oh, of course. But I cannot present a complete picture, because we are still in the middle of your therapy. I can give you some impressions. But they will be initial observations, since we have not looked at your experience in detail.

"In general, you do not like talking about what happened to you. You avoid speaking about it, resort to silence, make light of it, or even ridicule its significance. I believe there are several reasons for this. One—excuse my passion for enumerating things—you are frightened of being questioned because it reminds you of when you were interrogated in Iraq. Two, you choose to be silent because you want to free yourself from your constant sense that the world is a dangerous, insecure place, and silence enables you to continue living in it. You don't wish to appear weak, pitiful, or in need of help.

"You are independent. Proud. You do not accept charity or any form of assistance from other people. Three, some people resort to silence to protect themselves from recurring thoughts, to erase the effects of what happened.

"I also believe that you play down the cruelty that you have experienced by saying that it is a common occurrence in your society under certain circumstances. This is a very important point and needs to be discussed further."

Catherine stopped reading and placed the notepad on the table, then took off her glasses before continuing.

"Let us begin at the beginning. Let us understand the meaning of torture. Torture is an act of degrading physical or psychological abuse inflicted on a person who is being held prisoner. It has several objectives: first, to persuade the victim to supply the person in authority, who is represented by the torturer, with information which will be harmful to himself or to others; second, to intimidate and terrorize the victim to such an extent that he ends his involvement in political activity or confesses; and third, to humiliate the victim and deprive him of his belief in himself by shaking his self-confidence, identity, and will, reducing him to an impotent creature.

"As you know, there are several stages of physical torture, and they can sometimes end in the death of the victim. As for . . ."

There was a light tap on the door. Dr. Hawkins stopped talking. She excused herself and quickly got up and opened the door. The departmental secretary was standing outside. She whispered something. Dr. Hawkins turned to Adiba, apologized again, and said there was an emergency and she would only take a couple of minutes.

Alone in the office, Adiba avoided thinking about what the doctor had been saying, and instead occupied herself by looking around. It is said that every place reflects the personality of the owner or the person living there. This was hardly the case with this office. There was nothing to indicate that it belonged to a woman. In fact, there was nothing to suggest that it was Catherine's office. It had none of her warm and outgoing personality. Even the *ficus-indica* on the windowsill was one of those plants that did not need a great deal of attention. Untouchable. The office was utilitarian and only contained the bare essentials. She noticed there was a telephone on the desk. She had never seen it before. Perhaps it had never rung during their sessions. Was . . .

The door swung open. Dr. Hawkins rushed back in, in the same hurried manner in which she had left. She said, "I am so sorry. It was a real emergency. Now, where were we before we were interrupted? The objectives of torture . . ."

"Is this your own office?"

"No. The foundation doesn't have enough money for us to have individual rooms. At the moment I share it with two other doctors. And now, Adiba, where were we? I was talking about psychological torture, wasn't I?"

Adiba nodded her head.

"Psychological torture creates circumstances that have such an impact on the detainee that it makes the emotions they arouse virtually impossible for the victim to bear. Examples of such torture include long periods of detention in which the detainee is held without the knowledge of his or her family or is denied contact with anyone. Solitary confinement. Forcing the detainee to listen to the screams of other prisoners being tortured. Sleep deprivation. Forcing the detainee to watch friends, relatives, or other prisoners being threatened, tortured, or executed. Compelling the detainee to perform acts that are shameful to him or which he considers immoral or carry a social stigma.

"The essential point of psychological torture is that it places the victim completely under the control of the torturer. The victim surrenders his will entirely.

"If we apply this brief definition to your case, we see that you were subjected to both physical and psychological torture, as well as suffering the disappearance of your husband. We will discuss the matter in stages. I believe that you should start by not allowing anyone to minimize what you have experienced, or belittle your suffering. Deriding what you have been through makes you blame yourself. You come to think in the same sick manner of your torturers—that you have not been tortured enough, had your limbs chopped off or been executed."

"It's not only me. Most political detainees in Iraq have suffered similar treatment."

"You will not end torture by making light of it or accepting it as a normal social practice. The only way to end torture, even if it is just a slap on the face, is to reject it and refuse to accept it in any shape or form."

Silence.

"Oh, Adiba, you should have stopped me talking," Catherine

continued. "I should be listening to you instead of pursuing my own train of thought. It's a complex subject; it's an inhuman practice, though, ironically it is practiced by human beings. What do you think about what I've been saying?"

"I generally think slowly. I need days to think up an answer. Do you need a reply straight away?"

Catherine laughed.

"No . . . I think this is a step forward. And now, we still have a bit of time to read your nightmares."

CHAPTER ELEVEN

In the evening, Adiba went to the swimming pool. She yearned to immerse herself in the warm water. She shut her eyes and breathed deeply as she sank into the pool, feeling the water lap against her skin. She filled her lungs with air and started to swim. There were only a few women there. The stillness instilled her with a sense of peace and contentment. The smell of chlorine rose off the water and impregnated the swimmers' bodies with its distinctive odor.

She hadn't seen Majda in the changing rooms. She was late. She counted the people in the pool—there were eight women. Three of them stood in a circle at the shallow end, chatting and exchanging recipes. She recognized the faces. They said hello to each other every week.

She had been coming to the pool for five years now. Regularly. Every Friday evening at seven o'clock, missing her appointment only in extreme circumstances. As she swam, the thoughts that had been weighing her down lightened and melted away in the water. Do thoughts, like other material objects, possess an actual rather than an abstract weight?

Adiba looked about her. She was searching for Susan. She couldn't see her. Majda called her the crazy woman of the pool. She talked out loud to herself, and occasionally let out a shriek, startling and alarming the rest of the women. Once, Majda went to the management and complained, and demanded that they stop her from swimming. The manager frostily informed her that the pool was open to everyone without exception as long as they respected the rules and regulations. Majda jerked upright at that, and lashed back at him: "Regulations? Laws? What regulations? You apply the rules as you see fit; you bomb whom you want to . . ." She was about to embark on a long harangue on the British bombardment of Iraq, but Adiba took her by the hand and dragged her away, murmuring, "Sssh, Majda. We're at the swimming pool. It's not the place. You are shouting at the wrong person. Remember, we're at the pool." Adiba had apologized to the young man.

Adiba looked at the door leading to the changing rooms. It was closed. Majda hadn't come. She felt slightly perturbed. Majda was punctilious about coming to the pool, although she didn't take part in any other activity. Susan had not come either.

She stopped at the end of the pool and turned back, propelling her body strongly through the water, challenging the weakness in her leg. She turned on her back, and continued swimming in a relaxed way. She sighed with pleasure, managing to avoid splashing water onto her face.

She moved her limbs with enormous satisfaction. The swimming pool was now the only place where she could use her legs like she used to be able to. In the water she was no longer in pain; she was an able-bodied young girl. Would Catherine help her to regain her trust in herself so that she could live without nightmares? Would she help her put an end to them? She really did feel much better now that she had begun to see her on a regular basis.

Adiba thought back to the bitter argument she had had with Michael at the beginning of the year. She had arrived at the refugee office in Heathrow Airport gasping and out of breath. Michael had looked up from the papers in front of him and stared at her in surprise.

"I thought you had an appointment with the doctor this morning," he said.

"I did."

"What happened?"

"I got ready, got on the bus, got off the bus, walked to the clinic, sat in the waiting room. Five minutes before it was time for my appointment, I changed my mind about going, and left."

"You mean you ran away?" Michael asked.

"I could not stand the thought of any more questions."

"What questions?"

"Dr. Hawkins's questions."

"She's asking them to help you, to find out what's the matter with you," Michael argued.

"I know. I have told myself that a hundred times. But I cannot bring myself to face her. I feel she has some sort of control over me."

"You don't feel comfortable with her?"

"On the contrary, she is very nice and understanding, and I know she wants to help me, but I can't help it. I react subconsciously when I go to an office and am faced with someone sitting behind a desk, lobbing questions at me. My knees feel weak, my heart pounds, and I feel cold, even if it's very hot. I have tried telling myself that I must face up to my problems and accept them, but it's useless."

"Does Dr. Hawkins sit behind a desk?"

"No ... but the door to the office is closed. She's asking questions, demanding answers. It's awful."

"Adiba, let me give you some advice. If I were in your shoes, then I would think I had two solutions with three possible outcomes. I could either choose to face up to the problem, with all the pain that that entailed, in the hope that I would finally come to terms with it; or I could give in to it and live as a victim for the rest of my life until I committed suicide or went mad."

She remembered how on the same day, which was a Friday, she had come to the swimming pool and seen Susan. She was a skinny woman. She crept into the room where the pool was like a frightened child. She inched forward, then gingerly climbed down the three steps that separated the floor around the pool from the pool itself. She stretched out one foot. She found the top step, and then stretched out the other foot. It took her five minutes to make her way down the three steps. She stepped into the water carefully. She remained in the shallow end. She stood cautiously by the side. She looked around her as she clung to the edge. The other women stealthily watched her. Her eyes were glued to the edge, her back turned to the others. She didn't see them. She erected a screen around herself and denied their existence. She didn't want to see them. Head bent, she began to shriek, expelling a stream of words upon the surface of the water. She watched the words as they sank, then burst like bubbles below the surface. There was a regular rhythm to the sounds. They went on and on. For a whole hour. The length of the swimming session.

The sight of Susan aroused a deep sense of apprehension in Adiba. Susan was completely cut off from the outside world. Completely enclosed in the darkness of her fragile inner self. It was one of the reasons that Adiba had decided to return to therapy. She was afraid of becoming like her—terrified and clinging to the edge of life. An eternal victim to impotence and self-pity and nightmares.

Adiba stopped swimming to catch her breath. She wiped her goggles. She washed them several times to clear the fog from them. She must buy a new pair. She'd paid a lot for this pair, but they still misted up almost immediately. Perhaps they wouldn't mist up so fast, she thought, if the manufacturers spent money on improving the design rather than wasting it on packaging, and on leaflets describing how to use them, and on saying how unique they were.

She stretched out on her back. She felt her body gradually lighten. It lost the weight of ideas that, like rocks, dragged it down to the bottom. She realized she felt as light as she did on leaving Dr. Hawkins's clinic.

CHAPTER TWELVE

Majda attended the forty-day wake in memory of the poet Mihyar with Iqbal. She had hesitated for several days, afraid of leaving the house and going out on her own. Then, at the last minute, she gathered up her courage and phoned the members of the group. She desperately needed someone to accompany her.

She called Sahira first of all to get the duty call out of the way. Sahira was strongly disapproving. "Majda, aren't you ashamed of yourself? Me . . . me go to the wake of the writer of such doggerel, who attended Ba'athist parties and festivals? Are you mad?"

Majda didn't listen to the rest of what she had to say. She cut her off with a curt "good-bye," and banged down the receiver.

Adiba wasn't at home, so she left a message for her on the answering machine.

"Majda, let me be frank with you," Adiba said, when she called her back in the evening. "I met Mihyar in Baghdad several months after I had been released from prison. I'd recovered a bit and started to search for my husband. It was a very distressing time; the front was in power, which Mukhlis was opposed to, as you know. It was impossible to find anyone who would intercede on my behalf and find out what had happened to him. Then some friends suggested asking an Arab celebrity, someone like Mihyar. I was willing to talk to the devil if it would help me get news of Mukhlis. At that time, Mihyar was a real celebrity. They loved him in official circles."

"I know, I remember those days," Majda said.

"After a certain amount of effort, I got through to him. He had been invited to take part in some festival or other. Perhaps it was the poetry festival of al-Merbid or . . ."

"Was Mi'ad al-Salim there as well?" Majda asked hesitantly.

"I heard she was present, but the two of them were always together, weren't they? Why do you ask?"

"No reason. No real reason . . . Please carry on."

"We arranged to meet in the huge foyer of his hotel. I can still see Mihyar clearly. It's strange how clearly we remember such trivial details of our meetings with certain people. Was it because his situation was so different from mine?

"He was relaxed and gracious; the scent of perfume wafted of off him; he was smartly dressed in a white silk suit and was wearing a pair of expensive leather shoes of the same color. I noticed the color because I was shrouded in black and because at that time men in official positions usually wore dark striped suits, dark indigo in particular, in imitation of the President, if you remember?"

"I remember."

"I told him what had happened. I said he was a famous poet and that with all his influence would be able to intercede for Mukhlis. Do you know what he said? He asked me warily, 'Who am I to intercede for him? The country is currently celebrating the national front. Iraq has to regain its place in the Arab world. How can I intercede for someone who's under arrest at such a time, no matter what the reason?'

"I said, 'You are a poet. You are one of the most important intellectuals in the Arab world. Mukhlis is an academic, an intellectual like you. He has been arrested and has disappeared.'

"He interrupted me. He said, 'You've said it yourself. I'm a poet. Poets don't interfere in what doesn't concern them.'"

"It's true, he was a poet," Majda said.

"Majda! How can you repeat such words?" Adiba raised her voice disapprovingly. "If he were a real poet, he wouldn't have dirtied his hands writing odes and panegyrics for dictators."

"He believed in Arab unity, like Sa'id did."

"Well, as far as I am concerned, Mihyar was a second-rate poet, and man and death won't improve him one iota."

Majda sighed irritably and held the receiver away from her ear. The blood rushed to her face. Adiba's sharp words were like a slap across her cheek.

She said to herself, I'll try Um Mohammed. The phone rang a couple of times before the other woman answered. She sounded tired. She said she didn't feel well.

"Perhaps it's the change in the weather. Take some Tylenol and drink hot lemon and honey. Have you got some?"

"Yes, Mohammed bought some for me, and I've been drinking it all week. But I've lost my appetite, and I feel so tired."

"Well, you certainly won't be able to come with me to Mihyar's wake."

"No, it would be difficult, even if I were well. You know, Majda, whenever I saw him—may Allah have mercy and forgive him, because mercy is owed to everyone—whenever I saw him on television in Iraq, he reminded me of one of those 'bad women' who were famous in Sulaimaniya."

Majda wished her a speedy recovery and quickly put a stop to the conversation.

To her amazement, Iqbal agreed to accompany her.

"I'm amazed at you. Are you sure you want to?" Majda jeered. "Doesn't he remind you of some local prostitute or small-time pimp? Why aren't you against him like the rest of the group?"

Iqbal didn't understand the reason for the mockery and gibes.

"What . . . what are you talking about? Why should I be against him?" she asked in surprise. "He was a great poet, and I really like his poetry. His poetry's wonderful and that's enough for me. If we judged poets according to how much they praised governments, there wouldn't be a single Arab poet left for us to admire. Every one of them has written poems praising this or that ruler or political party."

"And what about his politics, then? I do hope you're not opposed to the role he played in politics?"

"Majda, why are you being so obstinate? However, I'll answer your question, even though it's inappropriate; as far as I can remember, Mihyar did take part in some festivals at the time when the front was in power. Ba'athist, Communist, Kurdish parties—they were all taking part. Why should we single him out for blame . . . if . . . am I wrong?" She forestalled an answer by asking instead,

"What makes you want to go, though? I thought you generally avoided going to public meetings, apart from demonstrations in support of Iraq?"

"Like you, I admire his poetry. I used to know him personally. He was a friend of my late husband's. He was the only person who helped me after I left Iraq. He helped me get a visa and settle here."

They sat in the back row to make it easy for them to leave early if they wanted to. But they remained to the end. They listened as people read some of Mihyar's poems and reminisced about him. Iqbal mouthed the words with them. She had learned several of his more famous poems by heart. The atmosphere of the evening was relaxed. The people who had come were united by their love for the late poet. They were mainly Syrians and Palestinians. There were only a few Iraqis present.

They were about to leave. The memorial service had taken place in a town hall in the west of London. Majda stood at the door for a few moments, waiting for Iqbal, who had rushed off to the toilet complaining of a sudden pain. To pass the time, Majda turned around and looked back at the people in the hall. Suddenly, in the middle of them, she glimpsed a familiar face. It couldn't be. She examined it carefully. 'Izat! Comrade 'Izat! That creep, that clerk in the Ministry of Education who had climbed up the party ladder, thanks to Sa'id. Become a member of the regional council and deputy prime minister! And . . . who was that with him? She could scarcely believe her eyes. Samira?

How had they gotten to London? Why were they here? Were they refugees? They didn't look particularly wretched. 'Izat was surrounded by a circle of men, just like he had always been in the past—dark suit and glasses, beads in one hand. His mustache as thick as ever, with one slight difference: it no longer grew down on either side of his mouth in the Ba'athist style.

He was just the same . . . full of himself . . . laughing and chatting as he used to in his office or surrounded by comrades . . . What had happened? Had he been transferred to London? But the embassy and consulate were closed . . . and there were no diplomatic links between Iraq and the UK. And anyway, he was the center of attention as if he was important and respected . . . Iraqi diplomats were disowned these days. No, he had to be a refugee.

Majda hadn't seen him since the day she received the devastating news. She had phoned their house a hundred times after that, asking to see him or to talk to Samira. She had desperately needed the help of her friends. She had desperately needed Samira's support, but her friend avoided her like the plague. Then the letter came appointing her as a receptionist in a hospital in Diwaniyya.

'Izat must have sensed her shocked eyes raking his face, for he turned and looked at her, then quickly turned back to the people he was talking and laughing with. She felt suffocated.

Iqbal, where are you? You've been in the toilet for a quarter of an hour? What's happened to you? she wondered, beginning to panic.

She wanted to get out. She was finding it hard to breathe. Her heart pounded. Her chest hurt. The image of Sa'id grew bigger and bigger. Her heartbeats grew louder. People would hear them; they'd smell her if she didn't get out immediately. She was drenched in sweat. The pores were opening up in response to her fear. She could smell it. It was disgusting. Was it coming from her? This stench of terror mixed with the memory of murder.

She almost screamed. Iqbal, where are you? If only she could move. If only she could shift her feet. But they felt as heavy as lead, rammed deep into the marble floor. She looked down at them and saw a chasm yawning in front of her. It was like a crack, in ground made arid by a period of drought, that opened up and threatened to swallow a human being. Iqbal . . . where . . . ?

A hand touched her shoulder; she swung around to find herself face to face with Samira.

"Samira!"

"Darling Majda!"

She pulled Majda's wooden body toward her and embraced her, loudly kissing her four times, twice on each cheek. Majda jerked herself free of the encircling arms and stepped backward. Without waiting for a response, and oblivious to her hesitation, Samira launched into speech.

"Majda, darling. Where have you been? We've been asking about you ever since we got to London. We've looked for you everywhere. Where have you been? 'Izat and I thought you must have gone abroad. How many years is it since we've seen you? Ten, fifteen? My God, I can't remember. And look at you! You haven't changed a bit. You look just the same, as tall as ever and just as pretty, and you've kept your figure. 'Izat's always remembered you with such fondness. My God, we've never stopped thinking about you.

"When we inquired about you in Baghdad, they said you had gone to Syria, then on to London. We heard that the late Mihyar helped you. We said, 'Thanks be to God! Praise be to God.' We said, 'She's well; she's escaped this terrible fate that's affected us all.' It was like being in prison. Then, three months ago, God in his mercy opened the door for us, and we fled on a dark night. We escaped to Amman. We were welcomed by members of the opposition. They organized everything for us and got us to London. I'll tell you a secret: they have an important delegation going to America, and they say it is absolutely vital that 'Izat should be a member. *Wa-Allahi*, Majda, you can't imagine how often we've thought about you and remembered you in the long nights of cruel oppression we endured.

"Do you know that that bastard's imprisoned all our relatives and friends? They've been tortured or have disappeared, just like the late Sa'id, but you won't be interested in that, my dear. Do you know that 'Izat has sworn on his honor to seek out and expose that murderer and his stooges? He's passed on everything he knows to the Home Office here and the leaders of the opposition. Only yesterday he was interviewed on a program on satellite television that lasted for two whole hours. He described our sufferings and mentioned the name of Sa'id, the martyr. If you want to see it, I'll send you a copy. We recorded it on video. But, darling Majda, let us get back to the present. We've missed you so much. Come and see us. We've bought a house in the suburbs near somewhere called Siri or Sari." She laughed gaily. "It's easy to remember it because it's like the Indian sari. God, remember the old days, Majda? The good old days. Do you remember them?"

Majda turned aside to hide the expression of loathing on her face. Her features were so contorted that had she seen her face in a mirror she wouldn't have recognized it. Her knees trembled. She felt close to collapsing under the weight of shock and confusion. What was she going to do? Where was Iqbal? She was aware of an intense ache in her belly and wanted to vomit. She had to be dignified and respect the memory of Sa'id. Get away from this tart and her miserable husband as quickly as possible. Stay calm. Remember she was in a public place. Turn around and leave before her nerves snapped. She didn't want to look at Samira. What was she doing with that hypocrite? Her face painted like a common slut, all that makeup, bright red stains on her teeth, and her expensive, vulgar clothes? Trollop! How should she behave toward her? How could she answer her boasts? She was still talking. Majda was not listening anymore. But she could see her lips moving. They didn't stop. Filthy cow . . . daughter of a bitch . . . vulgar little whore with her pimp of a husband . . . traitor. She noticed Samira holding out something toward her. What was it?

"Sorry. We were hoping to see you this evening . . . 'Izat is so busy and has been invited somewhere. But here's my card . . . It has my phone number and address on it . . . Get in touch so that we can meet up. 'Izat would so like . . ."

Majda looked down at the card that Samira had placed in the palm of her hand. She was icy cold. Her body trembled with hatred and rage, and an anger surged through her more powerful than anything she had felt before in her life. She ripped the card into tiny shreds and scattered them scornfully over Samira's carefully arranged hair.

"You bitch!" Majda screamed. The high, sharp words burst out from somewhere deep inside her. "You whore!" She hurled the insults at Samira as if upending a bag of rubbish over her head. "Now that you've run out of ways of making money in Baghdad, you've come to London to carry on your . . ."

No longer aware of what she was doing, Majda began to beat Samira about the head with her black handbag, raining down blows upon her. She was seized with a fit of madness. Consumed with feelings of revenge and hatred that had been suppressed for so many years. Unable to believe their eyes, people gazed at the tall black-swathed woman as she screamed obscenities and thrashed the other woman with a violence that was at odds with her skinny build and age, until the latter's husband finally came to her aid.

Majda then turned her handbag on him and aimed her blows at his head, launching a stream of invective into his face. "Traitors, spies, pimps! Who tortured Sa'id with his own hands, eh, who? . . . Do you think I don't know? Torturer . . . We all know how you enjoyed torturing people . . . Impotent bastard! Now you and your wife have had enough of money and being pimps . . . you've joined the opposition . . . I spit on you . . . Filthy bastard, bitch! You . . ."

'Izat was as pale as a corpse. He wiped the saliva off his face. "You're mad, you're insane," he hissed like a snake. "You're off your head. You obviously don't know who we are."

And somewhere there was Iqbal's white face and gentle voice as she put her arm around her and quietly whispered in her ear, "Majda, Majda. That's wrong, Majda. For heaven's sake, be quiet. Calm down."

With the help of the security guard in the hall, Iqbal took her out into the street.

"What did your family think?"

"My father and brother were fine. They helped me. They were enormously loving and protective. Mukhlis's family were fine, too, but they wanted me to get out of the country as soon as possible. They were tired of constantly being watched and questioned. They were tired of being afraid for me and worried about what might happen to the young people of the family as a consequence of what had happened."

"Do you have any friends in London?"

"Yes. I know many people, both Iraqi and British."

"What's your relationship like with your family now?"

"It's good. I am always on the phone to Mukhlis's family. We try as much as possible to exchange news and information about him. I've got a strong relationship with my brother. He finally managed to escape to Syria and has just been accepted for asylum by the UN High Commissioner for Refugees and is qualified to live in Europe or America."

"If you need a letter of recommendation to help him apply to Britain, I would be willing to help you with it."

"Thank you very much. That's very kind of you. He's younger than I am. He's forty now, but I still feel responsible for him. I feel I haven't fulfilled my duty to him. There are many things that I have not paid attention to. Despite being in exile for so long, I have not been able to forget them. It is as if I'm living in the past. The past! It has been perfectly preserved ... Any fresh snippet of news or event takes me back to the country as it was when I lived there."

"The refugee remains tied to his country emotionally," said Catherine, "although he is physically separated from it and from everything that is important to him. Thus, anything bad that happens there is reflected in his life; it worries him, makes him sleepless and afraid, and takes him back to the time of his departure."

CHAPTER THIRTEEN

Iqbal hurriedly read the newspapers. She stood behind the desk, rather than sat, so that she could scan the pages at speed. She had promised the director that she would help him gather information about Israeli attempts to rebuild the al-Aqsa Mosque, as the agency planned to bring out a book on it.

"We don't have enough money to allocate a special budget to it," the director said. "The information's available. All we have to do is collect it and organize it into chapters. I will get a well-known author to write the introduction."

We're just cheap labor, Iqbal thought. Overtime was included in the conditions of the work contract. But when the director told her that he intended to give her a bonus, which wouldn't form part of her monthly salary, she welcomed the idea. She'd receive the bonus in hand, so she wouldn't have to pay tax on it.

It was a strange situation in the office. The employees occupied the same space and unit of time. They were united in their need to work, but separated by their political beliefs, their reasons for working, and their native countries. They were all from the Arab world, and had left their countries through choice or coercion. Their days and their relationships remained completely Arab in spite of the historical and geographical distances that separated their countries of origin from the country they were now in. The social customs of their homelands had acquired the status of laws and creeds and were much stronger than the laws of the country they now lived in. They teetered between the original customs and the acquired. Practices. Traditions. Interests.

The director, for example, was a mild-mannered, generous, and sympathetic man, who tried to help them as much as he could. He'd lived in London for ten years now, but had only acquired a smattering of English, just enough to help him carry out his daily chores. He had transplanted himself from his country to London just as he was, wearing the same suit of clothes, believing in the same ideas and practices. He had remained like that, preserving the original casing intact for fear that it would be damaged.

At home, he and his family watched Arab satellite channels. In the office, he read Arab newspapers and only mixed with other Arabs. He bought *halal* meat from Muslim butchers, vegetables from Arab green grocers, and books from Arab bookshops. Sometimes, he raised his eyes to see what had brought about this rapid and huge change to the world about him, and then looked down again, saying: "Thanks be to God we are as we were. We know what we need to know, and we do not know what we do not need to know. We can dispense with the depravity we have heard about. May God protect us from the evil deeds of others!" And he murmured a *bismillah*, an "In the name of God," and other pious phrases, and returned to the safety of his time capsule.

Who says that travel teaches man anew and gives him knowledge and wisdom?

There was a varied rhythm to their work in the office. Silence reigned for a time until it was broken unexpectedly as one or another of those with their heads stuck in a newspaper burst out laughing, cursed, or swore, depending on the nature of the news or article they were reading.

Occasionally, one of them raised his head from the pages and made a sarcastic comment. He could not tolerate the sound of silence. He spoke out loud to hear the sound of his own voice. The voices of the others, for the most part, clamored internally as well.

Iqbal tried to avoid this game of extempore speechmaking. She kept her mind focused on getting the job done as quickly as possible so that she could get back home to Samer. Come on! Hurry up! She turned over the pages of the newspapers, the newsprint rubbing off on her hands and turning them black. She was careful not to touch her face or clothes. She smiled while reading odd bits of news; in passing, her eye lit upon a column devoted to readers' questions that appeared in *al-Wahda*, an Arabic weekly magazine published in Cyprus. It was her favorite column, and it made her laugh more than anything else in Arabic or English. One question was published repeatedly. Most of the queries were about rare sexually transmitted diseases that no one apart from the person asking the question and the publisher, who no doubt were one and the same, had heard of. She cut out an article from a page dealing with religious questions and *fatwas* from another magazine, folded it up, and placed it in her handbag. She would read it out to the group. She sighed contentedly. She had finished going through the papers. She put them on one side, and arranged the articles that had been requested on the other. She bent down and scrabbled around under the table. A magazine had fallen on the ground. She heard the director murmuring her name. She straightened up and looked at him inquiringly.

"Iqbal, there's a personal call for you," he said quietly. "You'd better take it in my office."

Her heart rate quickened. She went white.

"There's nothing wrong, is there?" she asked.

"Everything's fine, *in sha' Allah*. Hurry up," he said.

She hurried to the office and picked up the receiver.

"Hello. Can I help you?"

"Mrs. 'Allawi?"

"Yes."

"Samer's mother?"

She felt a lump in her throat; tears filmed her eyes. Samer . . . he was asking for Samer's mother. It had to be something to do with Samer. Samer. Was . . . ?

"Yes, has anything happened to him?"

"No, no. He's fine, believe me. But there's a small problem at school, and we would like you to come and see us as soon as possible."

They must be keeping something back from her. Her child, her son. What had happened to him?

"What's the matter?" she jerked out the question again. "Is he all right? Please tell me quickly."

"Believe me, Mrs. 'Allawi, he's absolutely fine," the teacher said calmly. "He's here in the office. I am Patrick Hand, the headmaster. I believe we met once before. We would just like to talk to you before the end of classes today."

"I'll come immediately."

In a trembling voice, she gave the director details of the conversation and asked permission to leave for the school.

"Of course, of course," he said. "Go immediately. *In sha' Allah*, everything will be fine. Don't worry. We will leave the work on the book until tomorrow."

Iqbal hurried away from the office, followed by the silent, sympathetic eyes of her colleagues. She was trembling with shock and fear. She forgot about the queasiness. What had happened? What had Samer done? Stolen something? Been in a fight? Hit one of the pupils? She remembered how they'd phoned her in just the same way when he was six years old; she'd rushed over to the school like a mad woman and found him covered in blood. One of the other pupils had pushed him over in a game, and he had fallen against the wall and hurt his head. She had taken him to the emergency room of the hospital, and waited while they dressed his wound and X-rayed his head to make sure he was all right. He had remained there for half a day under supervision in case he'd suffered a concussion. The doctor had stressed how important it was for her to watch him and bring him back to the hospital if his temperature went up or he felt dizzy. Samer had ridden out the crisis with the strength and vitality of a child, but she had spent many painful days going over the incident in detail and suffering hours of slow and soul-destroying agony. How she had longed to have a sister or other relative with her then.

What had happened to him? She felt paralyzed with fear. Tears started to her eyes. She was assailed by pangs of guilt at the way she had neglected him. These feelings rendered her almost immobile whenever she left him on his own or spent a night without him. Lovingly, she recalled his gentleness and obedience; she thought of how patient he was with her and their situation, and her eyes filled with tears.

She raced up the steps in Oxford Circus Underground station and down the steps at Kilburn station. As she hurried, she was blind to everything apart from what was going around in her mind. She clung to the memory of her son as if she were about to lose him.

She didn't wait for the light to change. She dashed breathlessly across the street. She turned left up Shoot Up Hill Street. She tried to remember what had happened that morning. To single out Samer's position in her morning. She had left home earlier than usual in order to reach work before her colleagues and get a start on preparations for the book, greedy for the bonus she would earn.

She had called Samer, and left once she'd heard him reply. Did he get up immediately? Or did he go back to sleep again, taking advantage of the fact that she wasn't there? What was he wearing? Supposing he's had an accident, she thought, with a stab of alarm. Supposing he's been kidnapped, like sometimes happens, and they ask me what he's wearing . . . How will I be able to help the police? She didn't know what he wore each morning.

She stumbled in her haste, as she continued to reproach and blame herself. Did he have breakfast before he left? Did he take his lunch with him or forget it, as he sometimes did, so that he had to stay hungry until he returned home? Was he late getting to school? Oh sweetheart, *habibi*!

With every step she took, she saw his face silently accusing her. He was nine years old, still a child. She should be putting out his clothes for him, preparing his breakfast, talking to him rather than shouting at him to hurry and get up before she left for work. What sort of relationship did she have with him? She didn't ask how he'd slept, or if he'd had any dreams, or whether he was going to school on his own or with a friend. When was the last time she'd played with him?

She thought about it and reviewed their routine.

It was the same every day. When she got home in the evening, she was tired from working all day and didn't have enough time to chat. Anyway, he was usually immersed in a television program and answered her in monosyllables. When she asked him something in Arabic, he would reply in English.

"Samer, how was school today?"

"*All right.*"

"What about your friends?"

"*All right.*"

"Have you got any homework?"

"*No.*"

There the conversation ended.

About an hour later, she would have another conversation with him.

"Samer."

No response.

"Samer!" she bellowed.

"*Yes, Mum?*"

"Supper's ready. Come and let's eat together."

"*Please, please . . . let me watch this program.*"

And because she was too tired to argue and couldn't face the trouble that would arise were she to insist they eat in the kitchen, she gave in to him. Agreed to eat in the sitting room, sitting on the floor in front of the television.

That was the end of that conversation.

An hour later, at eight o'clock, she would call him again.

"Samer, bath time! It's time for your bath."

Silence.

He never answered. She would have to go into the sitting room and press the on/off switch on the television. The images would be swallowed up in the darkness of the screen. Samer always protested. At first he would plead with her, then, as his voice got louder, he would advance forceful arguments and end up by reminding her that he scarcely ever saw her.

"Samer, *Allah halik*. You're tired. I'm tired. Just go and have your bath! Get it over with!"

Grumbling, he would stomp off to the bathroom. He knew that she was unrelenting on the question of early bedtime on school nights, and he knew he was fighting a losing battle. But every night he would come up with new arguments and points of discussion. He didn't give up. Perhaps she would grow tired and give in to him.

Iqbal opened the gate to the school and went in. Silence reigned in the playground. It was the last lesson before the end of the day. In half an hour the children would be free from class, and the hubbub would break out.

The secretary took her to the headmaster's office. Mr. Patrick Hand. She'd met him several times while helping to organize school fund-raising parties or taking part in jumble sales. She looked at him in surprise. He was so thin. So ill-looking. She couldn't believe her eyes. He'd changed so much. He was half as thin as he used to be. What was the matter with him? She was so struck by the sight of him that, for a moment, she forgot Samer and his problems. Mr. Hand had always been so active and alive. And now here he was, finding it difficult to get up from his chair. He shook hands, then introduced her to the social worker attached to the school.

Iqbal's throat was so dry that when she swallowed, it produced an odd sound.

She sat down and stiffly faced the headmaster like someone waiting for judgment to be handed down.

"Where is Samer?" she asked.

"In class. Don't worry. He's fine," Mr. Hand responded.

"What's happened, then?"

"He wasn't in class this morning during register, so the teacher marked him down as absent. At the end of the lesson, she decided to phone you to make sure that he was all right. But in the meantime, the school caretaker had found him by chance outside the school with a couple of older boys."

An iciness spread up her back and legs; the blood left her face.

"They were hiding out in one of the school shelters. When the caretaker found them, the older lads were sniffing glue. Samer seemed content to watch. He was more interested in hiding and skipping classes, pleased to be with some older boys.

"Mrs. 'Allawi, Samer has not done anything illegal, and I don't want to worry you unduly. I also realize you've had quite a shock, but we can't ignore what's happened, because it could lead to something more serious in the future. I think it would be a good idea for you to talk to the social worker, Mrs. Shair, to clear up some matters."

CHAPTER FOURTEEN

"What would you like to drink?"

"Peppermint tea, please," Adiba said.

Iqbal fetched a cup of water from the machine placed in a corner near the café.

"Do you want a coffee and a piece of cake?" Sahira pressed her, offering to buy something.

"No thanks. I don't want anything now," Adiba said.

They waited in silence for Sahira to return. They were sitting in the small café on the ground floor of the Royal Free Hospital in northwest London, where patients and visitors could buy tea or coffee, sandwiches, and simple kinds of cake. There was a cash machine to the left, and a small kiosk that sold newspapers and stationery, and another small shop which sold things that patients and visitors might need, such as paper tissues, fruit juice, bottled water, and get well and sympathy cards.

"It is worrying about Um Mohammed," Iqbal said.

"I know. Hopefully they'll soon find out what's causing the pain," Adiba responded.

"She wants to fast. Imagine. She wants to go back to her flat immediately so that she can pray and fast. Apparently, it's the first time since she was nine years old that she hasn't been able to fast during Ramadan."

"I hope she'll be able to go back home soon. However clean and organized hospitals are and however good the nursing care, the atmosphere is always difficult, even if problems at home are more complicated. I'm sure Mohammed and his girlfriend will take good care of her. It is possible that Mohammed has asked the social services to help. Anyway, as you said, we wish her a quick recovery without complications."

Sahira returned with a tray piled high with cups of mint tea and coffee and hot chocolate, and a piece of cake.

They gaped at her in surprise. Iqbal asked,

"Who's all that for?"

"For you. You look pasty, and you've lost about ten kilos. I've brought you a cup of chocolate and a piece of cake to put the color back in your cheeks."

"Sahira, I really don't want anything."

"Try eating something, even if it's just a crumb."

"God, I can't."

Sahira turned to Adiba.

"Well, Adiba, you try the cake."

"Thanks. You know I do not like sweet things."

"You mean you're going to let me eat on my own?"

"If you like cake, then go ahead and enjoy it," Adiba said.

"No, no, I don't like cake either," Sahira protested.

"You know, we should be sitting in our café now, drinking coffee and discussing the state of the world, and trying to decide whether to go to the cinema or for a walk in the park," said Iqbal.

"What café?" asked Sahira.

"The monthly meeting we agreed upon," Iqbal reminded her. "The café in Hampstead. Have you forgotten? The second Monday of the month. Two o'clock in the afternoon, as stipulated by the women's edict signed by Majda, Adiba, Sahira, and Um Mohammed. Today's Monday, November 16th. How can you have forgotten? You're the one who told me about the arrangement."

"*Wa-Allahi*, Iqbal, believe me, I'd forgotten all about it. Is it just a month since we agreed that? It feels like a year. What a month it's been! Disaster at home and disaster abroad!"

"Iraq! We all know what's happening there," said Iqbal. "It's one calamity after another. Or as they say in math, disaster squared. We're at the breaking point and our gathering is no more. Majda's locked herself away in her flat and has refused to open the door or answer the phone ever since 'the battle of the black bag.' I'm referring, of course, to her attack on the leader of the Iraqi opposition and his wonderful wife, whom she beat about the head with her heavy black handbag. Um Mohammed now lives on the sixth floor of this hospital. She's got tubes inserted the length and breadth of her body, and the doctors scratch their heads over her, mystified by her disease. As for me, well, I'll tell you my story in a bit, once Sahira has filled us in on her news. Let's lay out our problems in order of seniority. Sahira, it's your turn. Tell us your good news, *in sha' Allah*."

"Good news! What good news? Kadhim's kicked out the PhD student. He said he was an impostor and that he hadn't come to ask for his opinions or to document the history of the party, as he claimed at the start. No, it soon became clear from his questions that he was there to put the blame on him. Kadhim told him he was tired of arguing and discussing and philosophizing. Then Kadhim spent the next couple of days going around and around the house saying, 'It's all useless. Now they're blaming me and saying I'm responsible for everything that happened, after all the time and effort I put in.' He's decided not to have anything more to do with Iraqis and to retire from the world. He's become a recluse. He goes out once a day and walks around the neighborhood, and then hurries back home. He only stays out for half an hour. He won't answer the phone. If it rings, he just looks at it till it stops."

"What does he do all day?" Iqbal asked.

"He reads, and watches the news on the Arab satellite stations. Between one lot of news and the next, he reads. It's like he's making up for lost time and is afraid he won't find what he's searching for. I've started talking to myself because he refuses to talk to me. I'm worried about him, about his health. I don't know, I don't know what to do. If only one of you could tell me . . ."

Without thinking, Sahira picked up the fork and turned the thick layer of cream on the cake toward her. She lifted a bit of it to her mouth. As she gulped it down, the next morsel was already on its way. She didn't chew the rich pieces of cake; they slipped from the tip of her tongue and slid down her throat and esophagus. As she ate, she struggled against the burning tears that coursed silently down her cheeks. The edge of her tongue licked at a drop that had rolled close to the side of her mouth. It tasted of salt mixed with sugar and cream, spun through with chocolate. Sweetness and bitterness together. She gazed at Adiba and Iqbal through a film of fine tears that veiled her beautiful eyes; she was wary of their friendly eyes and sympathetic faces. "You know, Kadhim married me when I was just a teenager," she went on. "He raised me. I mean, Kadhim's everything to me. He's my husband and my family and the father of my children . . ."

She blew her nose on a fine white handkerchief, whose edges were embroidered with pretty red flowers. Sahira is the only one among us who has remained faithful to such feminine frippery as embroidered handkerchiefs, Adiba thought.

"I love him; my God, how I love him."

Sahira sang softly to herself, like a mother crooning a lullaby to her child.

> Of me who always has loved you
> You've never asked, O 'Abed my dear,

You've never asked

And me, who has suffered so much for you
You've cast into shame, O 'Abed my dear,
And me you've cast into shame

Iqbal gently touched Sahira's shoulder, and then put her arm around her in a show of affection and comfort. Sahira was silent for a moment. "It's like watching him melt like wax on a burning candle," she said. "I don't know what I'm doing. I've asked him to explain what's the matter, but he refuses to talk to me. It's as if he thinks I'm one of 'them.' One of his enemies. He doesn't say a word all day. I'm so worried about him. He's withdrawn from everyone, even the children. He doesn't ask about them. He walks from room to room and thinks; he appears to be living in a completely different world."

"What does he read?" Adiba asked.

"Books. In Arabic. To begin with, he just read English books. He loved English. But now, he's changed. He's begun to read books in Arabic—about Sufism and heritage and history. I've had a look at them. There's *History of the Arabs Before Islam* and *History of the Arabs After Islam*, and books about religion, whose names I can't remember. They weigh five kilos each, at least."

"Sahira, don't exaggerate," Iqbal joked.

"I mean, well, perhaps it's less than five kilos."

Adiba laughed.

"It's probably a temporary phase; he'll come out of it. He's searching for an identity now that he's lost the beliefs which he's held all his life. Perhaps he's frightened of facing emptiness."

"What do you mean by 'emptiness,' for God's sake? If he wanted to, he could turn our house into a football stadium and fill it with people from morning till night."

"No, Sahira, that's not the kind of emptiness I'm talking about." Adiba explained, "I'm talking about an internal void. When people reach a certain stage in their lives, they take stock of themselves—of their ideas and ambitions and achievements. Throughout his life, Kadhim has followed a particular path that he believes will lead to a dream destination, a free homeland and a contented people. Suddenly, after thirty years, he realizes—he discovers it for himself, or someone tells him—that he's been following the wrong road. The destination he has been making for is somewhere else, or perhaps it doesn't exist at all. He must go back to the beginning; he stops and looks back. What does he see? A long and rugged road, and he is old and tired and alone. He doesn't have the mental or physical strength to retrace his steps. What does he do?"

"He tries to be patient and convince himself to accept anything no matter how unreasonable," Iqbal answered.

Adiba went on, "Either he finds a new belief, or turns to religion, or clings on to his former identity; perhaps he does all these things, even though he knows deep down that he has turned his back on what he previously believed in."

"I believe that everyone has the right to change their ideas," Iqbal intervened. "It means they're developing and not standing still."

"As far as we are concerned, it is more than mere ideas that develop, change, grow, and are renewed. Our internal world has been transformed. The things we believed in so firmly, which we accepted without question, have gone. Once the solid core at the center explodes, then the reverberations reach us on the outside, and we begin to crumble."

Sahira looked at her in bewilderment.

"Adiba, 'aini, it all sounds very clever, but where do I fit in?"

"What do you mean?"

"Why does he neglect me and . . . and carry out this . . . this research into history and identity all by himself? Why doesn't he think about me? . . . I've shared my life with him, haven't I? Opened my heart and soul to him? . . . I've given him my youth . . . What does he do now? . . . After all this time, he goes off on his own and leaves me sitting on the doorstep like a mangy dog. You talk to me about things collapsing? What collapse? Why haven't I collapsed as well?"

"Sahira," Adiba said. "Don't get angry. I am not trying to defend Kadhim, and perhaps what I am saying is all wrong, an absurd analysis, but . . ."

"What about me? Why haven't I gone to pieces?"

"I think you have protected yourself. You've had the house and the children to bring up and Kadhim to look after, who is like your first child. It means you've had different priorities."

"And communism? Where's that gone?" Sahira asked.

"That is exactly what I have been saying to you. But I think you're too upset to listen. The collapse of the Soviet Union . . ."

"What about the collapse of the Soviet Union?" Sahira panted. "I thought he believed in communism, not in the Soviet Union! Just because the Soviet Union collapses, does that mean that communism is finished everywhere else in the world? Really! I mean, is it logical to believe that we must die because communism has died, or become Sufis instead, or turn religious and go to Mecca?"

"The question is not that simple, Sahira. The story is . . ."

Sahira raced ahead. Thoughts and words streamed out of her. She was like a runner nearing the finish line who lets loose an extra burst of speed to prevent her competitors from catching up with her. She exploded into speech. The words tumbled out of her in a manner they were not accustomed to hearing, as if she had glimpsed a far off light and was sprinting toward it.

"It should have been from the start . . . From the start . . . we ought to have been like our ancestors . . . praying and fasting and believing in God. Shame on them for cheating people . . . misleading them with promises of a happy homeland. Do we know how many people have died? . . . How many imprisoned and tortured? And now? Kadhim *effendi* . . . the leader who taught them all this magic . . . he's started reading all about the history of the Arabs before Islam! Isn't it too bloody late?"

"Sahira," Iqbal interrupted. "People change, we all change. The dead are the only ones who don't."

"People change? That's rich. Kadhim, change? You must be joking. And anyway, does that mean he has to stop respecting me? Even if he's changed, what's that got to do with me? Why has he left me, thrown me aside . . . without an explanation . . . as if he's the *only* one who's got the brains to understand . . . As if he's the only one who's been sacrificed and lost, and I'm just some silly follower."

"Why do you resign yourself to being a follower?" Adiba interjected. "You shouldn't spend so much time worrying about him and looking after him. You need to get out of the closed circle in which you have become trapped. If he is happy on his own, with his reading, let him be. I am not telling you to leave him or neglect him, but I am suggesting that you find something else apart from Kadhim to occupy yourself with. Find a course or a job, even if it's only for a few hours a week."

"God protect you, Adiba. Who's going to give me a job at my age and with my wonderful English?"

"Go to any center for volunteer work. I myself began as a volunteer for the Refugee Council."

Sahira began to cry quietly.

"What about your children?" Iqbal asked. "What do they think about it all?"

"They've got their own lives. ʿAdil's gone to Iraq as a volunteer with a British medical delegation; they've taken over medical supplies to those in need as part of an attempt to break the sanctions; Kadhim won't hear his name mentioned. Shakir phones once a week and has promised to spend Christmas with us instead of with his girlfriend's family. Nahid is occupied with exams, and we haven't seen her for three months. We've all changed. The family's falling apart. We're like an English family now; we only see each other twice a year—at Christmas and Easter."

"What are you talking about?" Iqbal protested. "There are English families who visit each other all the time, like some of us do, and others who only visit their relatives once a year, like others of us do. It's wrong to generalize, Sahira."

"That's what I've heard," she capitulated wearily.

"And have you seen it with your own eyes? Among your neighbors? How many English people do you know properly?"

"*Allahu Akbar*, Iqbal! Stop nagging, please. Have I said I am an unbeliever? We know you've got an English boyfriend whom you want to defend. Have we cursed the green grapes and said they're sour? It's just talk."

"I'm sorry, Sahira, you're right," Iqbal said, in an attempt to ease the tension. "Let's change the subject and get back to your children. Perhaps she doesn't come home because she's got a boyfriend."

"Who?"

"Nahid! You said that for some reason she's stopped coming to see you. Perhaps she's got a boyfriend!"

"Boyfriend! Of course she has friends—boys and girls—but . . ."

"Sahira, please don't pretend to be naive, because it doesn't suit you," Iqbal said. "You know what I am talking about. I mean, her own special friend, 'boyfriend' as the English say—a sweetheart, a close friend whom she prefers to spend her time with!"

Sahira went pale; she wiped away her tears and blew her nose loudly, then raised her voice in defense of her daughter.

"Boyfriend! No, ʿaini, no, no. Nahid's sensible and knows what she can and can't do. She's certainly not involved in anything like that. It's her studies; it's definitely her studies that are keeping her busy."

"It was only a suggestion. Now's not the right time to discuss whether she has the right to have a boyfriend or be treated equally, but . . . Oh, that reminds me of something I must mention before I forget. There's going to be a vigil in front of 10 Downing Street to protest the launch of the latest bombing campaign against Iraq. Will you come?"

"What's the point?" Sahira countered. "Can you tell me that? What's the point of it all? If they've decided to bomb the country, they'll bomb it, even if we're dying outside the prime minister's house. It's all a waste of time. We know what they're planning. They've bombed the bridges, the power stations, and the water treatment plants . . . But their agent's still there . . . *Wa-Allahi*, it's all a clever scheme to destroy Iraq and the entire region, and let him remain. Do you really believe that the whole of the CIA, with all its money and advanced technology, can't get rid of him?"

Iqbal glanced at Adiba, expecting her to reply, but she sat silently watching the to-ing and fro-ing of the people around them, so she answered instead.

"Don't tell me you're still relying on the Americans to save us from Saddam Hussein despite everything you know. We've heard them say that a hundred times . . . The important thing now is to save the people . . . Haven't you heard them say that the devil you know is better than the one you don't? Yes, I believe there is a point to demonstrating. We've got voices, and the people in charge in this country will have to listen to us and see we're not mindless sheep. I'm hoping to be there tomorrow." Iqbal then changed the subject. "Have you seen Mohammed?"

"I bumped into him while I was getting the tea," Sahira replied. "He was paying at the till at the same time as I was. Something strange happened."

"What?" Iqbal asked.

"Mohammed said hello to me and asked how I was."

They stared at her dully, surprised at her excitement.

"But he's a very polite young man. He always says hello to us," Adiba said.

"Yes, that's true. He says hello to us in English. But today he spoke in Arabic," Sahira said triumphantly.

"When they bombed Baghdad in 1991, I stopped speaking English," Adiba murmured vaguely, as if talking to herself. "If it was absolutely necessary to talk, I would answer in Arabic. I tried to tell myself that I was acting naively and it was a useless thing to do, but I couldn't stop myself. I did not talk to anyone for days, not even the people closest to me; nor did I speak to ordinary people like the green grocer or bus conductor, even though I knew that some of them felt exactly the same as I did. I was overcome with bitterness, frustrated anger, and a sense of injustice, which prevented me from understanding what was happening."

Silence.

Sahira swept the cake crumbs into a corner of the plate, then pinched them together with her fingertips, and lifted them carefully to her mouth.

"I've got a suggestion to do with Um Mohammed," Iqbal said. "Let's organize a rotation for visiting her. We'll be there if she needs anything, and we'll be helping her son as well. Because I work, I'll arrange to come in the evening after I've finished. I'll try and persuade Samer to come with me."

"Wouldn't it be better for Samer to remain at home watching television or playing with the neighbors' children?" Sahira suggested.

"I'd rather have him with me as much as possible. I'm afraid he'll get into trouble."

Sahira stood up. Despite her pretty pink dress and velvet coat, she was like a tree drained of its sap. She said she'd go up and see Um Mohammed for a bit. Iqbal reminded her of the heavy bag of shopping she had placed under the table. Sahira gave her a distant look.

"Sahira reminds me of Samer when she starts arguing and debating," laughed Iqbal. "Sometimes he surprises me by suddenly coming out with a whole sentence in classical Arabic."

Adiba contemplated Iqbal. Despite her apparent liveliness, there was an air of exhaustion about her. She hadn't put on any makeup and had neglected her appearance. Anxiety had scored two black rings under her eyes.

"Are you all right?" Adiba asked.

Iqbal answered instantly, as if shaking off a painful misfortune.

"I'm pregnant. That's my pressing piece of news. I'm pregnant."

They exchanged glances.

"How many months?"

"Almost eight weeks."

"Did you plan it?"

Iqbal laughed out loud.

"I read somewhere that three-quarters of human beings are conceived accidentally. Samer, for example, was conceived by mistake. And so was I. No, I didn't plan to get pregnant. I changed the pill I was on because of its side effects, and I got pregnant. There must have been a couple of days separating the two."

"Have you told the father?" Adiba asked.

"I haven't decided whether I want to keep the baby or to have an abortion."

"Wouldn't it be better to discuss it with him? He has a right to know, and you have a right to expect him to share the responsibility."

"I don't know. I don't want him to feel that I'm testing him, even though I'm sure he'll be overjoyed at the news and start planning the wedding immediately."

"What is the problem, then? Is it because he wants to get married and have a child, and you don't?"

"Yes. It's not John who's dithering, but me. I'm the one at fault. My son and I are completely free at the moment. I might work for long hours and not look after him as well as I would like, and we don't have much to live on, but we're free and that's the most important thing when all's said and done. I'm mistress of myself. I've gotten used to a new way of life. I only have to answer to my son for what I do. What guarantee is there that, if I get married, my life with John will be like my life now?"

"It certainly will not remain the same, but it might be better in other ways."

"Do you talk about your family and your country with your close friends?"

The question provoked a rare burst of laughter from Adiba.

"I beg your pardon. I did not mean to laugh. Perhaps the real question is do we ever talk about anything else? We spend most of our time pretending to be engaged with secondary concerns. We go around and around in a circle, hoping to get to the center."

"How do you feel now?"

"I feel I am getting better every day. I accept what life has to offer me day by day. Even depressing ideas. Like death."

"Your death, or other people's?"

"Most recently, my own death."

"Did you know that I came to study psychoanalysis late in life?" Catherine asked.

Adiba shook her head.

"I took an arts degree initially. In the sixties, I directed my energies into various kinds of political activity. Like you, I had huge expectations. I was not imprisoned or tortured, because I live in a relatively democratic country compared to yours, but my hopes were continually frustrated on a general and personal level, and I ended up suffering a nervous breakdown and undergoing a period of treatment. As a result, I began to look for meaning in what was going on around us." She chuckled. "I was on the point of becoming a philosopher, but I changed my mind. I left the field of arts and started to study psychoanalysis. Realizing that I would not be able to understand myself unless I could understand others was a very significant point in my life. This concept might appear self-evident to some people, but it was difficult for me to appreciate, and it took me a long time to learn and understand it. From then on, I became interested in people's internal struggles. These struggles perfect each other as well as contradict each other at the same time. Like good and evil, for example."

Catherine became aware that she was still wearing her reading glasses and took them off.

"No wonder you look so blurry!" she said. "And now, Adiba, since I have talked for so long and taken over your session, what do you say to my continuing my lecture and telling you about a theory that I read once and which you've reminded me of by bringing up the idea of death?"

"Please go on."

"First of all, I should make clear that it's not my theory. I'm not exactly sure who compounded it. It may have been Erich Fromm, the German psychologist and thinker. If you're interested in the source, I'll look it up in my books and tell you next time. The theory proposes that in every human being there are two dispositions: the love of life and the love of death. Parallel to them are good and evil. There are several factors that influence the hypothetical balance between the two. If a person spends his energy defending himself against certain attack or protecting himself from hunger, he will have a greater love of death than love of life. Other factors that can influence the balance are injustice in society and being used by or oppressing others. A love of life develops most naturally through freedom; but freedom in the abstract sense of the word is not sufficient. Freedom must be understood here as the freedom to act, the freedom to be creative—to create, to construct—or to roam freely. To enjoy such freedom, human beings have to be active and responsible rather than slaves or cogs in a machine."

CHAPTER FIFTEEN

Why do certain days have a bitter flavor you can't forget? It was an ever-present sourness in her mouth. If she licked her skin, it had the same taste, and when she washed, droplets of bile seemed to well up out of her and cling to the side of the bath. Was it possible to clean out her insides?

Iqbal sat behind her desk in the morning. She was still breathless from the rush to get to work—the hurried departure from the house, the walk to the bus stop, the race to catch the bus. (If she missed it, she would have to wait another quarter of an hour for the next one to arrive, which would make her late for work.) Then, at Kilburn Underground there was the forward push with the other commuters who, like her, were hurrying to get to work. And, finally, there was the squeeze into the train, which was already crammed full of bodies. There was the usual morning fug. The smell of people. Sweaty armpits. Overcoats anointed with the stale fog of winter.

She went to get a cup of coffee from the small machine near the director's office, as she had done every day before being cursed by pregnancy and morning sickness. She wished she could remember which night it had been, exactly, when the mistake had happened, but she couldn't.

Every night she spent with John was a pregnancy waiting to happen. She had abandoned vigilance and precautionary measures. She rebelled against them, freed herself from all the restraints—be they custom or tradition, religion or reason. She went to extremes to satisfy her desires, extracting the very last drop of pleasure she could. She was like a drunk who patiently and intently upended a heavy glass bottle of *araq* in the hope of getting a few more drops of liquid. The last drops were the sweetest and most pleasurable.

Wasn't it strange how physically she felt as if he were the first man in her life? Once, he'd asked if she had known how to make love before him, and she had retorted, "Don't have such a high opinion of yourself. Yes, I've made love and more!" Then Iqbal had added with a teasing giggle, "Don't forget, I am a wild divorcée."

Sex with her husband. How to describe it? One-sided exercise! Pinned to the floor like a mattress while he practiced push-ups on top of her—rising and falling, up, down, one, two.

Once, as she had lain there with her eyes closed, she calculated how long intercourse lasted. Five times up, five times down, and then break apart. Ten seconds and an "Oh, Iqbal, my love" before his eyes closed and he started to snore beside her.

How she wanted to forget! To erase their years together! Their arguments. Her rude answers. His slaps. His beatings. Her sobbing. His pleas for forgiveness.

Oh no! The blasted machine was out of milk and sugar. She couldn't bear black coffee. The smell made her feel sick. Before going back to the office, she turned right along the corridor, and went into the shared toilets. She threw her bag on the floor and began to vomit up a yellow liquid and the sour-smelling contents of her stomach into the toilet bowl.

When the retching had faded, and her stomach had settled down, she drew a deep breath and emerged from the toilet. She washed her face in the handbasin and rinsed her mouth to get rid of the persistent taste of vomit. She looked at her pale, tired face in the mirror and shook her head miserably. She thought, I look like a corpse.

Iqbal bent down to pick up her handbag and noticed several splashes of vomit on the hem of her long khaki skirt. Her eyes filled with tears. What a foul day! she thought. It has begun badly, may God make it end better. She lifted the hem to the washbasin and cleaned off the traces of puke. Curse long skirts and whoever invented them and wore them.

She preferred wearing long skirts at the office, though only in the office, as they made her feel less inhibited and less aware of the way she was sitting and moving. In fact, they gave her a greater sense of freedom.

Once, in the middle of a sharp argument, Sahira and Majda had looked at her in astonishment when she told them that she understood why women wore the *hijab*. In a strange way, she'd pointed out, the veil lent women equality in traditionally male areas of Arab society, such as the workplace.

"I don't understand your argument. Explain what you mean, please," Majda asked.

"Majda! Sarcasm won't get you anywhere. In my opinion, when a woman wears the veil, she immediately ceases to be the center of attention."

"In other words," Adiba interjected, "it negates her existence . . . her presence."

"No, I don't think so," Iqbal said. "It just means she's no longer an object of desire and interest. She still exists as an employee or in her functional capacity. I wear long dresses and skirts and long-sleeved shirts in the office, but I don't think I count for less because of that. On the contrary, I feel I'm more on par with the men. Outside the office I wear what I like."

Majda stuck out her neck and rested her elbows on the table that was between them in the café.

"You're a hypocrite," she said.

"I'd rather use the word 'aware,'" Iqbal laughed cheerfully.

"Aware? Aware that a man is free to look at you when and how he wants? Why doesn't he cover up his foul, prying eyes in the office?" Majda retorted.

"I really think he should do the same as Iqbal," Adiba smiled, "and change his eyes like she changes her clothes, when he goes to the office. He ought to put on a different pair of eyes from the ones he wears outside, and use these exclusively to look at his women colleagues in a neutral fashion. When he's outside the office, he's free to take them off and wear any other pair he wants."

"I am so pleased that my innocent remark has made even dear Adiba have a joke at my expense," Iqbal said.

Adiba chuckled. She touched Iqbal's hand gently and said, "I'm sorry. But you have to admit that such an invention would solve the perennial problems that exist between men and women."

"Why can't men learn how to be modest?" Sahira fumed. "Why do I have to go around covering up my hair and arms and knees while they swagger about, showing off everything they've got? Have you seen the men in *dishdashas*? They lounge about in the cafés or streets in their see-through *dishdashas* with their legs wide apart as if that thing they've got dangling between them is calling out, 'Come on and take a look at me.'"

"Let's stick to the subject," Majda said, leaning further forward over the table until she almost knocked over Sahira's cup of tea.

"What subject?" Sahira cut in. "I didn't know we were attending a formal meeting with Madam Majda as the chair."

"No, no. Of course it's not an official meeting. We're merely trying to understand why men sit with their legs so far apart," Iqbal said. "Do you want to know what I think? I think we should feel sorry for them, poor things. They splay their legs like that because they've got such a big problem between them. Imagine having a half-kilo weight swinging back and forth between your thighs as you walked. On top of that, there's the heat in Iraq, the humidity in Britain; I don't envy them, do you? And now Sahira wants us to imagine there's something calling out from down there as well; I say, God help them."

Um Mohammed laughed so much that tears came to her eyes.

"*Dishdashas* are the best," she added shyly. "They are wide and comfortable, like *shirwal*."

Majda turned on her.

"Even you, Um Mohammed!"

"Et tu, Brute?" Iqbal said, amid gales of laughter. They were like schoolgirls giggling about something forbidden, abandoning themselves to childish merriment.

"There is nothing to be ashamed about in religion," Um Mohammed said.

A loud, playful laugh escaped Sahira.

"I believe *dishdashas* and *shirwal* are best for both of them," she said. "I mean, men and women. It's like Iqbal was saying about her long skirt. It gives them freedom. Makes them quicker and more efficient at . . ."

Iqbal held up her finger as if calling for silence. Their laughter died away as she drew a newspaper clipping out of her bag.

"Listen," she said. "Lend me your ears, please. As I've done before, I will read you something that is mysterious, marvelous, and meretricious. I shall read you an item of news. I know this doesn't support what I've been saying about being 'aware,' but please listen. This question appeared on the *fatwa* page in *al-Din* magazine":

> I am a young woman who has recently gotten married.
> Before my wedding, my mother told me that a husband
> had the right to look at and touch the whole of his wife's
> body, but she said that he must not look at a particular
> place. Is this true?

"His holiness, the virtuous sheikh, answered the confused girl as follows":

> It is not *haram* for a man to look at or touch any part
> of his wife's body. But the sight of this particular place
> is distasteful. Certain sources say, "The action is not
> distasteful when they are together." Although this
> part of the body does not look desirable, nevertheless

it performs its task, and in a way defined in religious
practice. Everything in nature fulfills its purpose. God
is all-knowing.

They roared with laughter until tears ran down their cheeks and the
owner of the café looked disapprovingly at their noisy, girlish behavior.

"Now, if we turn the question on its head," Adiba said, "and imagine
that the young girl has asked the virtuous sheikh for a religious ruling on
whether it is appropriate to look at certain places on her husband's body,
what would be his reply?"

"Are you referring to 'His Highness'!" said Sahira. "The unique male
member! The sheikh would issue a *fatwa* ordering it to be treated like a
king. Venerate and respect it, he would say, and when it stands erect, be
sure that it is something nice to look at and touch . . ."

"Good morning!"

"Good morning," Iyad and Qassim replied, without looking up from
the newspapers and magazines they were reading.

She headed for her desk, covering the damp spot on her skirt with
her handbag. Where was everyone? It wasn't important. She couldn't be
bothered to ask after them. She wanted to start work immediately, before
she started feeling sick again. She was light-headed with exhaustion,
anxiety, and misery.

A pile of newspapers, magazines, publications, and press releases
lay in front of her. Her daily allotment. And extra. 'Aida was absent . . .
why?

The director wasn't there either. She speculated as to the reasons for
his absence. Personal reasons! He was probably embarrassed. He hadn't
shown up during the bombing in 1991. He wasn't brave enough to face
his colleagues. He went missing. He sat at home, holed up behind the
secure walls of his citadel, until the initial days of the bombardment were
over.

She shivered. It was cold outside, but the heating in the office had
been turned down to save money. For better or worse, the Gulf War
had had an effect on everyone. It had had a negative impact on their
office. The old furniture hadn't been replaced. The salaries arrived late. A
number of employees were made redundant. They cut back on expenses
and travel, and now had canceled them altogether. The director did his

job, his deputy's, and the personnel manager's. Everyone at the office did three jobs to make up for the people who had been there before the war.

Iyad refused to talk to anyone or answer his phone. Iqbal picked up the receiver four times for him, then left it and sat listening with the others to its irritating ring. The young girl who typed some of the translated articles had taken advantage of the director's absence and gone shopping. Qassim was crashing around the place like an angry bull, swearing loudly, waiting for her to come back to type his article so that he wouldn't be late leaving at three o'clock.

"Curse the fathers of the world," Iyad ground his teeth. "Fuck the mothers of the world. Bitches! Sons of bitches. First Palestine, and now Iraq."

Iqbal thought, swear words that involve men are basically respectful, such as "curse the fathers of the world." But swear words that have anything to do with women immediately involve the female sexual organs. Or is it because they think that women as a whole are 'aura?

She smiled, imagining herself discussing this point with the group. Why did they laugh and joke whenever they started discussing sex, and why did everything appear so funny? Laughter gave them courage and distanced them from the embarrassment that came with discussing such a taboo subject.

She drew a deep breath. She thought about her own problem. She had to calm down. It was a difficult time, and she must avoid slipping into depression. She had to get the better of her feelings and emotions. She had enough problems to deal with already: Morning sickness, the question of whether to tell John or not, Samer and all her worries about him, organizing someone to look after him during the long Christmas holidays, which were about to start and which she hadn't done anything about yet. And on top of the pile, the airstrikes on Iraq and the sanctions.

Iqbal read through a number of papers. She didn't feel like working, or living. She started flipping through the pages of a recent copy of *Time* magazine—the American weekly—published on November 22, 1998, after she noticed that the cover story was "Crisis in Iraq." There were various headlines inside: "The Whites of His Eyes" and "Yo-yo in the Gulf." And a colored map of Iraq that pinpointed the military objectives being targeted by American bombers.

Her eyes filled with tears at the wretched state Iraq was in. Its people suffering, fragmented, ripped to shreds. Her chest tightened with pain. A wave of heat passed over her, and she broke out in a sweat. Her stomach heaved in fear and pain. She felt sickened by the media hypocrisy in all its glory.

Nausea returned. She raced to the bathroom, and vomited.

"Have you got a new nightmare for me?"

Adiba gave her the notebook in which she had written down her nightmares.

"Yes," she said. "But I've noticed that the recurring nightmares I used to have have gone. We must have succeeded in burying them."

"Adiba," Catherine laughed. "You will soon be able to take my place. But you have used a nice expression. You interact with things as if they have a life of their own, as if they are alive."

"As far as I'm concerned, my nightmares are more alive than some people. As you know, I am a single woman—I am alone, at night in particular. I feel as if the nightmares—despite their ugliness, which is caused by something within me—are living with me. They like to force themselves on me and visit me at night. I don't know how to cut myself off from them. How to get rid of them."

"They will go with time. You won't get rid of them immediately, because they exist inside you and are a living part of you. I think nightmares are a necessary evil. They are essentially a form of therapy. They are not merely a symptom of exposure to a tremendously painful experience. They are more complicated than that. They are a mechanism of self-defense, a way of ridding oneself of feelings of grief."

"I used to think they were a replay of the trauma, because they took me back to what frightened me."

"They are a way of making you face the crisis—an alarm bell. They represent the struggle between what you are thinking about at the moment and your denial of what has happened."

"Their acuteness changes from time to time."

"When are the nightmares at their worst?"

Adiba thought.

"At times of despair. Loneliness. When I think about death. Political crises. The bad news coming out of Iraq. The bombing. The repression."

"What about when you have been in touch with your family?"

"I don't think they are directly linked to that."

"You told me once that you are in frequent contact with your husband's family. Do you think they are optimistic about him?"

"The position of people in Iraq is different. They despair. I always try to encourage them."

"What about his mother?"

"She's old and tired. Confused. Sometimes she asks, 'When will he come back, so I can see him before I die?' And other days she says, 'I'm sure they've killed him because if he were alive, he would have found some way of contacting me or telling me that he's alive.'"

"What about your mother?"

"She died five years ago," Adiba responded.

"I'm sorry. You must have suffered even more because you were so far away from her."

"I longed to be able to cry. I sat by myself for a number of days. I couldn't bear to see anyone. I felt so angry. I was drugged with bitterness and impotence. Grief was like a horrid animal crouching inside me. It took me over completely so that I thought it would remain there forever. It seemed the only way to get rid of it was to die myself."

"We want to die sometimes because we are unable to protect those we love, particularly from death."

"I wanted to be beside her. With her. To enjoy her company. I felt guilt and grief for all the pain she'd suffered, and because I had exposed her to so much pain and sadness and hadn't helped her. I was suddenly aware there was so much I didn't know about her. I hadn't looked after her as I should have. I hadn't paid enough attention to her. I hadn't listened to her problems. I found that I had many questions that I wanted to ask her about herself. When she died, I felt that I had lost my childhood as well—because I lived in her memories as a baby and a child.

"I wanted to bring her to visit me here. I had even organized a program. She loved plants and flowers, so I thought I'd take her to Kew Gardens, and we'd go for walks on Hampstead Heath. She liked rivers, so I'd take her to Richmond Park, and we'd walk beside the river and, and . . ."

"You desperately need to grieve for her. You need to cry for her. Dealing with the death of a close relative is a process. There are several stages—you feel disbelief at first and refuse to accept the death, then you feel angry, then, finally, great sadness. The tears wash away the grief bit by bit until you accept the death as a natural part of life."

"As far as I am concerned, she's still alive," Adiba said. "I have convinced myself that she's still living in Iraq. Far off and distant, and not allowed to travel."

"That brings to two the number of people who are missing in your life."

"Who do you mean?"

"Your mother and Mukhlis."

CHAPTER SIXTEEN

Majda suddenly remembered that Um Mohammed was ill, and decided to break her self-imposed exile to pay her a visit and bring her some comfort. On her way to Um Mohammed's flat, she realized that she hadn't brought her a present. What should she get? she wondered. A box of chocolates? Um Mohammed didn't like chocolates. A bunch of flowers? They were a waste of money. They'd be dead within a couple of days, and she'd chuck them into the dustbin. What about a magazine? She would buy her a magazine in Arabic, so she could read the funny, sad news of those backward Arabs.

She went into a small shop not far from Queensway station that sold Arab newspapers and magazines. She chose a magazine, then stood in the queue to pay for it. She occupied herself by looking at the shelves near her and noticed a stack of Arabic books between the notepads, exercise books, and envelopes. Old books, covered in dust and forgotten. There were no more than ten of them. She reached out her hand. She drew one out. It was about astrology and how to tell the future from the stars. She laughed. What future? The second book was about Moroccan cookery. It was almost her turn to pay. She tried to put the book back in its place, but her hand shook and it fell to the floor, bringing one of the others down with it. She bent down to pick them up and glanced at the other book. Her eyes bulged. Her heart gave a queer jump. Blood rushed to her face. She held the book out to the man at the till, together with the magazine, and paid for both of them.

At the door to the shop, Majda looked about her. Had anyone noticed her purchase? She placed the book inside the magazine and put it into her handbag. She clutched the bag and walked back to the station. From there she took a train back to her flat. She completely forgot what she was doing in Queensway and the huge struggle she had gone through to convince herself to go there.

She closed the door to the flat firmly behind her, then locked it and put the chain across. She made sure the curtains were pulled. She put on the light and, after sitting down, impatiently began to leaf through the pages. It was relatively old, she noticed. How come she hadn't heard of it?

Her heart quickened as she started to flick through the book. It told the story of his life and struggle, his ideas and his humanity. There were pictures of him. Loads of pictures. Showing his childhood and adolescence. Marking each stage of his life. He was there at the celebrations. In different poses. He looked just the same, just as she remembered him. Handsome. Tall. With piercing eyes and jet-black hair.

Majda took the book to bed with her. She leaned back against the wall. She needed to find a position that would keep her steady. Shore up her trembling body. She stretched out. She began to read. Paragraphs here and there. Dipping in and out of the pages. Suddenly, she paused at a line that seemed familiar, at a story that she knew in detail. The writer was describing what had happened when the President stayed in her house.

> One of them had recognized him. He had told the others that Saddam Hussein was in Tariq's house. And so he found himself unexpectedly surrounded on all sides. Had the moment finally arrived when the great knight would fall into the clutches of the enemy? Had it all come to an end? Had the time come for him to give himself up and allow them to place his legs in chains and bind his hands behind his back? He had to resist. But would he be able to? He had to find out how many men there were ranged against him, so he let off a couple of rounds of ammunition. He was answered by a hail of bullets. They came from all sides. There was no point in returning fire. This time resistance was impossible. It would only result in the deaths of innocent members of the police force. The people who owned the house, who had given him refuge, would also be punished severely. The doors and courtyard of their house would run with blood, and they would die. There was no escape this time. In a resounding voice, he called out, "Death to 'Abdul Salem 'Aref. Long live the Socialist Arab Ba'ath Party." Then he surrendered.
>
> When the soldiers reached the second floor of the house, where he was waiting for them, several officers revealed their low origins and inferior character by shouting insulting remarks at a young girl of fifteen and her mother. They were the sister and mother of

Comrade Tariq. He trembled like a madman, and without anyone seeing what he was doing, he seized a hand grenade wrapped in paper, which was lying on a nearby table, and shouted, "If you repeat that foul expression one more time, I'll explode this grenade and we'll all be killed!" The commander perceived the danger they were in and ordered the officers to stop their obscenities immediately.

Majda ground her teeth. What was this nonsense? He hadn't mentioned her name. He'd mentioned Tariq. Why had the writer changed Tahsin's name to Tariq? Tahsin the martyr. How had he become Tariq?

She sat on the edge of the bed with the book in her lap; unconsciously, she clenched her hands. She felt a sharp pain. She saw blood seeping out of her palm. She had dug her long fingernails into the taut skin. She re-read the single phrase pointing to her existence. With round eyes, she read it over and over, rocking back and forth with monotonous regularity. She couldn't believe what she was seeing. The lines and false words wavered in front of her. No, no. That was not what the President said. He was not a liar. Liars were feeble and weak and traitors. He was strong. He was triumphant and self-assured. So why was he lying? The details of the story were all wrong. The book was wrong and . . . and why had they changed Tahsin's name to Tariq?

She put her head between her hands. Squeezed it. Pressed her fingers against her temples. Rubbed them. She didn't understand a word she was reading. She must be tired. Worn out. Unable to understand the underlying meaning of the President's words. She had to sleep, to relax. She would read them tomorrow.

CHAPTER SEVENTEEN

Um Mohammed turned over in bed. She was childishly content to be back home again. Her home.

For the first time since coming to London, she called the flat home. What could be nicer than sleeping in your own bed? Clean cotton sheets, not the thick sheets they had given her at the hospital, which were a mix of cotton and nylon and made an embarrassing noise every time she moved. Then there were those nice nurses, with their white uniforms, who cleaned her and looked after her. They didn't let her sleep properly though, and were always coming to wake her up at night to take her temperature and blood pressure, and sometimes to force her to go to the toilet for a urine sample. Then there had been the old woman in the bed beside her whose moaning had been really annoying. What a shame! The nurse had spent ages cleaning the woman. She changed her clothes and sheets, and then she dirtied herself almost immediately. So they had to start putting nappies on her as if she were a child. The nurse had made signs to show Um Mohammed that the woman was suffering from incontinence and other illnesses.

"May Allah be compassionate! May Allah protect my self-respect and dignity, and keep me from such a state. Allah, let me die before I reach the misery of old age," Um Mohammed prayed.

Um Mohammed was the youngest patient in the geriatric ward. When Iqbal heard her say that she had grown older and that the important thing was to leave with dignity, she said, "Um Mohammed, you are still young and fresh compared to these relics who belong in an archaeological institute."

There was a senile old woman in the bed opposite Um Mohammed who slept during the day and woke up at night to begin the activities of the day. Her routine made Mohammed laugh. "Her biological clock is broken," he said. The woman wasn't content with just moving about at night. She ate and drank in the darkness. She walked around and then went to the bathroom, which was next to Um Mohammed's bed. She didn't do anything except flush the toilet. They tried giving her sleeping tablets to correct her sleep pattern, but she only slept for two hours, then woke up full of life and began her ritual visits to the toilet. During the two hours that she slept, the snores that emanated from her toothless mouth were like the noise and vibrations produced by an Underground train.

Adiba asked one of the young nurses who helped Um Mohammed to lie down and get up correctly about the old woman.

"She's perfectly strong and healthy," the nurse replied. "The only thing wrong with her is senility. She's in this ward because she's elderly and has no one to look after her. They are waiting to find a place for her in a residential home. This ward is her home, and the only place in the world where she can find someone to look after her."

Um Mohammed stayed in the hospital for two weeks. During the first three days, they examined her thoroughly. There wasn't a place on her body they hadn't poked or probed or taken a sample from for testing—weight, height, body mass, discharges, excretions. X-rays, tests, and exploratory procedures were all performed.

She felt as if her body had been taken apart like a car engine or a television set. "The doctors and nurses remind me of your late father," she told Mohammed. "Whenever he wanted to mend the television, he would take it apart and set out all the parts on the table and separate the good ones from the damaged ones. Once, may God have mercy upon him, he forgot to put some of them back. I pointed the parts out to him. But by that time he had screwed on the back of the television and really didn't want to undo it again, so he said they weren't necessary—they were surplus."

During her illness, she'd felt like such a burden on everyone. Oh Allah, may I not be a burden upon them, and grant me a normal death that will admit me to the ranks of the just, she pleaded now. You are powerful over everything in your mercy, oh most merciful of the merciful.

Mohammed visited her periodically with his fiancée and looked after her. (Um Mohammed was the only one who referred to Mary this way. She couldn't bring herself to say girlfriend.) Mary was a lovely girl.

Sahira and Adiba and Iqbal were always at the hospital as well. They had stood by her. Iqbal came twice with Samer. She'd asked permission for him to visit, and they'd said it would be all right as long as he didn't disturb the other patients.

Um Mohammed asked about Majda, and they said that she was a bit under the weather and would visit her as soon as she got better.

"*In sha' Allah*, it's nothing serious."

"It's nothing . . . Just a cold."

"May God grant her good health!" Um Mohammed said.

May God grant each of them a long life and give them health and happiness, she thought to herself. All of them had gone to such trouble for her. It was a long way to come, and they had so little time, but they'd still come to visit her. She felt full of gratitude.

Oh God, we praise and thank you. She still felt weak after the operation, but in a couple of weeks she would feel like herself again and start going out. They told her—how proud she felt as Mohammed did the interpreting—"You are very lucky, Um Mohammed. The cancer in the kidney is in its initial stages, and we caught the tumor before it spread to your second kidney or any other part of your body. It's slow-growing. Your second kidney is healthy and is more than strong enough to do the job required of it."

Praise be to Allah! Say: Nothing will afflict us save what Allah has ordained for us. His mercy encompasses everything.

Adiba had read Um Mohammed details about the kinds of food she should avoid. Adiba seemed happier and more relaxed. Better than before. She wanted to ask her if she had heard good news about her missing husband, but Iqbal's arrival had distracted her.

"Where's that angel Samer?" Um Mohammed asked.

"I phoned John and waited till he arrived so he could stay with him."

"But he's used to staying on his own," Adiba said.

"There's been a problem at school, and they advised me to try and spend more time with him or find someone else to look after him. The problem is that it makes me even more dependent on John."

Iqbal looked at the list of foods.

"How many kilos have you lost?" she joked. "Twenty? My God, Um Mohammed, you'll become as thin as Claudia Schiffer. If you follow this list of food, which is exactly like the one prescribed by Adiba—do you remember the 'three nos'? no spices, no fat, no taste—you'll turn into a professional supermodel, and we'll be deprived of your wonderful cooking."

"I will cook for you whenever you wish, sweetheart," Um Mohammed laughingly promised her, "so long as God gives me strength and grace."

The hospital had arranged for her to have home help. Someone would come to clean and organize the house and do the shopping on a daily basis. And they had also arranged for ready-made meals to be delivered to her flat and for a nurse to visit her regularly. There had been so many changes. Everything had happened so quickly.

Now, back at home, she was beset by a deep sense of loneliness and a longing for her family, her relatives, and her city. How nice it would be if her sister were with her.

She sighed loudly. Her eyes teared over, and then she got control of herself. She reached out her hand to the drawer beside the bed. She drew out a small book of prayers, which she read from time to time and had recently come to rely more and more on. She opened it at random and read, "He said God is the most high. Truly no one despairs of Allah's soothing mercy except for those who have no faith."

Her face relaxed and she said out loud, "I ask forgiveness of God. I do not doubt your blessings. At least I live near my son, I sleep in my bed, and I am much better off than millions of other people."

CHAPTER EIGHTEEN

Iqbal and John sat on the sofa, facing the television. Still as statues while pictures of troops massing and the beginning of the bombardment flashed across the screen. The bombing of Baghdad ... No one had believed it would happen, but it was happening. They wanted to think it was a lie, but it was happening. It was being shown on television, transmitted live from the top of the Ministry of Information building, in a city that was about to be subjected to massive air raids. A journalist narrated the live feed. The level of adrenaline in his blood rose until he began shouting excitedly at the act of destruction.

"Wow!"

He screamed like an excited child at the sight of the night explosions. His infectious excitement spread to the other journalist sitting in the studio, who was connected to the live broadcast via an enormous screen that had been erected specially in the studio to enable British viewers to see what was happening in Iraq. The American correspondent (who was being broadcast live from Baghdad) repeated the scanty information he had. The British correspondent (in the studio) repeated the information relayed to him by the American. Audiences all over the world watched the same film clip.

The picture showed the roof of an undistinguished building with a mosque and a bridge in the background and some buildings in the distance. The night in Baghdad had a strange hue. The sky and air appeared a foggy green through the filter of the night vision lenses. The color diminished the reality of what was happening and the destruction that was taking place. Rocket explosions lit up the sky unexpectedly so that the color wavered for a second and took on a reddish tinge.

Iqbal felt desperately lonely. Isolated. A long way away from her family and city. John reached out his hand to draw her toward him, but she edged away from him.

"You look exhausted," he said. "Go to bed. Try and get some sleep, and I'll call you if anything new happens."

She leaped to her feet and turned on him, barely able to conceal her anger.

"New! What do you mean 'anything new'? Is there anything more new than bombing a city and destroying it over the heads of its inhabitants without any reason whatsoever?"

He fell back, biting back what he was going to say.

"I am sorry. I didn't mean 'anything new' in the way you understood it. I just want you to rest. I know how difficult this must be for you."

"Don't be stupid. Why do you British keep on telling me, 'I know how you feel,' and 'we know what you mean,' etc.? If you really understand, why do you go on causing this destruction? . . . Which you don't want, apparently . . . which you don't agree with."

"Iqbal . . . Iqbal, calm down! You are right about me . . . I am sorry."

She shouted as loud as she could,

"Don't say 'sorry' . . . don't pretend to be sorry just to please me! Who says you're sorry? Look at the television and you will see what the British really feel. Do you see how the presenter stops the discussion to point at more rockets falling on Baghdad? Can you hear how pleased and excited he is? That's how you all really feel."

"Darling . . . listen to me, please. Who do you mean by 'you all'? I'm John; I was your friend before I was your lover. I am not some silly, excited television presenter. Why don't you compare me to Tony Benn, for example? He's British as well, and you respect him. Why? Because he's different, as you're always telling me; he's searching for justice for everyone. Why are you so scornful of me and so full of hatred? I know I don't feel exactly the same as you do when I look at the bombing of Baghdad. I don't have the same direct ties to it as you do. But I still feel angry because of the injustice and repression and political hypocrisy, just as you do. You know very well what I think of the sanctions and the airstrikes. Do I still have to prove myself to you after two years of being together?"

She kept her distance from him, staring fixedly at him with blank, unseeing eyes.

"Darling," he entreated her. "Come and sit down. Calm down. I'll make you a cup of chamomile tea, and then I'll phone Howard to find out if there is a demonstration against the bombings tomorrow, so that we can rally the people we know and go. Let me turn off the television, just for a short time, while you relax. What good will it do if we both suffer nervous breakdowns?"

Like a sleepwalker, she allowed herself to be led by his soothing voice; she sat on the sofa, facing the television screen, and with desolate eyes stared at the desperate image of herself reflected in the empty screen.

CHAPTER NINETEEN

Majda was wearing her black hat. She peered at the street through the window. It was empty. She peeped from behind the white blinds. She had to make sure that no one was watching her house or following her movements.

She noticed a white spot on her black jacket. It must be Greek yogurt, she thought.

She rubbed the spot. It didn't come off. She headed toward the bathroom and washed it.

She hadn't changed her clothes for days. She'd slept in them, woken up in them. Why bother to change them? She didn't see anyone, and no one visited her. Anyway, she was clean. Her body always smelled clean. She didn't sweat like some people. There was no need to change her clothes. They were all black.

She returned to the window. There was no one there. The road was safe. She put on her coat and went downstairs. She stopped at the outside door to the building. Checked. The street was empty. It was ten o'clock in the morning. The best time. Most people had gone to work, and the pensioners generally left their homes at half past nine to do their shopping—the liberal happy hour when they were allowed to use their free transport passes. She laughed out loud as she took her first steps in the street. She was laughing at the pensioners. Poor things. Miserable souls. They woke up at five and were imprisoned in their homes till they left at half past nine exactly. Ha, ha, she laughed to herself. They deserved better; they should learn ... learn what? The lesson! What lesson was that?

It was a clear day, but Majda still carried an umbrella. To protect herself. She never knew when she might need it. Her handbag had gotten torn somehow, and she had had to sew it up by hand. She remembered using it to hit someone. Now, who was it? Some thief probably, who'd wanted to rob her. She had hit him on the head. Did he think that she was going to be parted from her bag? She'd bought it in London the first time she'd come to the city. She'd take it to the cobblers, but not today. She'd go to the post office first. She'd buy some stamps for the postcards she was writing to Baghdad, or no, no. Perhaps it'd be better to buy the stamps later. Go to Brent Cross first; the child was more important. The letters could wait. She shivered. It was cold. There was no wind. Where was the bus? Why did she always have to wait for it? A few days ago . . . What had she been waiting for then? In a faraway place in a hall filled with Arabs.

A black youth came into the bus shelter to get away from the bitter cold. She edged backward. She stood outside the confines of the temporary shelter. The young man drew out a rolled up newspaper from his coat pocket and started reading. She thought, I'm sure he's pretending to read. When will the bus come? She watched him out of the corner of her eye. Why didn't he turn the pages over? Had ten minutes gone by? She grew more afraid. Ten minutes, and he was still on the same page! He'd been sent to get her. She'd have to go back home. Postpone the shopping trip.

Majda turned around to go back the way she had come, but then noticed the young man stand up unexpectedly. She followed his eyes. She saw the bus approaching—a double-decker. She gave him a chance to get on first. He climbed to the top deck, and she chose a seat near the driver. It was important to be careful.

Once in Brent Cross, she strode confidently into John Lewis. She did what she always did when she arrived: she made her way to the corner where they sold expensive perfumes like Chanel. She chose Coco Chanel. First, she sprayed herself behind the ears, then on both wrists. She took a deep breath and inhaled. Oh, there was no perfume like it! It was the first perfume Saʿid had given her as a present. It cost fifty-four pounds, which was about equal to her weekly income. It was way beyond her budget. She was always using that expression: beyond my budget. Where had she gotten it from? It was not an Arab expression. It was foreign. It was bloody English. When she was younger, she never thought the day would come when things would be beyond her budget.

As she gave herself a final spray, she cackled with laughter. The woman behind the counter glanced at her, and asked very politely, "Does madam require any assistance?"

Majda looked at her angrily and didn't reply. It was a waste of time. Talking to them was a waste of time. They were all pampered and spoiled. They've destroyed our lives; they've ruined our country, and then they ask if there is anything I need, she thought angrily.

Was it wise to have come to Brent Cross? One of them could sneak up on her out of the crowds and attack her. Who knew what their plans were? They might want to kidnap her daughter.

She proceeded to H&M. She went into the children's department and looked at several dresses. The clothes were arranged according to age—from zero to one and from one to . . . What age should she choose? Which dress? She lifted her hand up and held her wrist to her nose. She drew a deep breath. Mmm! How lovely it was. Sa'id used to smell her neck like that—drawing a deep breath, saying how much he loved her. If only he were here, she wouldn't feel afraid. But then she remembered. It's all his fault, she thought . . . It's his fault we're ruined and have had to flee, and he . . . He's escaped from this tiring life. He's sleeping peacefully. Now, which dress should she choose? Perhaps she needed pajamas. She had so many dresses. She remembered now that what she needed was a new pair of pajamas. She wouldn't buy her a nightie, because she was like her and didn't like being enveloped in a garment. She would catch cold. Pajamas were better. She picked out a pair for a two- to three-year-old. Was that the right age? How old was she now? She stood there helplessly, her eyes darting this way and that.

She remained standing there for a long time. The other customers bumped into her, but she didn't move. One of the security guards covertly signaled to an assistant, who came up to her and gently asked if she needed any help. Majda emerged from her stupor with a frightened start. Quick as a flash, she smiled at the assistant and said, "Thank you very much, my dear. I'm dazed by your beautiful showrooms."

She turned toward the section for older girls. Would pajamas for seven- to eight-year-olds fit her? Perhaps they'd be too small. No, perhaps they'd be too big for her. Oh Lord, what was she to do? How old was she?

Majda stood among the brightly colored pairs of girls' pajamas swathed in black from the top of her head to the tip of her toe, with her black umbrella in her hand. She put the umbrella under her arm and tried to work out how old she was on her fingers. She lost all sense of time as she counted: She started. She stopped at the thumb. Four. Then went back to the beginning again.

Did she really need pajamas? She had ten pairs of new pajamas. She had bought different kinds of clothes in the sales. She'd made her two beautiful dresses. She'd embroidered sheets and pillowcases. No! No! Not now. That was years ago.

She suddenly felt exhausted. She had better rest a little. She left the shop and sat down on a bench outside. She opened her bag. She must take it to the cobbler to have it mended. Majda al-Sheikhly couldn't go around with a broken, shabby bag! She'd tell anyone who criticized her it was an antique. Ha, ha, she laughed to herself. They call anything old an antique here. An objet d'art! Threadbare carpets that are eaten away by time! Ha, ha! Yes, yes, Sa'id, don't tell me I'm wrong. It's quite correct to say that. Copper utensils. Time's been eating and drinking off of them for hundreds of years!

She took out a pill to settle her stomach. She swallowed it without water. The letters and postcards! Where were they? Had she written them? What about the stamps, the cobbler, and her daughter's pajamas?

Her head was spinning. She didn't know where she was, or why she was sitting in the middle of this strange place. She had to go back home. Sa'id could buy the pajamas. She sighed contentedly. That was the best solution. She'd send Sa'id out to buy what she needed. And she'd stay at home with her daughter. If Sa'id got back early, they might go out to Nadi al-Sayd in the evening. It was Thursday today, the best night there. What about the little girl? What was her name? She'd forgotten her name.

Majda leaped to her feet. She had to get home quickly. Her bag and umbrella fell off her lap onto the ground. She bent down to pick them up, and a man tried to help her. She gaped at him in terror. She snatched the things out of his hands and raced outside to the bus stop. She was bareheaded. She had forgotten her black hat.

"Who is your best woman friend?"

Adiba thought for a bit. She smiled before she answered.

"I've never thought about that before. But I think that the person I am closest to now is a man rather than a woman. He's named Michael. He was the one who advised me to come and see you."

"I know." Catherine was silent for a moment.

"Are you close to him?"

"You mean, am I in love with him?"

"Adiba," Catherine laughed, "I'm not used to equivocating with you. I apologize for not being completely frank with you. Yes, are you in love with him?"

"No, he's a friend. I trust him and feel relaxed with him and don't need to prove myself to him." She laughed cheerfully. "He's exactly what I say he is—the best friend I have."

"What about Mukhlis? Was he a friend as well as a husband?"

The laughter faded. Facial muscles returned to their habitual position. The tired face changed; the person who was wearing it tried to school it in expressions it had forgotten. At the edge of her mouth were etched lines of age. Sad. Deep. Like furrows.

"We were happy together. We were older when we decided to get married. I had finished my doctorate in Moscow and gone back to Iraq hoping that the political situation had improved. I met him while I was finalizing my appointment papers at the college of education, where he was a lecturer.

"It wasn't love at first sight. We grew closer gradually. We had the same political beliefs. In that sense, we were more than friends. We were comrades."

As she peered back into the distant past, she screwed up her eyes like someone struggling to contain what she was seeing.

"We used to laugh a lot," she added. "At stories of friends . . . how they got arrested and were released and coped with prison, at stories of his arrest and imprisonment. He would find the funny side of the most dangerous situations. He was so full of life. He was so optimistic; he regarded everything as auspicious. He infected me with hope. He took pride in his students and was happy in his role as educator; his students gathered around him and our house became a student club, where they discussed ideas and philosophy. Now, I think I have such a treasure chest of memories of him that they will last me for the rest of my life. Sometimes I feel as if I'd lived with him all my life. Do you know how many years we actually lived together?"

Catherine shook her head.

"Two years. Just two years. Then they arrested us. They arrested him at home because he was ill. He had a bad case of influenza, and the doctor advised him to stay at home. They took him out of the house in his pajamas. They arrested me at the university. Two men from the security forces asked me to go with them to answer some questions. They were soft-spoken and polite. They said it would take a quarter of an hour. Just the time it took to go down the road. They said they'd bring me back personally. One of them joked, 'We'll even save you the cost of a taxi.'"

"Was that the last time you saw him?"

"No, I saw him once more, a week after we were detained. Why do you ask? I've answered this question several times before."

"I know. But each time I hope that you will remember something new. I am trying to prompt you to remember by asking the same question in another way or by coming at you from another angle. Adiba, for perhaps the tenth time, I want you to go back to your prison cell. I believe that we have a better chance now of finding out what happened to you on that night, the night you can't remember. I think it holds the key to unlocking your memories. It was a night on which you underwent more than just physical torture, wasn't it?"

"I don't know."

"Adiba, let's try. We've overcome many difficulties by working together. You've become stronger. Your nightmares are not so dark. You're spending longer periods of time asleep at night. Therefore I urge you to return to that prison cell, even though you know it will cause you terrible pain. What do you think? Will you help me?"

"I don't understand what you're asking of me. What's the point of going back again and again over the same old story? Especially when I remember most of what happened. What do you want from me?"

"Adiba, I want you to take me with you to the cell. Close your eyes if this will help you to picture it. Take your time. First of all, tell me about the place. Let's suppose it's the first time you've been there. What happened? How did you go in? For example, what were you wearing?"

In spite of herself, Adiba smiled slightly—a smile soaked with pain.

"Is this a new psychological strategy to help me make progress?" Catherine laughed.

"It's no good. You see through everything I try to do. You're right, though. It's another strategy of mine. Nevertheless, let's play the game together. Let's join forces. The strategy you've exposed might help us unlock your memory and reveal what's still hidden. Do you remember what you were wearing the morning they came to arrest you at the university?"

"Final examinations were being held on that day, and it was extremely hot. I was wearing a blue medium-length skirt, a gray cotton over blouse with half sleeves, and a pair of low-heeled white shoes. I had a black handbag and a black briefcase. When I was taken from the examination hall, I tried to go back to the teachers' room to fetch my bags, but they wouldn't let me. One of the men politely reminded me that I didn't need to take them with me, as I would only be away for a quarter of an hour."

"Weren't the students and teachers surprised when you were taken out of the hall? Wouldn't it have been better for the security men to wait and arrest you quietly?"

"They didn't bother much about what people thought. The way they behaved when they arrested me was different. Usually they tried to benefit as much as they could by terrorizing people. They wanted to establish an image of terror and aggression that would intimidate anyone who opposed them or had different opinions from them. That was, and still is, one of their ways of operating."

"Let us stand together in front of the cell," Catherine said. "Was the door made of wood or iron? Was it open or closed?"

"I don't know. I was blindfolded. Don't ask me to be like one of those blind people in a Hollywood film, and to show you around the place using my supernatural senses. My senses were all blindfolded. They were paralyzed. The only thing I can remember is being thrown into the corner of a relatively large room. It had a tiled floor. There was a tiny window boarded up on the outside with a thick wooden plank. My briefcase was beside me. It hadn't been touched. The pens and papers and exam timetable and the teachers' invigilation table were all there."

Adiba laughed. "There was also a recipe for preparing spaghetti sauce still in it. We had a friend who was an artist from the Jil Rawad, the Pioneer Generation, who had studied art in Italy during the fifties. He had learned how to cook spaghetti and macaroni like the Italians. Once a month, he invited us to a huge banquet where we ate spaghetti with him and his wife and a few other lucky people. I asked him for the recipe once, and he gave it to me and I kept it. But I didn't have a chance to try it out. That's all I remember. You know the rest."

"Good. I know the details of the following days. What about the last night? What can you remember?"

"The picture is not very clear. It's confused. Like a television screen that breaks up during transmission. There are tiny fragments, like very fine particles, that swirl around and around. The sound's like that, too. My ears were muffled. I couldn't hear clearly. It was as if the noise inside my head was louder than the screams of the people being tortured outside. I was weak with exhaustion. I would have collapsed if I had not been propped up in a corner. I sat on the floor without moving, clutching my bag to me as if it were the last life jacket.

"How many days passed? How many times did they take me to be interrogated? How many people did I meet? How many blank faces loomed up in front of me, belonging to bodies that were being carried past or in the last throes of death on the floor? Mukhlis . . . When they brought me face to face with him, I didn't want to look at him, but they forced me to. One of them volunteered to turn my head toward him. In the beginning I pretended to look at him, but I was really looking at the color of the wall behind him—like I do when I see a violent scene in a film. I look up at the ceiling or at the walls without moving my head so that the moment of violence passes without my having to reveal my fear."

She stopped speaking for a moment, and then said,

"You asked me about the door to the room. I remember it now. It was made of wood; it was quite ordinary. Old. I was in one of those large traditional Baghdadi houses. There was a courtyard. There's no doubt it was an old house."

"Was the door locked?"

"I don't know. I had been in detention for fourteen days by that time. I must have dropped off to sleep immediately after I returned to the room. It was pitch-dark. I could just make out the blur of my white shoes. My shirt was the same black color of the wall. There was darkness, dirt, blood. My hair was matted with dried blood, dandruff, and dust, and saliva and mucus. I was soaked in sweat and fear.

"The door opened suddenly. Yes, the door must have been locked. I came to abruptly. I put my hand up to shield my eyes. The sudden beam of light hurt them. I heard the sound of something crashing as it was thrown into the room. When I was able to see, I noticed that there were two guards. Usually there was only one. There had only been one guard during my period of detention. They stood there arguing like a pair of quarrelsome dogs. They were shouting obscenities because they couldn't get the door shut. My heart quickened. I started shaking with fear when I realized that the thing which one of them was kicking was actually a person. The guard kicked the person harder, but he didn't stir. The other guard cursed when he was forced to help move the person a bit in order to close the door."

"Did the person move? Did he make any noise?"

"I don't remember. I just remember shaking like someone with a high fever. I was so afraid that I thought my limbs would drop off because I was shaking and trembling so much. I was hot and cold. One moment I was shivering, the next I was bathed in sweat. If the person did make a sound, I didn't hear it, because my teeth were chattering so loudly and there was a roaring in my ears, which was all mixed up with the sound of people laughing and joking on the other side of the door."

"Joking? Are you sure? Don't you mean the sound of people being tortured?"

"No, no. They were different voices from the ones I'd heard the previous nights. The men were deliberately standing on the other side of the door. They were laughing, like kids waiting to see the result of a practical joke. I leaned against the wall, trying to make myself as small as possible. There was a sharp pain in my back where the wall dug into me. I drew away slightly and fiercely hugged my bag against me to stop the trembling. I buried my teeth in the leather, afraid that the person would hear them chattering. What should I do? I wanted to vomit. The muscles of my stomach contracted, and I retched . . . then . . . all of a sudden . . . I went blank. I was no longer there. Out of time. It was like falling into a deep well of darkness. I wasn't able to remember anything after that."

"What happened to you was a defense mechanism created by your body and mind. You were pushed to the utmost limit of what you were able to endure that night. Adiba, why do you always refer to the person who was thrown into the cell as 'the person'? Is it because you don't know whether he was a man or a woman?"

"Did I say person? It wasn't clear. He was far away and in the dark. He had his back toward me. I mean, they threw him in like that. He didn't move."

"Did you hear him breathing? Was he breathing?"

"No, no!" she cried out nervously, rubbing her hands. "I told you I couldn't hear anything. Why do you persist in your questions? She was there ... I mean, perhaps it was a woman wearing trousers—a person curled up like a fetus—with her back toward me. A woman or a man—what's the difference?"

"This man or woman—did he or she have short or long hair?"

"Short."

"Like a man's or a woman's?"

"I don't know. Why are you going on about this?"

"How big was he? Was he tall or average sized?"

Adiba was beginning to show signs of exhaustion. She slumped back in her chair like she had in her first session. She was agitated, her hands rubbed against each other; her eyes darted from place to place as if searching for something she'd lost but didn't know what it was.

"I don't know!" she cried out even more sharply.

"Was he about your size, or bigger than you?"

"Bigger than me."

Suddenly, Adiba got to her feet. She felt she was standing on the edge of an abyss. She reached out her hand and drew her stick away from the edge of the desk. She looked drawn. She avoided looking at Catherine. She was shaking. Darkness swirled around her. Her stick fell out of her trembling hand, and, with great difficulty, she bent to pick it up. She mumbled something incomprehensible.

She walked toward the door, born down by the invisible weight on her shoulders.

She closed it decisively behind her.

CHAPTER TWENTY

She'd write him a letter. She'd bought the stamps. Forty-four pence for a normal letter weighing at most forty grams. She'd make it short. A letter of apology. She should buy postcards. Like Adiba. *Adiba* didn't write letters. She sent cards. Beautifully colored cards. "If they get bored of my words," Adiba had joked, "they'll look at the photograph or painting, and enjoy it." Adiba had started laughing recently. The last time Majda had seen her, she had laughed twice.

Previously, she couldn't remember when exactly, Adiba didn't know how to laugh. At best, she smiled; she bobbed her head back and forth and smiled. Once, Iqbal observed, "Majda and Adiba are chronically hostile to laughter."

What was happening to Adiba? She was happy.

Majda shrieked with laughter, "Ha, ha!" She went in search of a paper tissue. Wiped the tears away. Shrieked again, "Ha, ha!" Adiba's happy, she said to herself. She's *sa'ida. Sa'ida's* feminine; *sa'id's* masculine. Sa'id, Sa'id. Curses on you in this world and the next. You've left me on my own. Get out of my head. Haven't you done enough?

He pursued her from place to place. "Don't laugh," she heard his voice warn her. "Don't be happy! If you so much as think about being happy with someone else, you will conjure me up and I will return to you." Sa'id, *ba'ied, ra'ied, na'ied, qa'ied, a'ied, sai'ed.* Happy, clappy, nappy, flappy. She had a problem with Arabic grammar and its derivatives. Sa'id had been the one who wrote her speeches for school. Sa'id had been the one who wrote the editorials for *al-Thawra.*

She looked at her reflection in the mirror fixed to the back of the bathroom door. No makeup. No Coco Chanel. She said to herself: That day when we stood before him, they recited poems in his honor ... But I stood there like a deaf-mute ... Now I must find the right words ... to tell him how much I respect him ... venerate him. Yes, a few eloquent phrases, that's what it'll take. Ah, ha! How can I be as eloquent as that pimp 'Izat? What was it he said in that speech of his I read?

She hurried over to a side cupboard piled high with bundles of old Iraqi newspapers, papers, publications, and opposition leaflets. She searched among the newspapers until she found a photo of 'Izat, and an interview in which he said:

When His Excellency says we are victorious, I am
confident that the matter is concluded. We are
victorious, therefore, and I will not discuss it further
... because I know the emotions, the ideas, the
possibilities, and the considerations that make His
Excellency able to say this. Therefore, we have to carry
out his sayings.

How would she be able to carry out such sayings? She'd forgotten how
to feel and how to love. She didn't know how to write. Ah! But she could
quote sentences about love and whispered conversations from Catherine
Cookson, couldn't she? She could address him, divulge her feelings to
him—her fears, and the pain of living in exile in a strange land. Her
loneliness, isolation, and longing for her life as it once was.

She wanted to turn the hand of the clock back to those days. Should
she write and ask him, in his mercy, to turn the clock back to the past?
He alone could do such a thing. Who else had the power to restore her
happiness, her sense of security? And Sa'id? Would he return Sa'id to
her?

If he forgave her and allowed her to return, he would pardon Sa'id
as well. For the rest of her life, she would live in his shadow, under his
care and protection. She thought, why don't I write this down while I
am still able to think about it? She sat facing the window. She set out
the writing paper on the table. It was very light. It wouldn't weigh more
than forty grams. She grasped the pencil eraser by its tip. An eraser. She
needed an eraser. She certainly needed one. Then she started writing the
introduction:

To His Excellency, President Saddam Hussein, may
God save and protect you,

I am Majda al-Sheikhly, the sister of Tahsin al-Sheikhly
the martyr. Do you remember ... ?

Majda furiously chucked the pencil aside. She didn't know how to write
properly. This was nonsense. She couldn't write like that after being
separated from him for so long. She pushed the notepad away. Perhaps
she should write a couple of postcards and ask Iqbal to correct them for

her.

Then, a thought occurred to her that pleased her. She remembered what Sa'id had once advised her to do when she asked him to help her write an official speech. He had handed her copies of *al-Thawra* and *al-Jumhouria*, and said, "Quote what you want."

She'd cut out some paragraphs from old newspapers and then go back and arrange them in the form of a letter.

In a fever of enthusiasm, she set about ransacking the newspapers. She turned the pages and read the speeches, interviews, and telegrams of congratulation. She extracted and pruned words from them with which to express the inner turmoil she was going through.

POSTCARD DRAFT ONE

My health has improved to some extent after a relapse, which grieved me, immediately after I had taken part in a demonstration calling for the victory of Iraq and an end to sanctions. The weather was very cold, and I did not wrap up well. My zeal overwhelmed me. I was oblivious to everything but the warmth of the nation. I had eyes only for the image of our beloved Leader, and it is only for the sake of the nation and my beloved Leader that I have recovered my health.

DRAFT TWO

I envy you the air and water of Baghdad. I envy you your choice of homeland over comfort and contentment. I envy you Saddam Hussein. I shall return. I cannot bear to remain here. When the year ends, I shall pack up my cases and return. My days have been transformed into a nightmare that pervades my breast. I cannot breathe. I am insensitive to the beauty of objects and nature. I do not go to the shops. I do not want anything. I have just realized ... I want nothing more than to return to the bosom of my country. I love you all. I even long for the grief and suffering you have experienced in the past, and I long to share the hopes for what is yet to come. With my soul, I shall redeem you all—you, the

nation and the Leader . . . Anticipate my return, *in sha'
Allah.*

She ripped up the drafts. She scattered them on the floor. Who would
she send them to?

She walked up and down the room. She set the pile of newspapers
back on the cupboard. It lacked poetry, she thought. Perhaps . . . he'd
forgive her if she wrote like Mi'ad al-Salim. He admired Mi'ad al-Salim's
poetry . . . He called her *al–Majda*, didn't he? Didn't he say . . . she was a
woman unlike any other?

How could she compete with Mi'ad's unique position without
poetry? But she didn't know how to read poetry, let alone write it. She
decided to ask Iqbal for help. She was the only one in the group with any
intelligence. She wasn't resentful. She had an honest heart. She reminded
her of herself when she was young. She was a beautiful girl. But how
could she arrange to see her? She'd have to phone and ask her to come
and visit . . . No! She couldn't do that . . . The phone might be tapped . . .
The last time she'd lifted the receiver, to call Adiba, she'd heard a buzzing
sound and a slight noise. They were probably watching . . . her house.
How could she contact Iqbal, then? She'd use the public phone, that's
what she'd do.

She stopped suddenly. The pencil dropped to the floor. She bent
down to pick it up. She came across a child's sock in the dust under the
table. Oh to think she would have bought another pair for her if she
hadn't come across it. Majda folded it lovingly after shaking the dust off,
then put it in the pocket of her jacket.

Oh the place was so dirty . . . She was covered in dust . . . She would
be buried in a cold country . . . The weather was cold here. The people
were cold. Unfriendly. Fear was like weeds and dust . . . She ought to
give the flat a quick clean. Quick . . . quick . . . Why quick? Ha, ha. What
was the urgency? She was on her own . . . An alien. She sang in a strong
voice:

> Oh mother, how alien I feel,
> Now that your eyes have left me,
> Lost in time, lost in time

She stood in the middle of the room. She didn't know how to finish the song. She had been about to do something . . . but what? She remembered. She had gotten up to open the window. It was stifling. Then, she quickly changed her mind, afraid that someone might attack her through the window—even though she didn't live on the ground floor. She decided to phone the council and ask them to put iron bars over it. That way the flat would be safer. She was on the alert. Was the door locked? She rushed over to it, and drew a deep breath and smiled with satisfaction when she saw it was locked and the chain was in place. No . . . they would not be able to catch her out.

She was caught up by a wave of turbulent thoughts from which she was unable to escape. She thought of her daughter. She had to protect the young girl . . . She ran to the bedroom . . . She made sure it was locked . . . It was safe . . . The place was safe . . . in this safe country. She remembered a verse from the Qur'an. She recited it as they used to do at school: "In the name of God, the merciful, the compassionate. By the fig and the olive and the Mount of Sinai and this city of security. Thus spoke the Lord God." Her eyes filled with tears. She didn't know why this verse always made her cry. She thought of Um Mohammed's glowing face. Her goodness shone through her. She loved everyone.

Love . . . love . . . they circled and turned, and always came back to love . . . Love of the mother . . . love of the homeland . . . Iqbal loved John, and he was English. The English were destroying her homeland and making people hungry . . . and Iqbal loved her homeland . . . How could she love her homeland?

She and Sa'id . . . they'd loved their homeland . . . She and Sa'id and the comrade qa'id, the Leader . . . She was filled with longing for him . . . How handsome he was! And what about the way he'd joked with them that night? This was Arab unity, he'd said, as the four of them stood together, each one from a different Arab country. He saw the future in them. They represented Arab unity to him . . . If we represented Arab unity, my love . . . then why did you do it? No, no . . . it wasn't possible. It wasn't him. He was the Leader. He was above wrongdoing. It was the thugs around him. Stooges . . . pimps like 'Izat . . . They informed on us. They told lies about us. The memory lay heavy upon her. Garbage . . . *qul wa la taqul* . . . to say or not to say . . . She pressed her hands to her head. If only she could remember proper Arabic syntax, she would write a beautiful letter to the Leader . . . But she had to be careful. She mustn't say things that might mean something bad . . . She must say . . .

Her head whirled . . . She sat down to recover . . . She put her elbows on the table and looked at the end of the road—at two people, a man and a woman, who were walking along together, side by side. The man was tall. He stood up straight. The woman walked in his shadow. The man helped the woman to cross the road. And Majda wept. She wept in agony. She wished she were in her place.

CHAPTER TWENTY-ONE

Majda froze behind the curtain, her fingers clinging to its edge. She held her breath, afraid that the people ringing the bell would hear it. She was going to suffocate. She forced herself to turn slowly away from the window.

Terror gnawed at her. Who was ringing the doorbell? It was evening. It couldn't be anyone from the social services or the housing department. It couldn't be the postman or the milkman. They usually came during office hours. Anyway, she had gotten rid of them all. One by one, they'd stopped coming to see her.

She tiptoed away. The bell rang a third time. She bit her thumb. Tasted blood on it. Why couldn't they leave her alone? She peeped out from behind the curtain. It was difficult to make them out because they were standing under the porch, and she couldn't see them from above. If only they would move back a bit, so she could see who they were.

She was watchful. Her suspicions were proving to be correct. Her telephone was tapped ... The house was being watched ... And here they were at her door. Urgently ringing the bell. Threatening to attack her. The bell rang a fourth time ... Who'd sent them? 'Izat? Samira? Muwaffiq? ... What were they called? Hypocrites and slanderers. They'd deserted the sinking ship ...

Pimps ... He's the dearly beloved, the person who sacrificed his life for us ... We competed to betray him ... Even Sa'id ... Sa'id, the pimp poet, who cheated me and cheated everyone ... He must have been a traitor; otherwise, why was he executed? Our Leader can't be wrong. Let the despicable be despised. He can uncover treachery just by looking into someone's eyes ... If he's such a bloody tyrant, as cheap propaganda claims, then why didn't he kill me? Ha ... why not? Because he knows ... he knows I'm loyal.

CHAPTER TWENTY-TWO

They came back worn out by the demonstration. Exhausted by a sense of injustice and general despair. It was freezing cold. But it hadn't stopped them from going. The three of them went—Iqbal, John, and Samer. They'd met up with Adiba there, opposite No. 10 Downing Street.

At the start, they stood side by side handing out leaflets protesting the airstrikes, which had started two days previously. Iqbal argued with some of the passersby. John joined a group that was standing near the prime minister's house and shouting. Samer zealously handed out an enormous pile of leaflets.

As soon as they got home, Samer went off to play with their neighbor's son. Iqbal told him, "Just for an hour, and no pestering me and asking to stay longer."

Samer agreed immediately, hoping that she would be so preoccupied with John that she'd forget to watch the time.

John sat down on the floor by himself. He sipped a glass of mulled wine. He offered to make her a drink as well, but she refused.

"It's a wine you like," he said.

She didn't answer.

Iqbal busied herself by cleaning a shelf of knickknacks. She could feel his eyes watching her as she moved around. She wiped the small statues and the brass coffee cups several times. She wasn't thinking about what she was doing, and wiped and cleaned mechanically. She thought, why haven't I told him yet? Was she afraid of being tied to another man? Or losing her independence by forming ties that she wouldn't be able to break easily? Or was it because she didn't want to recognize that she needed him—loved him—after swearing never to get married again when she got divorced?

John considered her as she circled around nervously. She was avoiding having to sit down beside him. He noticed the way she devised imaginary jobs about the place. She wiped the dark television screen, picked up one of Samer's books, which was on a side table, and immediately went off to put it in the bedroom.

She was talking angrily to herself in Arabic, mumbling while walking. During moments of anger, crisis, and bitterness, her mother tongue always returned to her. Once, when a drunk attacked her in the street, she'd forgotten herself and poured out a stream of angry Arabic words. The drunk had stood and stared at her in bewilderment, as if she had drawn a machine gun on him. Then, after a couple of moments' hesitation, he'd fled, leaving her on the dark sidewalk, her obscure words pursuing him.

She heard John calling her affectionately.

"Iqbal!"

"What?"

"Come and sit beside me."

"I've got a lot to do before Samer gets back."

"Tell me what needs doing, so I can help."

"No, no . . . Just sit and relax. I've got enough to worry about."

"Iqbal, please, come and sit down and tell me what's on your mind."

She submitted to his pleadings. She didn't sit on the floor. She sat on the sofa. She stared at the television screen with exhausted eyes. She hadn't watched the news today.

"Tell me how you spent your day off!"

She answered him mechanically.

"It was Samer's last day at school. So I took him to school in the morning and promised that I would collect him at the end of classes so that he could eat *shwarma* from a shop close to the station. Then I phoned Adiba. She told me she had an English friend who was going to Iraq as part of a delegation that is trying to break the sanctions. I wanted to send some money to my family. So we agreed to meet. I asked her about Majda, and she said she hadn't heard from her. That she wasn't answering the phone. We decided to go to her flat in Burnt Oak. We stood on the doorstep of the building and we rang the bell again and again, but there was no reply.

"We stood there for about ten minutes. We were sure she was there. I told Adiba that I had seen the curtain flutter a little, but she said she hadn't seen it. Nevertheless, we stayed there hoping that she would open the door to us. We were disappointed."

CHAPTER TWENTY-THREE

She addressed him with cloying sweetness.

"Samer, sweetie. Hold on tight to my hand so you won't get lost."

Samer avoided her. His face had gone pink with embarrassment. He glanced around. What would his friends say if one of them saw him holding Sahira's hand like a child, or heard him calling her Auntie Sahira!

He pretended not to hear and politely carried on walking beside her.

"Samer, the streets are so crowded that a father wouldn't recognize his own son," Iqbal said. "If we get separated, where will you go?"

"Mama, I'm not a kid," he said heatedly, in a voice trembling with the anger he felt for her and Sahira. "I know my full name and our address AND our telephone number."

"Good, good! You don't have to shout. Will you please remember we're not at home now?"

Oxford Street was impossibly crowded. Lights. Brilliant rainbow-colored decorations. Trees decorated with gaudy lights. Merchandise gleaming red, gold, and silver and all manner of glittering colors. The lights were reflected in the faces of the crowds, who pushed and shoved each other as they hurried to buy their presents—everything from soaps and shoes to handbags, scarves, and silken underwear.

It was a few days before Christmas. A time for shopping and exchanging gifts. For lights and fireworks. For stuffing oneself with food and drink, and lighting tons of candles. For jingling bells. A time for banishing the dark specter of winter. For celebrating, not mourning, the descent of *Tammuz* to the underworld. Long nights and short, cold, dark days. Night fell at three o'clock in the afternoon and wrapped them up in its ʿ*abaya* and overcoat, scarves, hats, and gloves, and persisted till eight o'clock the next morning.

The decorations and lights on Oxford Street had been lit since the middle of November; a whole month had been devoted to preparing for the arrival of the New Year.

"How many more days are there left till Christmas?" Samer asked.

"Today's December 21st. Therefore, there are four days left, completely and utterly," Iqbal answered.

Samer swung on his mother's hand, favoring her with snatches of well-known Christmas carols, "Completely and utterly . . . we wish you a white Christmas . . ."

Then he turned to her and asked,

"What does 'completely and utterly' mean?"

"To cut a long story short . . . It means exactly. Come on. Do you want to go into Selfridges so that you can choose your present from Father Christmas?"

"Mama, Mama! You know that I know that Father Christmas is just a story for kids, and he doesn't exist. How many times have I got to tell you how old I am? Every day? Every hour?"

"But the whole purpose of coming here," Sahira intervened, "and letting ourselves be pushed and shoved around by all these hordes of people was so that you could enjoy yourself and look at Father Christmas and see the Christmas trees and lights."

"Thank you very much, Auntie Sahira, but I don't want to sit on the lap of a fat old man wearing a cotton wool beard, so I can ask him for a present I know my mother's going to buy."

"Children today!" Sahira muttered. "They know everything."

"You know, Sahira, sometimes I think that most of the things I do for Samer I'm actually doing for myself. Take today, for example. Samer would have been quite happy staying at home, glued to the television. But I made such a fuss that he finally agreed to come out with me to look at the lights and decorations, and buy presents and walk and eat roasted chestnuts."

"Adults obviously need lights and festivals more than children. We long to please ourselves, more than others, with happiness and feast days. To forget our dark days," Sahira replied.

"Have you bought any presents?"

"Kadhim won't allow it. He says we should only celebrate our own feast days."

"Our feasts, their feasts! Who cares! If it were up to me, we'd celebrate the lot of them."

"We used to celebrate Christmas, when the children were at home. He liked buying presents then. We would wrap them up and cook turkey. We'd get together and eat, and sing our own songs, and celebrate in our own way. Then, gradually, the holiday began to annoy him. He now regards it as a purely commercial occasion."

"To tell you the truth, I agree with him. People in this country start shopping for Christmas in October, and spend the whole year slaving away and saving their money, just to buy presents. Sometimes, they even take out a loan. And what happens to the presents? They generally end up being returned to the shops or exchanged, or they're thrown away, or given as presents to other people. People here spend money as if it were a duty. They must buy. They must eat and drink more than necessary, and they must enjoy themselves to the fullest, even if they don't want to."

"Kadhim will be pleased to hear that you agree with him and are opposed to the festivities. By the way . . . what are you doing on Christmas day?"

"John's driving us down to his mother's house in Hove."

"Hove?"

"A small town outside London, on the coast near Brighton."

Sahira didn't feel particularly comfortable when Iqbal mentioned John. Personally, she would have preferred it if Iqbal were going out with an Iraqi or Arab man, but she forced herself to show a bit of interest.

"*Khair in sha' Allah!*"

"John's been on at me for ages to meet his mother. But I've always put it off. Finally . . . I agreed . . . I said it would be convenient. We'll spend the holiday with her. She lives on her own. She's a widow. John's father died five years ago. I've spoken to her many times on the phone. When John told her about the engagement, she called to invite me. Oh, I mustn't forget to buy her a present."

Startled, Sahira came to a sudden halt in the middle of the jostling crowds.

"Engagement? What engagement?"

Iqbal grabbed her hand and dragged her away from the entrance to John Lewis, which was swarming with people, to somewhere where they could protect their backs against the wall.

"It's old news. I thought you knew. Come on, Sahira, let's walk. Get a move on. We can't stop in the middle of this crowd. Come on, I have an idea. Let's go to the café in John Lewis." Iqbal turned toward Samer, who had almost broken her arm in his repeated attempts to get her attention.

"Samer, would you like to eat supper in John Lewis?"

Samer welcomed the idea with a shriek of delight. He would eat whatever he liked and at the same time get out of the cold and away from the coats and umbrellas, and bags crammed full with shopping. His mother would certainly give in and get him what he wanted while she was busy talking to Auntie Sahira.

"But the shop will be closing shortly," Sahira remarked.

"No, it's staying open till nine o'clock. We've got two hours."

They struggled up to the fourth floor where the café was. They waited until a table became free, and Samer raced off to reserve it, calling loudly,

"Mama, Auntie, hurry up!"

Sahira sat down while Iqbal and Samer headed toward the food counter. Samer walked close to his mother, gripping her hand; he laughed in embarrassment when she reminded him about what he had said about not being a child and how he had refused to hold Sahira's hand. He pestered her to get him his favorites. He wanted fish and chips, orange juice, and a large slice of cake.

"Are you sure that will fill you up?" she joked.

"Thank you very much," he replied very politely. "I believe that it will be enough to last me till nine o'clock."

They returned to Sahira carrying two trays filled with food and drink.

"What's all this?" Sahira demanded. "I thought you weren't eating?"

"The tea's for us, and the rest is for Big Belly, Samer *effendi*."

"And so . . . ?" Sahira asked, a couple of minutes after they sat down.

"What?" Iqbal asked, confused.

"The engagement . . . have you forgotten?"

"Oh! The engagement. To put it briefly, we, I mean John and I, began seeing each other two years ago. He's been pressing me to live with him for ages. But I refused. I wasn't sure what to do. I was afraid of commitment and the ties and the complications of marriage, and I was very concerned about Samer's relationship with John. But things have changed, and I felt satisfied enough to give it a try. John's convinced me to become engaged. He's suggested that if we don't agree . . . if things don't work out between us, then we can cancel the engagement, or get divorced. So we're going to give it a try. If we get divorced, it won't be the end of the world."

Sahira shook her head in amazement, then sang in a subdued voice:

Lost indeed I am, my dear, so guide me
Show me where the station is, so guide me

Then she said, "My God, Iqbal Khanem . . . You make me feel dizzy. I don't know where I am today with you young people. If you want something big, it's big; and if you want something small, it's small. In any case, a thousand congratulations, my dear, and I wish you all good luck."

Iqbal laughed. Samer took advantage of his mother's preoccupation to add a vast quantity of salt and vinegar to his chips, licking his fingers as he ate each morsel.

"Everything is in the genes and inheritance," she said, glancing at him out of the corner of her eye. Then she turned to Sahira.

"Thanks, 'aini Sahira, and what about you? What are you doing for Christmas?"

"It'll be a normal day. We'll stay at home. Shakir and Nahid will come on Christmas Eve. 'Adil is still trapped in Baghdad waiting for God to open a way out for him. I am so worried and frightened for him; I can't bear to think about it."

Sahira hesitated.

"Iqbal," she added. "Do you remember how you and Adiba were trying to persuade me to enroll in a course or do something outside the house? Even the doctor gave me the same advice when I went back to him two days ago."

"Of course I remember, and I wish you'd listen to what we're saying about taking it easy, or you'll get depressed."

"Well, yesterday, while I was walking along the main street in Edgware, I noticed that they had opened up a new Oxfam shop there, and it had a poster asking for volunteers to help manage the shop. I went in and spoke to the manager. He was pleased to see me. They agreed that I should work in the shop twice a week, on Tuesdays and Thursdays, for a half a day each time. Of course, the work is voluntary, but they'll pay the cost of transportation. I said to myself, you'll be helping the needy on the one hand and keeping yourself busy on the other. I'll be mixing with people, and I'll improve my English. It's an experiment. If it doesn't work, I can always leave."

She looked cautiously at Iqbal before going on. "It's like you say, I'm giving it a try. If your marriage is an experiment, then I'm experimenting with a job, and I've decided . . ."

"*Ma sha' Allah*, Sahira!" Iqbal interrupted with a laugh. "It's as if the door to heaven has opened and decisions are tumbling out. There's no stopping you: 'my decision this,' 'my experiment that . . .' May you find life in decisions and experiments!"

"I've also decided that at the beginning of the New Year I am going to enroll in the college near me and take some suitable courses."

"God is truly great, Sahira! What's happening? . . . All these wonderful changes! *'Ashat yadaik!* That's the best thing I've ever heard you say . . . apart from when you sing, of course," she added with a smile. "*Wa-Allahi,* you've really made me happy. We must celebrate. Do you know . . . we must tell Adiba? No, no! You must call her yourself. She's been worried about you . . . She'll be so happy at this news. Let me sing instead":

> The world is beautiful, sweet, and happy, oh so happy,
> oh so happy.

CHAPTER TWENTY-FOUR

Adiba hadn't expected her day to be so tiring. Basically, she hadn't expected to be called out to the airport on a job. Like everyone else, she was getting ready for the beginning of the Christmas holiday.

The night before, she had mapped out every hour of her day down to the last minute. She had written down what she needed to do on a piece of paper, listing the tasks in order of importance. The tasks were not particularly difficult or complex, but she enjoyed seeing the details of her day written down for her to look at so that they acquired the force of certainty.

WHAT NEEDS TO BE DONE DECEMBER 24TH, AS WRITTEN BY ADIBA

> Breakfast. Remember to take calcium and vitamin E tablet.
> Defrost the fridge. Clean and tidy the kitchen, especially the floor.
> Throw out all the bottles and bags of spices that you've been keeping for years.
> Put the chipped plates and cups on one side and take them to the Oxfam shop.
> Have a rest. Drink a cup of coffee.
> Go to Camden High Street to get presents for Michael and his father.
> Buy Christmas cards.
> Lunch.
> Siesta.
> Clean the bedroom. Change the sheets.
> Organize the wardrobe. Sort out your clothes. Put the unwanted ones into a black plastic bag.
> Rest.
> Phone Majda.
> Phone Um Mohammed.
> Go through the pile of newspapers and magazines. Get rid of those you don't need. Check the bookshelves.

Sort out anything written by Marx and Lenin in
Russian. Should you hold on to them?
Get ready to go to Michael's.

She felt tense and welcomed the trivial household tasks, which provided a
distraction from her thoughts. She relaxed as she organized the timetable.
She really had to defrost the fridge, as she could hardly open or close the
door at the moment.

She wanted to buy presents for Michael and his father. The presents
were an unexpected addition to the list. Michael had telephoned her the
evening before, right after she had gotten back from her weekly session
with Dr. Hawkins, and invited her to have Christmas lunch with him
and his father. She was surprised by the invitation but accepted at once,
without thinking about it, glad to have an escape from the sense of
loneliness that was particularly acute at Christmas. A day for families. It
would also enable her to get away from the new and troubling thoughts
that Dr. Hawkins had raised in her mind.

Michael was going to cook a festive lunch the next day. His father
was elderly, and he had looked after him for years. She had offered to help
him—to do the shopping, or share the expenses, or prepare a dish and
take it with her—but Michael had been adamant in his refusal. He'd said,
"Your coming to us will be sufficient present."

She would go to Waterstone's in Camden High Street and buy a
book for Michael. She hadn't decided what yet . . . and she'd get a bottle
of brandy for his father and a bottle of good wine for them all from
Sommerfield's. She also needed to pack her small suitcase because she
would have to spend the night at Michael's, since the city's arteries came
to a standstill on Christmas Day and there was no transportation. It was
a universal holiday, the only one on the public calendar.

She thought back to what it had been like a few years ago when
Sunday was a bit like Christmas Day. Shops were closed, people stayed
at home. It was a rest day, a day for the family and shared family activities.
A day for going to church. Today, shops and markets of all kinds were
allowed to open, and shopping had become the new religion—the
shopping malls the new churches. Individuals and families flocked to
them. They went shopping; they ate, and read the Sunday newspapers
in cafés. They met their friends and families. They had a good time. All
under the one roof, which protected them from the rain and snow and
cold.

Now there was only one day in the year for family ties and religious beliefs, and that was Christmas Day. And only one meal. Christmas lunch.

Michael's invitation came as a relief from the pain that resulted from her retreat into herself. She dreaded and desired it at the same time. She had put off thinking about her last session with Dr. Hawkins. She had spent longer hours at work, clinging to any activity that would stop her from brooding. If she happened to find herself on her own, she invented cunning mental tricks to distance herself from the basic fact, the essence of the problem.

December 24th as It Happened

The night before, she had slept for a few troubled hours. She woke up once, drenched in sweat and frightened, instantly aware that the nightmare had returned. Gradually, the fear diminished. She knew she was in her home, in her small flat in Camden Town, in London. She was not in Baghdad. She was here, in the present. The past was far away and would not harm her.

She did not open the window. The temperature outside was around zero. People's wishes for a white Christmas might come true, and she was worried about catching cold. She limped to the sitting room—her book of nightmares in her hand. She had added a secondary title in the last month and written "and diary" in her childish handwriting.

She liked writing. So she had recorded other events and thoughts in the nightmare and diary book.

She sat on the sofa, enveloped in her brown robe, and started writing immediately. It had been her first nightmare in two weeks.

> I was somewhere that was swarming with people. As I walked about, I listened to a radio program. It was a live broadcast. Listeners phoned in and discussed current issues with the presenter. The issue that day was the growing number of refugees in Britain. Despite the noise and constant interruptions in the street, I strained to hear what they were saying. Soon the people around me turned hostile. I didn't understand what I was doing there. I just knew I was heading toward some kind of island.
>
> The radio discussion continued, and an official

suggested that refugees should jump over to the island to prove that they were genuine and that they really wanted to return to their countries of origin once circumstances had changed. "We will not be able to help them unless they pass the test," he said. I said out loud, "But I want to return." I found myself at the edge. The weather changed. It had been cloudless before, I remember. Now it started raining heavily. It poured down.

I didn't hesitate. I leaped across to the island. But because of my leg, I was unable to make the distance. I slipped. I gripped the muddy edge of the island with one hand. It was like being in an action movie. I very slowly began to slip back into the abyss. I begged a woman to help me. She was wearing a long flowery skirt and a headscarf made of the same material, and she was carrying a baby in her arms. I begged her to hold my hand. She spoke in some foreign language, pointing to the baby, indicating that she had her hands full looking after him. I slipped further. The firm ground changed to mud, and I was only able to grab handfuls of sticky earth. I was being dragged further and further down.

Adiba looked at her hands. She could almost see traces of dirt sticking to her fingernails. What struck her and distressed her in particular was the woman's failure to help her. Why had she refused?

She made a cup of chamomile tea. She wouldn't think about the nightmare. She didn't want to. She would read it with Dr. Hawkins. She walked about the room. Shelves of books in Arabic, English, and Russian lined the walls of the flat. They would soon reach the ceiling. She must clear things out. She looked out at the silent street; the lights shone yellow. The street was empty. The local paper the *Camden New Journal* had recently carried a report about the growing number of thefts and robberies on the streets of Camden. The report attributed it to the rise in unemployment and the increased use of drugs among the young. She put her face up close to the glass so that she was almost touching it, and peered out as if searching for the homeless in the empty street. Should she give up walking around Camden from now on? How would she get home after work? How would she manage? She felt cold, and returned to bed. She wanted to block out her thoughts by going to sleep, or at least by trying to. She prepared herself for the restlessness and anxious thoughts she usually encountered, and got ready to defend herself against them. She girded herself for a campaign that had become a quintessential part of her night.

But . . . she fell asleep.

She gently slipped into a valley of calm. She slept deeply until morning.

MORNING, DECEMBER 24TH

The telephone woke her. It was half past eight. The duty clerk was on the line from the immigration office at Gatwick Airport. They rarely called her from there because she was attached to Heathrow Airport. But due to the disarray caused by the holiday season and their failure to find another interpreter, they had been forced to phone her.

The clerk sighed with relief when he heard her voice. "I've tried ten other people," he said, "and you're the first person to answer the phone."

He explained,

"I've got an Iraqi family here. Five persons—husband, wife, and three children. If you can't make it, don't worry, I'll understand. We'll send them to a detention center until Christmas is over."

"No, no," Adiba gabbled, as if she would be able to prevent them from being arrested and sent to a detention center by speaking quickly. "I'll come immediately. Just the time it takes to reach you. Please don't send them to the center. We'll organize something for them in town."

It was an exceptional situation.

She put off her plans for the day. She looked at the paper on which she had written out her list of things to do, and that she had stuck on the calendar. She thought . . . it doesn't matter. I'll do them another day. She'd buy the book for Michael after the holiday. He would understand. But his father wouldn't. She flung on some old clothes. She put on her long coat and went out into the street. She bought bottles of brandy and wine from the first supermarket she came to. Two good bottles for a special day. She wanted to make Michael's father happy. He liked presents. He took a childish pleasure in them although he was almost eighty years old. She put the bag in the flat, then set out for the airport. She arrived at half past eleven. By twelve o'clock she was sitting in the immigration officer's office waiting for the refugees to arrive. She drank coffee from a machine, served in a paper cup.

She finally left the airport at ten o'clock at night. It had been a long ten hours. Standing, sitting, translating, listening, trying to calm the family's fears, humoring and distracting the children, fetching food and drinks, urging the examining officer not to send them to the detention center near the airport, with its awful reputation, making phone calls to people they knew, friends and relatives in London, summoning their guarantor and waiting for him to arrive and sign the official papers.

Finally they were released and allowed to enter London.

She felt as exhausted as if she had just completed a marathon, racing against well-known athletes despite her crippled leg and persevering to the finish. It had been a marathon of competing agitated emotions. She had been asked to calm down people arriving at a strange airport. She had spent hours explaining, elucidating, making clear, setting fears at rest, and giving them a certain sense of security and peace. She had given everything she had. She had used up all her energy.

She felt faint on the way back home. She dozed for a quarter of an hour on the train. She woke up and felt joy flood through her, a sense of lightness of being. It spread through her body, soothing her aching muscles and smoothing the lines on her face. She thought back on her tiring day. She remembered the previous night and recalled in amazement her deep, untroubled sleep. Adiba murmured joyfully over and over to herself, "I slept like a baby; I slept like a baby."

She looked out the window of the train. She could see her face reflected in the night—a happy face. She felt afraid. She heard her mother praying (as she did each time Adiba laughed or was happy), "May God make your laughter good."

The train took its time as if, like everyone else, it had already begun to celebrate the holiday and had started drinking early. A slight tingle ran through her own body and refused to go away. She was intoxicated with the memory of sleeping for several hours without waking up or being afraid. Her mother's voice faded. Without realizing what she was doing, she smiled to herself.

What had happened? What had brought about this change?

She thought back to the closing minutes of her last session with Dr. Hawkins. She had been angry with her after the previous session. She had left the room the week before without saying good-bye. It embarrassed her. She had never behaved like that before in her life. It disconcerted her. She decided she would never go back to see her. Never. But after spending a terrible night, which had been much worse than usual, she changed her mind and attended her final session before the Christmas and New Year break.

Her Session Was on December 22ⁿᵈ, at Four o'clock

She arrived in a state. For the first time in her life, she had seen a robbery take place. It had happened near Camden Town Underground station in the middle of a crowded area and in broad daylight. The thief had grabbed a girl's handbag and run away, leaving her screaming and crying in vain.

With an effort, Adiba wrested her attention away from the shock she had received. She didn't want to mention the incident to Dr. Hawkins.

"I am sorry that I left so abruptly last time and didn't say good-bye," she said.

"No, it was my mistake, and I must ask you to forgive me. I hadn't given sufficient attention to your state of mind. I was wrong about how much progress you had made. I thought you were psychologically ready and prepared to take the final step."

"What do you mean?" Adiba asked.

"I miscalculated. We will talk about the subject after Christmas in more detail, if you wish. I recognize that my timing was wrong. Generally … let's forget about it." She added brightly, "What are your plans for Christmas?"

"I don't have any. It's a family holiday, and I don't have any family. I'll stay at home like on other days." She laughed cheerfully. "I'll cook a special meal for one from a recipe I cut out from a woman's magazine. Then I'll sit down contentedly in front of the television so as not to miss the Queen's speech."

They laughed.

"Actually, my husband and I hate Christmas and all the fuss around it. Every year we try to escape it and go somewhere where Christmas isn't celebrated. But this year, because of all our work obligations, we aren't able to get away."

"Am I one of them?"

"You're the easiest of them."

Silence settled over them. A silence heavy with the unsaid matters that hung between them. Matters that needed to be discussed.

Looking directly at Catherine, Adiba said very quietly,

"It was a man."

Catherine immediately picked up the thin thread.

"Did he look like anyone you knew, or remind you of anyone?"

"I don't know. It was very dark, and I was not able to think or make comparisons."

"I am relying here on what your subconscious mind registered at the time. At present, you are like someone walking around in the dark armed with a small flashlight. I'm hoping you will direct it at places that exist, but which you can't see and whose existence you are unaware of."

"I have tried . . . I am trying. I am unable to walk. If I walk into that room with a flashlight in my hand, as you suggest, then the only thing I can see is myself. I see myself frightened and scared to death, crouched in a corner."

"Why did you run away last time?"

"I was tired. Exhausted from constantly going back to the same hole, to the past. You take me back to a place, then you leave me there and lock the door behind me."

"That's true. But I think it's much deeper than that. Last time, I believe you came close to remembering something very significant. It's as if you felt the psychological barrier was about to come down. You're scared that if it comes down, you'll see something behind it that you don't want to look at. You'll see something so terrifying that it'll destroy you if you're not ready to face it."

Adiba's face paled. She looked at her hands. She lightly ran her ring finger along the lines in her left palm. She traced the lines as if seeing them for the first time. Then . . . with similar caution, she looked up. Her eyes were covered with a transparent film of tears. They were the wounded eyes of a caged lioness, whose spirit was laid bare in the eyes of the woman opposite.

"Adiba," Catherine said. "I think you know who the person was who was brought into your cell. You knew him in spite of the darkness and the terrible state you were in—despite your fear and sickness. You recognized him the moment they threw him in and kicked him and when you heard their voices mocking you outside. He was someone so close to you that you would have recognized him anywhere in the world, however dark it was. But you refused to believe it. You refused to know him. Losing your memory protected you from going mad during interrogation, but it also protected you from death. The idea that your husband was still alive gave you a vital reason to continue living."

Adiba noticed she had arrived at Camden Town station. How had she managed to change trains and reach Camden so fast? She looked at the station clock. It was a quarter to midnight. The ticket collector had left the exit unmanned. She smiled. He'd left early to celebrate.

Only two people left the station at the same time as she did. It must have been the last train. She recalled the incident of the robbery with concern. It really disappointed her. She had always thought of Camden as a safe place and refused to believe the stories of robberies and muggings that she read in the newspapers. At heart, she wanted Camden to remain a safe haven, an oasis for refugees. Was this refusal to look reality in the face, with all its pain and evil and disappointment, a basic trait of her character? Was this what Catherine had meant when she said, "You refused to recognize him to protect yourself"?

She glanced about her. The street was deserted. The other passengers had disappeared. A lonely street. Anxiety beset her. It was hard to imagine the Camden she knew, which was always so unbearably crowded, now that it was empty of all the young people and beggars and street traders.

She would tell Michael tomorrow that, after years of living in Camden Town, she had finally come to see its other side. Its hidden face. Silent, dark, and menacing. She crossed the street to the other side, to where the lit-up window of Superdrug announced a sale that would begin the day after Christmas.

She hesitated. She couldn't remember when she'd been so late returning home on her own. Should she go along Inverness Street, then turn right, or go along the main road until reaching the turnoff to her street? She gathered up her courage and decided. She turned in to Inverness Street. What was the difference? All the roads looked the same when they were empty. Darkness. Hadn't she spent enough of her life being afraid of the dark? Wasn't it time to face it?

Her uneven footsteps echoed audibly as she limped along the street, which was usually filled with vegetable, cheese, and fruit stalls. Luckily, she'd bought the bottle of brandy for Michael's father. She realized she didn't know his name. She treated him as she would an Iraqi. Abu Michael. Father of Michael. If she wanted to know how he was, she asked Michael: "How is your father?" She would ask him tomorrow. She didn't know Um Mohammed's name either. No, she was wrong. She had seen her name once when she was translating for her, but had forgotten it.

Adiba tried to remember what it was. Amina? Khadija? Something Kurdish? Haibat, perhaps? She would visit her after the holiday . . . She would go the day after tomorrow, in the evening. Michael had promised to drive her back tomorrow evening. She would phone and arrange to see Um Mohammed the following day. She had become very fond of her . . . She had been preoccupied in the last couple of days, but she would make it up to her, ask after her . . . She would also try and resurrect the notion of a monthly meeting. It was an excellent idea and might help them get to know other women—widen their circle of acquaintances.

She was deep in thought . . . She might be able to convince them to invite other nationalities into the group . . . liberate them from the stranglehold that Iraq had over them. The ghetto . . . Suddenly, she was roused from her thoughts . . . She heard the sound of footsteps behind her. It abruptly woke her from her pleasurable dream. She ignored the sound. She didn't glance back. She forced herself not to look around. She pretended not to be worried, but in spite of herself, changed her pace. She limped faster. Her steps became increasingly confused. The panic-stricken face of the girl who'd been robbed rose in front of her eyes. With her free hand, she grabbed the handbag dangling from her shoulder. She clutched it against her chest. A picture of herself came into her mind, cowering in a corner, alone and friendless, with nothing to hold onto but her bag. She shook the image away. She told herself encouragingly, now . . . I am here. I am now.

Now . . . Her walking stick hampered her. The steps drew closer . . . No, she would not turn around. It was some passerby like herself . . . He would not harm her. Why should he harm her? Tomorrow she would tell Michael and his father about her little adventure, and they would laugh at her fears. What was that? The steps continued . . . They marched in time with her, without overtaking her . . . They had a nightmarish quality about them. If she told herself it was a nightmare and nothing else, it would be over. It wouldn't harm her.

The footsteps kept time with the sound her stick made as it struck the ground. Her heart started to pound. Fear took hold of her again. It was a fear she was familiar with. The footsteps possessed the affliction of fear.

The footsteps were now keeping pace with the frightened pounding of her heart.

He was close behind. She was sure he was following her. She clung on to the last straws of hope. Perhaps he lived in the same street as she did . . . Perhaps it was one of her neighbors.

If only she had the courage . . . to rein in her agitation . . . If only she could face him ... perhaps ... she'd see that he was like her. Someone returning home late. Despite herself, tears started to her eyes. She felt unable to continue . . . She limped on. Her steps grew heavier and heavier. Her body trembled; fear and alarm stiffened her legs and made it difficult to walk. She gathered her newly regained willpower; she decided to face him. She drew a deep breath. She came to a stop. She turned around. The gas soaked her black searching eyes and closed them forever.

CHAPTER TWENTY-FIVE

Camden New Journal, the local newspaper, published the following item on its front page:

> Lawyers at the Maidstone court heard details of the assault on Mrs. Adiba Baghdadi that resulted in the loss of her life. Building worker Steve Wood, of Phoenix Street, Somerstown, was charged with first spraying her in the face with a CS gas spray, and then knifing her in the chest.
>
> The incident took place about 100 meters from Camden Underground station, in northwest London. The doctors did everything in their power to save Mrs. Baghdadi's life, but were unable to do so. Mr. Wood was arrested immediately after the incident when they found his pocketknife. When Wood was arrested, he joked, "Sure I killed her, and you can also record that I killed Stephen Lawrence."
>
> In his summary to the court, the council for the prosecution said that the incident took place at around twelve o'clock at night on 24th December 1998. Mrs. Adiba Baghdadi was returning home to her flat in Beardsley Road after finishing work at Gatwick Airport. She had left Camden Town Underground station, turned right along the main road, and crossed over to the other side. For some unknown reason, she had decided to turn left down Inverness Street, then right in to the relatively dark Arlington Street, where Steve Wood was waiting for her.
>
> Mr. Whitecar, a passerby who was in the vicinity at that time, heard a scream and went to investigate. Mr. Whitecar found Mrs. Baghdadi on the ground, bleeding heavily. He immediately phoned the emergency services and an ambulance. The wounded woman was

transferred to University College Hospital's accident and emergency department, where she died two hours later on 25th December 1999.

Mrs. Baghdadi was British, of Iraqi descent. She had lived in London since 1979 and had no family.

'abaya. A cloak-like wrap, used by men and women.

'aib. Naughty, wrong, shameful.

'aini. Term of endearment; literally, "my eye."

al-hamdu lillah. Praise be to God; phrase used in many different situations, particularly when completing an action.

Allah ghalib. Literally means "God is victorious"; phrase used particularly in North Africa to denote that the speaker does not want to take responsibility. Similar to "God knows."

Allah halik. May God grant you a long life.

Allahu Akbar. God is great; phrase used when a person has run out of patience and to put an end to an argument.

'aqal. A headband, traditionally made of camel's hair, holding the male headdress in place. Usually worn by men from the Gulf and Saudi Arabia.

'ashat yadaik. May your hands live. Phrase traditionally used in Iraq and Iran in praise of another's actions.

Ba'ath Party. The Ba'ath Party is an Pan-Arabist Socialist party that emerged after World War II. While this movement was formed to unify all Arabs in one movement or nation, it has two main branches, one in Syria and one in Iraq, which have been rivals since the 1960s, when they split along national lines. The Ba'ath Party ruled Iraq continuously from 1968 until the U.S. invasion of Iraq in 2003, when the Ba'ath Party, along with its head Saddam Hussein, was overthrown.

baukum. Sweetheart, darling; Kurdish form of endearment.

bismillah. In the name of God; frequently used when beginning an action.

chalgi music. Also known as chalgi Baghdad; a popular form of Iraqi music in which a singer, accompanied by a small ensemble, sings traditional songs about love, sadness, and nature. The ensemble is usually made up of oud, fiddle, drum, and qanoon (dulcimer).

dalala. Traders, usually women, who sell their goods in people's houses rather than in the market place.

al-Dharba. Term used by the Iraqi Communist Party to refer to Saddam Hussein's decision in 1979 to break with the Communist Party and put an end to the National Progressive Front, thereby initiating a period of savage repression against members of the party.

dibke. A group dance in which the dancers line up with locked arms or holding hands and stamp out the rhythm and sing.

dishdasha. Long full-length tunic, usually made of cotton, and often worn by men. Traditionally worn by men from the Gulf and Iraq.

djadjik salad. Salad made from yogurt and cucumbers.

halal. Allowed by religious law, legitimate, permissible. Opposite of haram.

haram. Proscribed by religious law or sharia', forbidden, taboo.

ibni. My son.

istikana. Device used for keeping water hot; similar to the samovar.

Jil Rawad. Pioneer Generation.

khair in sha' Allah. I hope you're well.

khatia. Term meaning "poor thing"; used particularly in Iraq and Palestine.

kubba, also kibbeh. A mixture of fine minced meat and onions wrapped in a shell of crushed wheat.

klaicha. A form of pastry stuffed with dates or nuts.

lahmacun. A form of pizza made with a very thin crust—popular in the eastern Mediterranean.

ma sha' Allah. Literally means "What God wills!" It can also mean "How beautiful/wonderful, etc.," when used in exclamations about something good.

madih. Poem of praise, panegyric, ode.

maqam. A set of notes in Arabic music. The nearest equivalent in Western classical music would be a mode (e.g. major, minor, etc.).

narinj. Bitter fruit of the orange family.

National Progressive Front. In 1973 the secretary of the Iraqi Communist Party, 'Aziz Mohammed, signed a National Action Pact with President Ahmed Hassan al-Bakr, forming a national front together with the ruling Ba'ath Party. This allowed the ICP to operate legally, but was regarded by some Communists as a betrayal of the thousands of party members who had been killed during and after the 1963 Ba'athist coup, which toppled 'Abdul Karim Qasim. The front officially lasted until 1979, but by 1978 Saddam Hussein had already renewed his repressive campaign against the party.

nefarat. Shared taxi.

qaimara. Very thick cream, traditionally made from buffalo milk.

qasida. A classical poetic form having a rigid tripartite structure.

rebaba. A stringed instrument of the Arabs resembling a fiddle with one to two strings.

salimtik. May you get better; said to someone who is ill.

sharia'. Religious as opposed to civil law.

shebab. Literally, "young men"; term used for torturers in Iraqi jails.

shirwal. Large baggy pants, usually worn by men but in certain regions also worn by women.

tar music. Traditional Iranian lute music.

NOTES ON THE TEXT

In Chapter Ten, as well as in Chapter Twenty (Postcard Draft One and Draft Two), I have used articles that initially appeared in Iraqi newspapers—*al-Thawra* and *al-Jumhouria*.

The book referred to in Chapter Sixteen is *Saddam Hussein: The Fighter, the Thinker, the Man* by Dr. Amir Iskander. It appeared in various Iraqi media outlets.

Stephen Lawrence, mentioned in the newspaper article in Chapter Twenty-Five, was a black British teenager who was killed in London in 1993 in front of a group of white youths. Until now, no one has been sentenced for his murder.